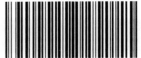

Normal Chaos
A. V. Smith
Without Chaos
Peace Cannot Exist
LEDOMA - BOOK 1

Normal Chaos: Ledoma Book 1

Book Cover: SEVIINTH DEGREE PRODUCTIONS LLC

Editor: AMY VRANA

Editing Consultant/Interior Design: ASCRIBE COMMUNICATIONS

Warped Writing and Publishing LLC, Columbus, Ohio

ISBN: 978-1-7351069-8-4

82879

DEDICATION

To my children, Devan, Naiya and Christian:

My prayer to The Universe for you has been sent. You are my life source; greatness awaits you.

I Love You.

TABLE OF CONTENTS

LEDOMA

BOOK ONE

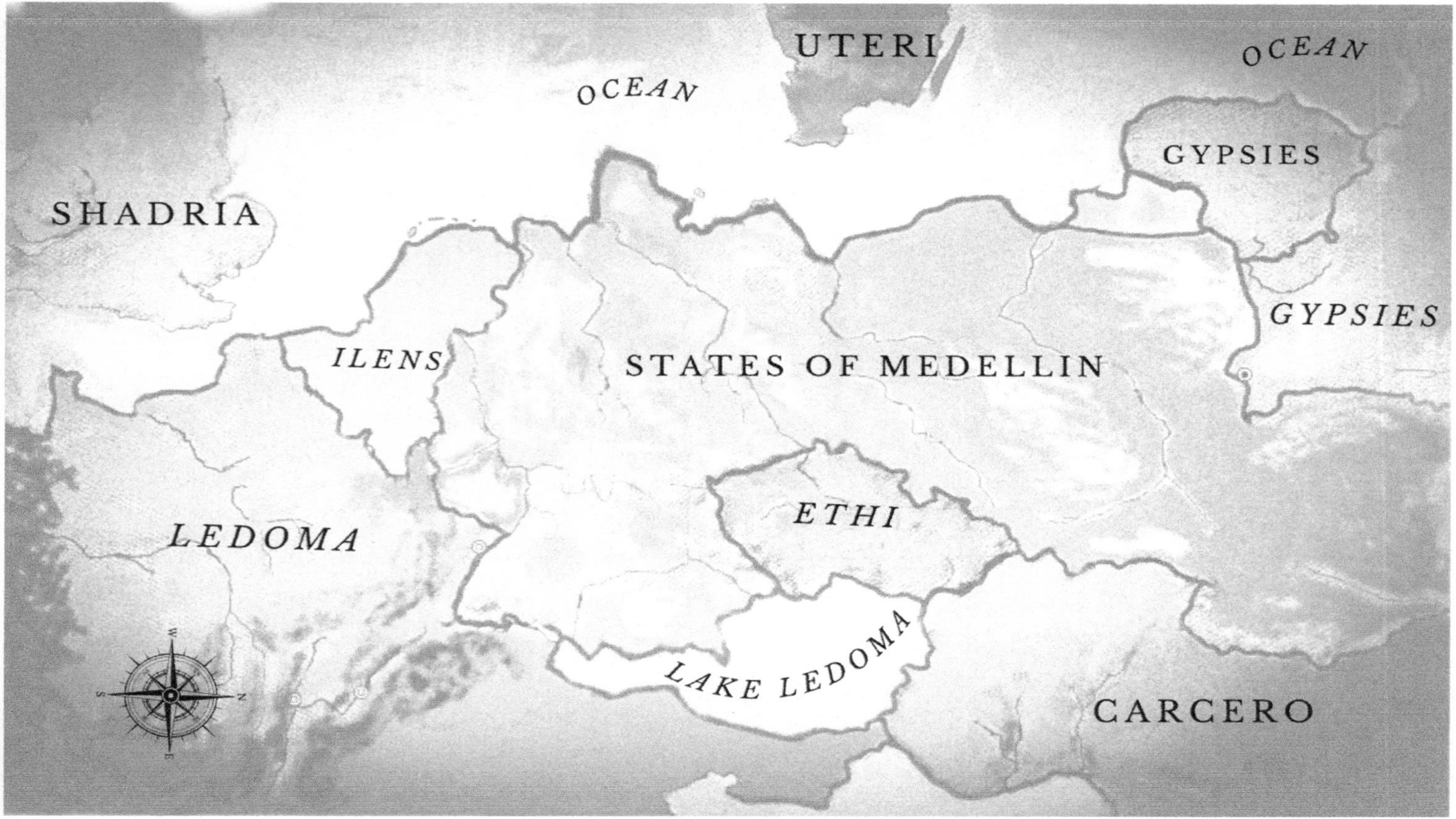
UTERI
OCEAN
OCEAN
GYPSIES
SHADRIA
GYPSIES
ILENS
STATES OF MEDELLIN
ETHI
LEDOMA
LAKE LEDOMA
CARCERO

PROLOGUE

In the moments after time and space came into existence, the war between the light and the dark was born. The furious battle escalated when the Creator formed the Earth.

Every thousand years the earth and humanity went through a cycle of transformation. For a series of seven cycles, each one lasting a millennium, the balance between shadow and light tilted. During this transformation, those of the shadow were ruled by dark magic, and they wielded it to satisfy their greed for coin, power, and dominion over all others. Ogres, Wyverns, and Soachim were a few evil fiends unleashed to turn the world into chaos.

The Creator gave the world the Light of the First Mother, the bridge between humanity and the heavens. She bound with the Original Giants and Dragons of the earth to stave off those of the darkness. It would be her bloodline that fought against the shadow, but as her visions became clearer, she also knew some of her descendants would succumb to the darkness. Now, the Light was represented by the Tree of Life and protected by the Order of Petals.

The Seventh Age was drawing close.

AE 781

"Every step we've taken since the armed guard surrounded us has been treacherous. The Tree of Life abducted and placed us into the lower earth. It has brought us nothing but death. We had no choice but to walk aimlessly inside these tunnels, and it's been over 7 months. The occasional traces of sunlight that we actually get glimpses of have been seen less than 40 days. We have been attacked by a virus which took out two of our sisters, five guardsmen, and almost took you and the babies you carry into the afterlife. And who would've thought that a beautiful, peaceful body of water would turn out to be an ogre's watering hole when no one has seen these monstrosities in almost a millennium? What would've happened if there had been more than one patrol of them? Do you think we would've lost more than an additional four?" Drahni was no longer biting her tongue. She had kept her voice minimal, but she had reached her limit. Her chestnut brown hair was more frazzled than curly, her green eyes seeming deeper than usual after the strain of watching people close to her die.

The air in the space circulated only by the magic they possessed, and their power was used scarcely. There were things tracking them, and magic made their group easier to locate in these tunnels deep beneath any city of the living. History had shown that the Earth at one time had been an ally to humankind, but that was long ago. All living entities had a right to self-preservation, and when Magicians used it inappropriately, the Power of the Earth drew back from humanity.

Drahni tugged on the leather baldric strapped across her shoulder and shook her head. She was formidable in her own right and a Petal of the Garden, a sister among sisters in the fight against the shadow. Humans had always resisted against the darkness that wanted to consume them, and Drahni was prepared to fight against it until her very last breath.

It was accurate, everything she had said when addressing the group, but the truth was they had no other option except to keep pushing forward; however, saying what everyone else had been thinking was long overdue, and the words kept piercing her lips.

"...and now, now we have shadows moving as we move, following us!"

Movement from the rear of their group shifted their attention as she was interrupted by another who held just slightly more rank.

"Yes, we do, and we may lose more. I may be next, or you, or you... and abduction is a bit over dramatic, don't you think?" The woman, nearly three inches taller, had presence. Her black pants looked greyer from fading as did the leather belts across her waist holding her daggers. Her hair, in two ponytails, was just as black and just as tattered.

The eyes of the group followed the taller woman as she paused to scan each of their faces, everyone except her sister Elanah—the very reason each of them were in this life and death predicament.

Elanah carried within her the last two descendants in an ancient bloodline of the First Mother. The eternal war was waged between those in the light and those of the shadow. Once during each age, it was foreshadowed a battle would ensue that either brought peace or chaos across the planet. Two ages of darkness had already been survived out of the six. Could humankind survive a third as the Seventh Age progressed?

Elanah was unsure if her older sister's "*they*" included her, but she held no reservation that her life was void for the children she would give birth to. She wondered if this was the Universe's way of punishing her for having an affair with the king. Even if she was his first and only love, his responsibility and honor was to his land, his people. She knew this.

He married another from a prominent family to unite the Elemental Houses—to forge a greater unity through bloodline and prepare for the beginning of battle coming in under twenty years according to prophecy. A few years into the marriage he found out his wife was barren.

Now the king, the father to her children, was presumed dead, murdered the very night the Great Tree of Life lowered this party into the hidden chasms deep into the earth. Elanah's group couldn't be certain of anything that happened since the large branches had wrapped them whole, making them disappear beneath the very ground the ancient tree had existed since the beginning of time as it opened large mounds of earth bypassing its network of roots. They were lowered into gaping tunnels that had not been traveled. This rare act of protection extending from the Tree of Life saved their lives in the moment as the queen sought them out to question for the murder, even though she had been the instigator of her husband's death. Now the only certainty for those remaining alive was to keep moving, and Elanah, although the youngest, had assumed the leadership role.

"Yes, *all* of us are disposable if it means 'they' survive." Elanah's hand ran across the stretch marks on her belly, leaving no doubt that only the unborn children, nearly formed inside of her, mattered.

"We leave within the hour." It took her a little time to scoot upwards from the makeshift chair before beginning to organize what she could, occasionally making eye contact with her sister who shared a strong resemblance. Elanah was an inch shorter than her older sister, but they held the same brown eyes traced with blue. Their skin like caramel seemed muted against the dark clay walls. Elanah didn't always follow tradition and thus had cropped hair, nearly shaven in the back with longer twisted black strands hanging towards the front.

The silence in the space was heavy before being accented by feet moving to follow suit. The eleven-person group was made of the leftovers from a party of over forty that were "chosen" by the Tree of Life for this journey.

It wasn't a path anyone of them would've taken voluntarily. Each minute of chaos, each confrontation with creatures long forgotten, each death they suffered had been involuntary.

Watching members of their party being killed by either disease, ogres, or snakelike creatures was always a reminder to be ready.

There had been no separation between night and day. Their body's natural sleep rhythm no longer existed, nor any schedule to find sleep. The anxiousness of being confronted by another dark entity was enough to keep them awake, even when it wasn't their turn to stand watch.

What other creatures dwelled in the shadow? Had they always

secretly lived deep in the space beneath the living? How did those in governing positions downplay prophecy simply because they could not believe what their eyes failed to see?

Elanah was able to sense a change in energy only moments before each attack. Initially she believed it to be the progress of pregnancy, but she came to understand that the twins she carried were special. She surmised that her children's ability was being extended into the power of her magic.

The two in her belly had to survive. The prophecy would require three from the First Mother's bloodline, and with the king dead, this prophecy would not favor the light, but she would do her duty. She wondered if the First Mother had challenges like this.

The First Mother had an internal struggle, but she also had full control of all five elements of magic. She could see into the future in glimpses but could not decode what her visions always meant.

The First Mother and her children, and children's children, would have the power to shape the world.

The communication between the divine and humans was non-existent until the First Mother was given agency. Shared knowledge given in visions and left to decipher was just the beginning of her journey into becoming the bridge between the heavens and earth. She learned that the propensity of her lineage would do great things, but she was certain some would follow the path of the shadow. Even more distressing were many visions, elucidating that true evil existed outside of humankind and would do everything to breathe energy into this world.

The First Mother scribed her recurring visions, seven in total. Each one of her foretelling's described the battle between the light and shadow in each age. Each scribe became prophetic. Now, in the Seventh Cycle in the Seventh Age, the next battle was beginning.

Each land held some form of knowledge relating to this prophecy. However, the weight of it had been lost over a millennium ago, and only the hardcore believers held onto the past. The group members pressing forward were not hardcore believers, but they knew the unborn children were part of that prophecy.

Tiques admired the resolve in her younger sister. She had been forced to mature a little more than eight months ago after finding out Elanah was pregnant. Tiques marveled at the bond still holding between the ragged group after the challenges they faced, even as the silhouette of death hovered around them.

They couldn't be certain how many days had passed as they pressed onward without incident. It was Delda, a third sister of High Rank that made out the ocean presence first. She was the strongest in the element of water, but she held her tongue until she could get a better sense of distance. When she saw the tree roots spread wider than they were deep, she giggled loudly.

"What's so funny?" Tiques asked slowly. She had no energy to join in the laughter.

"It was a tree…" Delda paused to correct herself with a sense of accomplishment as she ran her hand through her hair. Her skin, once like alabaster, was even more pale without the energy of the sun. Her voice, however, carried vigor.

"A most ancient tree that got us into this mess, and it will be trees that get us out. Oak tree roots." She pointed to a series of extremely wide lateral root systems.

"The oak tree can survive almost anything, high winds, sandy soil… salt spray. I've made out the ocean for a day or so but wasn't certain. Now I am. We are not in the same type of tunnels we had been traveling. These passages have been created by much newer magic than those of our homeland. Can't you feel it?" Delda waited for confirmation. She had been best friends with both Tiques and Drahni, crossing into the sisterhood in the same ceremony. The shortest of the bunch, she once had golden locks that hung down her back. Now she wore her hair at shoulder length and dark flaxen, having cut it after their preceding skirmish. She was almost towed deeply into an ogre's watering hole by aquatic-snakelike creatures.

"I do. I can sense it too." Drahni paused to tap into her magic.

"I can't be certain, but I would say we are on the lower continent and near Ilens. There are multiple air currents circulating. We are close." Drahni scratched the side of her head and laughed loudly as Delda had.

Exhales could be heard as a sign of relief that their ordeal was coming to an end. No words were spoken as Drahni and Delda continued to use their magic to move the group forward, zeroing in on the scent of salt water.

Elanah could feel something wet running down her leg. It took her by surprise, and she wondered was wetting herself something due to pushing herself harder to get them out of harm's way? She was overwhelmed with the responsibility of each life lost thus far. Many were her sisters in the fight against the shadow, and she knew all the guardians who had perished.

Elanah had pains and an intense tightening and release in her abdomen. It wasn't her losing the function of her bladder; her water had just broken.

"Damnit, or blessings, looks like you're going to be an aunt very soon!" she exclaimed loudly.

Her older sister began to give instruction on setting up an impromptu delivery station. That's when a different smell permeated the space, overpowering the salt water.

The joy was short-lived as Elanah's eyes went wide and she observed the same precursor of energy present each moment before they were attacked.

The group searched out, attempting to pinpoint the overwhelming scent of rotten eggs and burnt ash, and that's when the ground shook behind them as if the earth itself had detonated.

Rodents and insects skittered along the same course the group traveled before a large dark mass swooped towards them.

Those with earth magic agreed that it appeared to be the residual of an earthquake some far distance away and the eruption not as great as it seemed.

Elanah gave a sigh of relief and aimed to reassure them, even when she was still uncertain.

"It doesn't feel like we are near the epicenter, but we should be close to finally escaping. We can follow these winged varmints to the promised land. I will hold on until I can't because I don't want my children to be birthed in the dark." She removed her hand from her older sister's and pressed forward with assistance from two of the other women.

The sisters who claimed it to be an earthquake were hesitant to follow behind the others in the group. They could sense something else, another presence fading in and out of the vibrations. That's when they saw *them* forming from the cave walls.

Cave creatures had been formed in the past by the most powerful magicians in the history of their planet. These abhorrent creations could take the form of that which they hunted. Some were shaped as humans, but others looked like hybrids only written about in history books—animal heads with human bodies or the very opposite. The unseen power being used to form them had to be in close proximity, and if so, the group needed to travel faster, or they'd never make it out of that tunnel.

The remaining guardsmen turned to face the onslaught with special trinkets to protect them against magic. These ornaments were created to deflect mystical energy. Worn as necklaces or jewelry, their power acted as a protective barrier, and for now, it would be the skill and honor that each creature would meet at the end of the guardsmen's blades.

"No, keep moving!" The oldest remaining sister turned to see all five ready to greet death by their own choosing, but only one guardian turned ever so slowly to face the sister. His eyes spoke everything he could not say, and they could not be deterred.

"Nissa!"

The elder woman turned from him as her name was called. She ran to her sister, feeling guilt, but Elanah's children surviving was paramount.

The two women who trailed sprinted to catch up with the others who were still advancing, ushering Elanah forward while she fought deepening contractions.

Her children were conduits of pure magic, and all of the spectrums were visible: amber golds, crimson reds, aqua blues, emerald greens. Her power increased each time her contractions occurred. She had not had the gift of vision to see or use these additional forms of elemental magic before, but now she did.

The guardsmen could be heard fighting against the hordes, but the small barrier they held was being overrun as the wards in their charms diminished with each attack. They were surrounded. The first guardian went down and was pulled into the same earth being used to create the horde.

Nissa understood the sacrifice the men were making. It was no less than the one she was willing to make for the children's safety.

"Juli, stop!" Nissa called out.

Nissa met her sister's eyes and saw the confusion.

"We are right there, Nissa. Come on! Let's go. We can make it too!" Juli was adamant they could catch up to the group, but the last guardsmen fell.

"They can. We cannot," Nissa said without emotion. She reached out for Juli's hand and waited.

Hesitantly, Juli took it and dove into their magic. Each of them accepted their fear and embraced it, allowing it to reach into their magic. They would be the shield they were created to be.

Higher level magicians could bond their energies to form new vibrations and frequencies that individual magic could not. Visually the hues of each energy could be seen in minimal traces but as their connection strengthened, the colors of magic intertwined. The exponential increase in power was enormous as the colorful strands deepened. These Petals were the highest-level magicians.

Elanah looked back as the last guardian yelled out before being pulled into the abyss. She could make out the intensity of cerise reds and golden yellows extending from her two sisters now sacrificing themselves as the guardsmen had.

"No!"

Elanah broke free from the trio of women still hauling her forward and crumpled under the loss of her home, the man she loved, and those who had been killed during this trek. Rage fueled the magic coursing through her veins. She pulled in energy from each element. Like a puzzle the various elements intertwined and bonded together to form a complete magical ensemble.

A large portion of the cave creatures had been shredded by Juli and Nissa, but for each one killed, another two advanced.

Tiques knew it was out of her control, the responsibility of protecting her younger sister and the children that she carried. She rushed to Elanah's side as did the final two sisters. They embraced their power as the elemental magic was still attaching.

The vivacity of the power was visible to the sisters remaining. Swirls of blue green energy blended with intense sun fire-reds. She glowed like a golden yellow-amber sun. The elemental magic was pushed forward through all the darkness, and in that moment, Elanah had complete authority over all the magic inside their tunnel.

She moved forward, ahead of the remaining women who were now in stasis. She closely connected her hands and fingers, casting a spell none of them had ever seen. The pressure was noticeable as the magic she controlled forced the cave creatures back into the walls, leaving behind only the large silhouette of a shadow still advancing. For the first time they could see their adversary, the power controlling those beasts, the darkness.

Elanah was bombarded with all the emotional sadness for the people that had died or been killed since the journey began.

As she continued advancing through the chaos deep beneath the earth, a bright light emitted from her hands. The brilliance of the light shot outward into the entire cavern, lighting the space and revealing additional passageways.

As the light traveled towards the dark agent, there was a momentary hesitation in the black profile, and that millisecond was its demise. The intensity of white light dazzled around the silhouette of the shadow, and that's when the ground grumbled more violently. The organism of evil began to pulse as the light penetrated through it.

Elanah pressed forward until she was less than three feet from the creature.

"You are the first sacrifice for my children who will protect the light and destroy your dark master!" She stared into the shadow before turning her back as it began to finally cry out in agony. The spell she cast combined precise amounts of elemental magic in balance, creating white light which burned the shadow agent with illumination from the inside-out.

After one last surge of white light, the shadow no longer existed.

Elanah began to wobble.

Tiques was first to reach her sister before she crashed into the earth floor.

The remaining sisters held their tongue, having just witnessed the force of the bloodline.

"Don't just stand there. Help me. We have less than a half-mile until we are free from these caves." Tiques altered their course after sensing the open ocean air from a separate tunnel that had been illuminated.

Elanah could barely walk; her contractions had been minimized while controlling the magic, but now they were even more frequent.

Her children could no longer wait.

For the first time in over two hundred and forty days, they had a reason to believe they would be free from this perilous journey and the task they were set on would be accomplished.

Nissa was first to smell the sulfur stench again, and Drahni could sense the vibration beneath their feet shaking the space. They were not out of harm's way yet.

Elanah yelled out, but she was in no position to repeat the greatness she had just performed.

Tiques looked at Nissa and Juli with an emotion in her eyes they instantly understood. This was the final sacrifice each of them would make.

Nissa and Juli bonded again. Delda separated herself from those carrying Elanah. She added to the bond of her sisters. An intensity of vibrancy overpowered the large tunnel, illuminating the cylindrical chamber. Their magic appeared in crisp sapphire and rich jade colors streamlined into sandy yellows and bolts of crimson. Their magic strengthened exponentially. This trio would be enough to give those now carrying Elanah ample time to escape. Once out in the open, their magic would intensify, and the shadow would not pursue.

A scream ripped from Elanah's throat. She was trying not to push, but her body had other intentions.

"They are coming whether we want them to or not!" Elanah

bellowed.

The walls began to shake all around them as they kept moving.

Drahni glanced back less than ten feet from the exit. Nissa, Juli, and Delda held the line. Their magic, displayed by their practiced hand movements, had pin-point precision. The force of their magic emitted an energy shield with enough pressure to thwart any advancement from the entities returned to kill them all.

It was Tiques trying to slow down as they crossed the threshold of the cave. Drahni turned, but it was too late. The momentum carried them out of the tunnel, but Drahni edged them too far and their next steps had them falling downward towards a fast-raging river forty feet below.

AE 798

CHAPTER ONE
Morning Salutations

The toll of the bell from the first tower told Anel Improvi that soon others would be waking, starting a fresh new day.

The darkness of dawn was slowly erasing, still hanging on to its last moment of passing. Anel had not slept last night or the night before as she balanced the weight of full disclosure.

'Should answers be given to a question not posed?'

With the heaviness of knowledge she now possessed from the historians and with the new age looming around the corner, concern filled her. Her black shoulder length hair, frazzled, hung loosely like the reading glasses on the chain around her neck.

Anel looked over the aged parchment. It was filled with symbols and names long forgotten, written by a 'crazed mind' as others called him. With the bundle of documents the historians had drummed up, she noticed her heartbeat flutter and her palms begin to sweat. This was different than political maneuvering with the Speaker of Carcero or Emissaries from Medellin. It would be personal.

Taking one final look at the ancestral tree of the writer of the scroll, she understood that today had to be the day. She rolled up the faded parchment and then fastened the original green vine around it. This vine, if the stories were true, was substantially older than her one-hundred and four years.

'*It must be true.*' Anel removed her glasses and laid them on the table next to the scroll. She looked around the small enclave. Memories flooded back to herself as a child, with her twin sister. It had been over fifteen years since they had seen each other, but through their unique magic, they could sense each other when they slept. Anel smiled, thinking about her sister Somerset, and exhaled before sliding her chair back under the table.

The oxygen always remained fresh inside this study area; her magic was useful in closed spaces like this. Air was the breath of life, of ideas and action. This lesson had been drilled into the very fabric of her being since a child.

She pulled an empty glass from the table and then reached down, lifting the pitcher containing only traces of the orange blossom tea she drank as the night passed into day.

This room was unknown to all except for her sister. With the combined power of their gifts, they carved out the space when they were children to get away from the seniors and their teachings.

Now she was grateful to be versed in the history of all the known land and their multiple prophecies. Some were just superstitions traveling from generation to generation, each time being slightly altered until only fragments of the original scripture remained.

This was different.

What she had studied each night over the past year held so many words and symbols—symbols that she recognized from the people of the First Nation before it split. Words in other languages long forgotten, but as she taught herself to decipher portions of the texts, one line always gave her pause.

"In the seventh cycle of the Seventh Age, two will leave, yet three shall return." This minor sentence stuck in her mind like the pebbles and worn stones holding their community together, always shifting but forever standing strong through war and the changing landscape. This was the time of the seventh cycle in the Seventh Age. The rumors that the king sired two outside of wedlock could never be substantiated, but with the ousting of the Rose of the Garden over fifteen years ago, anything was possible.

Anel made plans to speak with the Emissaries from Medellin when they came to honor the First Master's dinner. Specifically, she would seek the counsel of an original Petal she had forged a friendship with a long time ago. If her daughter was a descendant of the First Mother, all was not lost. The children of the king hadn't been found in the fifteen years after he was murdered, and one descendant was better than none.

Reaching the top of the small incline, she closed the bookcase behind her. The coldness of the stones beneath her feet sent a chill through her body. This secret room was thought out carefully when she and her sister created it for many of the exotic, forbidden, and banned literature to be kept secured. They placed wards on the eight by ten-foot space and kept it simple—a table and two chairs with multiple candles. It was the best place to hide since the room was in an area that many would not frequent.

Anel and her sister Somerset were right. They would disappear for hours, and no one found them.

Her home took on a different feel this morning. Typically, she woke and had her entire day planned, but she was uncertain if she would need time to process her emotions, as well as calm her daughter's feelings after the ensuing talk.

The land of Ledoma had not yet been invaded by any yearning of returning to its glorious days when the Magicians were plentiful amongst them. A few buildings and other remnants remained from nearly a half-millennium ago, only held firm by the magic used to create them like the great circular assembly hall itself. She was still in awe of the governing chamber becoming a source of energy the night before as the Assembly of Senior's contemplated if they should sell land to a neighboring country. An elder had insinuated another wasn't speaking truthfully, raising conflict. In what she believed to be a measured response, the *lifestick* Anel carried emitted a power source that charged the entire chamber with elemental energy never seen before.

Ledoma was one of two lands that held onto tradition, but the number of those able to wield magic was diminishing. The States of Medellin had the highest number of initiates studying in newly constructed elemental houses. These new age magicians had taken on the ways of their ancestors and those who had previously been taught in the shadow of the Tree of Life. Those taught in the Motherland were called Petals once their training was complete. They contained a wide variety of secret knowledge passed down over generational cycles and were led by the Rose of the Garden—the leader selected by the Tree of Life.

Anel heard the pitter patter of a small animal run across the hatched roof of their home, and it brought her back into the present moment.

The cypress wax that had been left burning throughout the night on her mantle had invigorated the room with its scent. Her attention was drawn to another set of feet scurrying across the roof, making its way across the interconnected homes of common citizens.

The early song of the morning birds drew her attention. For those who listened intently, the chorus between the early blackbird and robin created a rhapsody. With each ascending moment of the sun rising, other feathered friends joined in. The tawny owl and chaffinch always followed their feathered companions in the melody. Every now and then various warblers made their presence known.

Anel found many answers when listening to the voices of nature, and her thoughts rose and fell with each note.

Her head throbbed, so instead of pressing the thought, she dipped her finger into the large metal basin to heat the water in it. She did not have the magic of fire needed to burn brush or an amulet to enhance her magic to clear new acres for crops. Only a handful of individuals had ever wielded that much natural power in Ledoma, and only one was still alive.

Anel had enough of the fire magic that she would never have to wait for a tub of hot water. As she disrobed, she paid closer attention to her scars—some from playing with others as children and some from accidents when learning how to use her magic.

However, it was the scar at her hip that kept her attention. It was the source of her greatest loss and most significant gain. The textured reminder of when she and Somerset had been separated as conjoined twins.

She slid into the basin, closed her eyes, and yelled for her life-daughter Nana. Nana should have been awake, but Anel knew that she had been up gambling with her sister-friend Ransa.

...

Nana rolled over and put the pillows over her head when she had heard the first bell. The morning had come too soon, and just as she settled in, she heard her name being called and dreaded to answer.

"Yes, Mother." Nana paused, knowing what her mother was going to say next. It had been the same for nearly two decades.

"Bathe and get dressed. Today begins anew." Always constant and consistent was her mother, and that was why many had called for her over the years to settle both minor and major disputes.

"Yes, Mother, I will be ready within the hour!" she exclaimed before watching her friend shift the covers down to reveal her face. Their home was a larger cottage, adjoined by a single door and a fireplace.

"I don't have the energy to listen to your mother this morning. After yesterday morning and the ten thousand questions she asked, you have to count me out." One of her closest friends Ransa rolled out of the bed and put her leggings on. She let her cotton shift drape down and pulled her worn leather boots onto her feet. The two younger women had slept less than two hours after spending time in the gambling quarters.

"Bogus, like I want to listen to her thoughts on what my future with the civilian council will be. I'm trying to get enough coin, so when you've completed your studies, we can go. All three of us." Nana sat up in her oversized bed and propped her back up against the stuffed quilted pillows.

"Uhm, yeah, I know. Who's been burning the candle at both ends for you? The first thing I need to do is go climb in my bed and sleep the last few hours before I return to…" She paused to change voices:

"*Little girl, if it takes you this long to make tea, you'd never make it as a healer, or Who do you think you are to question what we have done for the past…* blah blah blah." She let out a laugh louder than intended and hoped Anel didn't hear her.

"You're still bogus." Nana scooted off her bed, nearly tripping on the corner edge of her blanket to give her friend a hug.

"Until the children return."

"Until the children return." After grabbing her small travel bag, Ransa unlatched the door to leave. The four words were an essential prayer known across all lands. It was the way to acknowledge that the First Mother and her descendants were the only conduits to return the planet to peace.

Ransa inhaled slowly and stretched one last time.

"Come find me this afternoon." She closed the door behind her.

Nana was still dragging about; it was the cost of winning coin against gamblers, and it was a price she was willing to pay. She won more often than she lost, and when she did lose, it was Ransa picking up the currency. Nana knew that games of chance were more about luck, so she gravitated towards cards. Calculating odds was important with cards, but knowing opponent's habits was even more critical. The stash she had accumulated over the last two years could buy two horses or perhaps a horse with a wagon along with other provisions for when she got the courage to leave Ledoma with her friends. The three of them did not share the same parents, but they were more sisters than friends. They were family.

'*One day, Mother will have to let me see the world, even if she thinks that I am not ready for it.*'

The chill of the morning was slight as the seasons were changing. Nana's eyes scanned for the fire starter salve and found it laying on top of a bundle of wood stacked in the corner of the room. It would take two logs, thrown into the black stone hearth to heat the water for her basin. Staring into the flames, she remained by the fireplace with eyes half open.

The oranges mixed with red and yellow like notes to music. Each dance of fire seemed to change before her eyes, flashing with images of past events: mages riding dragons and giants who stood nearly twenty feet tall. These visions were not limited to only this morning. She was swarmed with faces of those she didn't recognize personally, only in the books she had studied. She envisioned relics of creatures that patrolled the deep seas during the Great Battle that split the world.

Nana would not disclose any of it, including to her mother. Strange visions were often seen as the onset of a mental ailment. Being touched with the 'crazies', as her father had been labeled, was an association she didn't want.

A dog barking was an indication the neighbors were moving about. With her basin of water now heated, she retrieved a face cloth and the rosemary soap she had taken from her mother's room previously.

'*Why do people wake so damn early? I'm definitely not a morning person.*' The water continued to heat as she bathed.

Nana dressed after washing, choosing a blue cotton dress and gray leggings. The gray cloak wrapped around her shoulders was held together by a gold clasp her mother had given her the day prior. She sat at the edge of her bed and slid her feet into deep blue leather sandals.

Her dark brunette hair was braided and pulled into a ponytail that blanketed the small tattoo on her neck. It was covering a birthmark, the only thing she had taken from her father that she could remember.

Nana smoothed on the last bit of golden aloe to moisturize her copper-toned skin. She put a mixture of yogurt and apple paste on a fresh leaf to clean her teeth and then gargled with mint water. After pouring the remaining dregs into the fire, she opened the passage between her mother's space and her own.

"I see you have gotten your usual amount of sleep. We will see how the new buds have opened this morning. This afternoon you must attend the lessons of the Assembly and stay until they are complete. Tomorrow, you can join me for dinner with the First Masters. Your time for games will be passing soon. There is such a beautiful and exciting life waiting for you." Anel met her daughter at the door and kissed her once on each cheek.

'*After a full day, my daughter will beg for sleep if she is not broken.*'

It was a foregone conclusion that it would lead to more questions. She grabbed Nana's hand and walked out of the front door of their adjoined cottages.

CHAPTER TWO
In the Blink of an Eye

The wind pushed gently across the morning hours, and the sunlight that extended from sky to earth became more frequent. Two brown and white patched dogs fought over meat scraps thrown from the window of a neighbor's home before looking up to notice the two women approaching.

Anel could have chosen to live amongst the other Assembly members in more modern abodes, but she was born of the people and would remain with the people. It was essential that her daughter understand the lives of those she had been chosen to help govern. Even as she aged to over one-hundred years, she never believed herself as separate from the people.

As the two women moved from the housing area, a husband and wife passed them, walking hand in hand. The love they shared after ninety-years of marriage was still present. Initially startled, the couple greeted the mother and daughter with grins.

The husband perked up. "Good morning to you both."

"Indeed, it is when surrounded by good friends." Anel smiled and secured her staff across her back strap. Her *lifestick* was a branch from the Tree of Life. It amplified the magic of those who were selected to receive it, and not all who in the Order of Petals had received the gift.

In the distance four guards were seen. Their task was to monitor the worn-down cobblestone roads at night for safety. The job simple, as there had been no violent crime for over fifty years. Those who performed lower-level criminal acts were sent to a prison colony to pay with time to be served.

The guards bid Anel and Nana good morning. Two of the men went back to talking while the other two smiled and followed Nana with their eyes, hoping to gain her attention.

Anel understood that with her daughter being of age it was more than conversation most men sought after. The older woman didn't know if Nana held interest in men yet, but she held no reservations that her daughter had learned about value and worth by sitting in on various council matters from childhood to now, or by witnessing her mother lead the group of seniors by always putting the community of Lake Ledoma first. The value of the many outweighed the individual.

As a parent, Anel knew she could point in the right direction, but she could not walk the steps for her. Anel had prepared her daughter physically because she was skilled in 'haishu', secret techniques of combat, as were their closest friends. The art form of fighting had been lost except for a few gypsy clans who still practiced. She worried she had not prepared her enough for those moments of unexpected emotion.

Black squirrels ran up trees and hid their morning forage while some of the carts were being set up to get a head start on today's buying and selling in the marketplace. Another group on horseback were headed deeper into the woods for a three-day hunt. Each day was like this, and it was this unchanged mode in their day-to-day lives that solidified this land. Tradition was always within reach and always used to fall back on when uncertainty presented itself.

Surprises were saved for the festival of games, whether they were the small yearly festivals of the villages that surrounded the lake, or the Great Festival, which took place every ten years within the very grounds of the ancient temple. Timed with the rise of new seniors into the Assembly, the ten-year festival brought tens of thousands to witness.

Nana detected their walk to the lake seemed a little different this morning. The surrounding grass and shrubs were all the same. The trees with the morning dew were in the same place as they had always been as she took in the wholeness of the moment, but she realized her mother had not paid attention like she always had before. On most days she called out the various birds and spoke about historical facts. Instead, on that morning, she stared forward as if something stood before her that she could not calculate.

Nana tugged on her braids. Her natural tanned, brown complexion was nature's gift. Her hazel eyes had blue specks along their outline, creating a stunning effect.

'This business with the Council must really be pressing.' That must have been the reasoning behind why she was ordered to attend the gathering later with her mother.

A raccoon emerged from an area of waist high bushes with an ear of purple corn in its grasp. It stared at both mother and daughter before quickly running across the dirt trail into another random set of shrubs.

Nana laughed and tugged on her braids again. She hadn't developed too many habits in her eighteen years, but pulling her hair was one of them.

"It will simply require time and pressure to make you the diamond you are." Anel spoke out of nowhere, catching Nana off guard.

Nana had no idea where the comment had arisen, but she let the thought fade. She didn't want to have a long discussion on how she could help the citizens of Ledoma, especially not as the day was just beginning.

Music always calmed her, so she began to hum a random melody.

As they neared the fork in the road, Anel reached back and took her daughter by the hand before beginning to sing along as the younger woman, rounding her eighteenth year hummed. It appeared that Anel understood she didn't need to press anything right now; she would wait until they settled at the lake. What she had to share with her daughter wasn't something she looked forward to.

It had taken Nana time to accept that she would never have a traditional family with history and stories to tell. It wasn't until the fifth year of being in Anel's care that she understood love. Love was complete acceptance.

Immense trees surrounded the outer banks of this abundant source of life of the Lower Continent. B'nobi, the first daughter of the First Mother, had blessed this lake herself.

Along its shoreline, plants and flowers grew. The Mandarin bellflower had wedge shaped petals that turned brilliant orange as it blossomed. Purple heart-shaped plants grew alongside the Mandarin. These rounded flowers were just small pieces of a larger puzzle that merged into one.

The birds sang, greeting the sun as it made its grand return for another day. They communicated to each other in a flurry of chirps that somehow sang together in unison. Multitudes of wildlife ventured in, adding more life to this majestic landscape.

Anel, an elder, was also the High Priestess of B'Nobi, and began each morning here at the lake before diving into the business of politics. She had done so nearly every day for her entire life, one hundred and two years. For over the past eighteen years, her life-daughter Nana had accompanied her.

Nana was not a child by any means, save one. Standing nearly as tall as her mother she knew much of the ways of the wind and water, but she held no magic to manipulate the elements. Her birth mother died when Nana was only one year of age, and her father was forced to leave shortly after she was conceived. Over the years the distinction between natural mother and life mother had been lost.

'*The first sun is always beautiful.*' Anel watched Nana move away to take her sandals off to dip her feet in the southern end of the lake. Arriving close to sunrise, the sun had already started its day. Its glow manifested brilliantly, bringing light across the land. Anel would allow her daughter to enjoy one more lovely moment before their talk.

Nana believed they were here this early to survey the long-pointed sundews and the new flowering plants scattered around the crystal blue water.

Anel knew otherwise.

For a while she had debated on telling Nana the truth of her parents, that her father believed himself to be of the First Mother's bloodline. After receiving the parchment from the historians, Anel wasn't certain if what he said was completely accurate but knew it had to come from her lips. For this reason, she scribed what she could remember along with all that she knew of Nana's parents to give to her to read. She even wrote down the words Nana's father had spoken on the night he was forced to leave Ledoma.

'If I do not find a way across the fog, she must. I shall name her 'Bearer of Harmony'. A name mentioned in the Prophecy of the Seventh Age.

Nana was old enough for the truth; Anel would tell her all she knew and give her the notes left behind by her father that had come into her possession.

Fish jumped in and out of the water, seemingly reaching for heaven. The height and frequency of their jumps decreased as the larger birds soared through the sky to eye their morning meal.

A different scent wafted in the morning wind than the floral fragrances.

'*Pungent.*' Anel wasn't sure what caused the pervasive smell. There were no dead carcasses of any animal within her view.

'*Something is not right.*'

The hair on her arms and neck stood up. A large obscurity caught Anel's eye moving slowly from the pocket of air made under the gushing stream to where the water fell onto large smokey almond boulders and spat back up towards the edge it rushed over.

Grave concern fell across her face as she watched the shadows transform into figures.

A mental picture of the beast flashed in her mind before she saw them.

'*Soachim.*' Aberrations created to serve the Dark Master.

The beasts shook the water from their hairy coats and crept closer. Larger than cart horses, they resembled oversized canines but with six legs. Where each paw touched, the newly sprung willows lining the bank began to wither. The hounds sniffed through the air and caught the scent of their human prey.

Her gaze shifted from the base of the waterfall to the area Nana had occupied last. She wasn't there; Nana had moved away from the shoreline, towards the thicket near the trees, her sandals in hand. Her viewpoint, partially blocked, kept her line of sight minimal.

'*If we can just make it to the trees for some type of cover.*' The thought moved through Anel as she looked back to the sprightly moving waterfall. As she did, the horrendous stench from the beasts followed the same course as the wind. The odor, like thousands of dead bodies piled one on top of another, was insufferable. These beasts came from ancient evil, given life through sacrificial flesh and the dark magic of their Creator. The Soachim would attack any being or creature in the area that was present, and they were designed for one purpose only: bring death.

"Nana, run!" Anel's voice rang out loudly.

Anel came from the same Assembly that fought these beasts and the evil that produced these creature's many centuries before.

'*These creatures should not be.*' She reached for the currents in the air that she would soon be using to fight them off. She could hold three, maybe four in this open area. There were six.

As the six-legged canines sprang from the base of the waterfall, two of the beasts circled around her as if to bar Anel's exit.

"Stupid creatures..." she said coolly with a smile that would break ice,

"I will never run from you!"

The animals that weren't agile or quick were slaughtered by two of the beasts separated from the larger pack who advanced, destroying everything in their path. The horrific shrieks shook Anel to the core, but it did not slow her. She needed a little time to help Nana escape.

Anel composed herself, twisting her cape and using the force of the wind to hurl the first hound into the lake. She required total concentration. She pulled her *lifestick* from her back and reached deeper into the magic at her call.

The Soachim, being earthborn, were somehow elementally protected against water. Anel needed fire. At best she could transfix them into a bundle held together with the dynamics of the wind but containing all six would require every source of her power.

The air in the valley shifted wildly as miniature columns of air circulated to elevate her high above the earth, using the currents to guide her body back and forth.

Anel would not turn back; she was fully engulfed in the power radiating from the midst of her spirit. The leaves and plants flew in the wind, circulating in small pockets like oval staircases.

The Soachim edged forward, fighting the swirling winds to reach her. Nothing of this world could stand against such power.

Vicious snarls revealed their razor-sharp teeth. Now that they had tasted blood from this realm, they would not surrender. Their low growls could be heard and felt deep within the earth. Their hindquarters tensed as they moved forward.

One touch from them would paralyze, and then she would be at their mercy, of which they granted none.

The water rose above its inner banks to flood the surrounding grounds. Its color began to change from crystal-blue to murky earth. Anel pulled from the energy created by the surrounding waves crashing against the bank of the shore and boulders. Air magic was her primary element while water her second. The maize and pale blue strands of her spell-working faded in and out as she maneuvered the currents of air. It was rare for actual elemental magic to be seen. Only those supremely powerful had this ability. Her movements were quick and dynamic to complete the binding. She commanded the flows of air securing them together. She had four of the beasts connected when she suffered pain on her back.

'*How could they have reached me?*' She considered her options.

The burning was faint at first, but it grew quickly like a brush fire.

She felt the yellow mist, saw the flowers and wild-leafed blue grass dying all around. The energy she commanded was returning to a different form, no longer under her spell.

She would not feel sorrow now. She would hold on until Nana escaped.

Anel struggled as her hold on the beasts loosened. The flame red eyes of the Soachim displayed hatred of being born again into this world of humans.

The wind subsided as Anel reluctantly accepted her strength departing and her binding undone. The beasts sent were free to claim her soul for their master.

Darkness fell across the lake, and the sun disappeared.

She fell.

As the Soachim leaped to claim her, their bodies were jerked back and forth. Fire erupted all around Anel, but she had no awareness of heat. The Soachim were on fire. They tried to plunge into the lake, yet an even more ferocious wind bound them. The howls echoed from the trees all the way to the limestone castle walls. Tiny fragments and only the charred remains of the earth were left in the place they had stood.

Anel's vision blurred… She knew she was dying.

Nana approached her side out of nowhere, panting, her chest heaving. Fear colored her words as she looked down.

"No, Mother, you cannot die. You must not. I forbid you from dying!" Nana was hysterical, reaching out, placing her mother's head in her arms; Anel was the only mother she had truly known. Tears streamed down her face.

"You need water. Let me get you some water!"

Anel was burning from the poison seeping through her veins and dragging her into the void. She coughed, her breathing labored. Anel's voice was weak, barely a whisper as she held onto her daughter's arm.

"I am Anel Improvi, daughter of Elya, eldest priestess of B'Nobi, mother to Nana. I live as you… with you. I am wind bound and waterborne." Her voice seemed to strengthen as the air returned to its original state. The oaks and hickories stood upright, and the lake waters calmed, but the damage had already been done. Peace fell over Anel as she looked up at her life-daughter.

"You have a task. You will choose to accept it as I and others have. Inside the second bedroom chamber, behind the bookcase, you will find an entrance to the room where I study the great mysteries. There are scrolls. One written by the hand of your father. They belong to you now. You have a role to play in the battles coming and the knowledge within them will help to prepare you for what comes next." Anel paused, grabbing Nana's hand and her fading voice spoke measures beyond wisdom.

"Today begins anew just like the seeds from the Tree of Life. As the seed bears roots, it grows independent, standing on its own. You are no longer Nana, standing in my shadow. You have become Naiyan Amitsa, Bearer of Harmony, Priestess of B'Nobi, daughter to Anel." The final words her mother spoke, were followed by Naiyan screaming out loudly before she lost consciousness.

CHAPTER THREE
Nourishment

The clasp her mother had given her was made of solid gold. As she passed the clasp back and forth between her fingers she realized it had never left her possession once it had been given. For nearly three weeks, Naiyan refused to venture out into the city. Not since the life ceremony was held in her mothers' memory.

Dignitaries from lands far away came to pay their respects. The Speaker of Carcero sent delegates to express her deepest condolences, vowing to keep the two lands relationship the same. Anel Improvi was revered for her unmatched power in air wielding, yet even more so in the wisdom she possessed and friendships she had made.

The musicians made Anel Improvi's passing a light-hearted tribute; however, Naiyan remained sullen and heavy-hearted. Ransa, and her other sister-friend Imani, shielded Naiyan from over-indulgent guests who were more interested in the ancient books her mother had than in Naiyan's well-being.

Ransa stopped short of cursing at a Senior who attempted to enter Anel Improvi's home without permission. Everything that Anel owned was passed to Nana—no, *Naiyan*. Now anyone wanting anything, regardless of their stature, would have to get them with her permission.

"*Naiyan Amitsa*." The change in name mildly baffled her. Although some name changes were common among those who graduated into higher levels of magic, she hadn't received one. It was her new task that added to the confusion brought on by the death of the only mother she remembered. She was empty of emotion, a chasm that she did not know how to fill.

A few elder priests and members of the community came to pay a personal respect to Naiyan after the life-ceremony. She accepted them into her portion of the home because it was expected; her mother would have required showing hospitality.

"*Manners are nearly as important as hygiene*." The words seemed to echo louder each time she reminisced about little sayings her mother offered randomly. Naiyan bathed but had not fixed her hair or cared to change her clothes daily. Today, she had mustered the energy to not only bathe but clean her teeth.

She appreciated all that was done for her but could not get the image of her mother falling out of her mind, nor could she undo the words echoing through her spirit. "*You have a task ahead of you... Bearer of Harmony*."

Naiyan had no formal training in manipulating the elements. She understood a few of the hand movements required to cast certain magic. She was able to read various languages as an adolescent, and over time, she was able to decipher ancient texts and symbols like Anel. This skill had proven invaluable when travelers from lands far away arrived as she often interpreted. Her mother understood how powerful knowledge and language were, even if application of said power wasn't feasible.

Now, she was given a name, full of expectation. Naiyan was certain that she could not meet the task and would be ridiculed in time.

'*Bearer of Harmony.*' A title she didn't earn. She would be made a mockery by both senior and citizen. The more she thought about how her life was no longer the same, the more she cried.

She attempted formulating plans to leave Ledoma in the first two weeks. After all, she had money to support herself. She was unsure what would happen to her home after she left.

Strangely enough, she still had not entered her mother's side of their joined cottages, let alone the room behind the bookcase where the items her mother said were left for her.

Now watching the only father-figure she had known pace her living space, she was finally able to breathe slightly.

Iver Balent was also a dear friend of Anel Improvi just as his wife had been.

His belly stuck out slightly at his waistline, but his body was sturdy and strong. Iver maintained his position in the armed guard even though he had been welcomed as a senior. He walked back and forth between the fireplace and one of two square eating tables, figuring out his next move.

His black linen draw string pants were a new design his daughter created. Stopping short at the ankles and cuffed, he accepted most men his age would say he was foolish but had learned a long time ago to let go of his ego. The matching linen T-shirt was hemmed at the elbows, and the V-neck design around the chest was fastened with delicate drawstring. Once a strapping young youth with the world at his feet, he fell in love and married, and now he had the world in his heart.

"I see Imani is still making you her fashion test subject. I kinda actually like this although I think a more natural color would be better with your hair changing." Naiyan relaxed her mouth and attempted to smirk, not letting this perfect moment pass to remind him he wasn't as spry as he once used to be.

"I think this will have to grow on me. I'm a traditionalist. Full length garments for me are sufficient, but my daughter has a lot of her mother in her. Telling her no was not the answer, and if my family's genetics tell me anything, I can't hold off the argent change in hair color no matter how much I try." He smiled and pushed a small silver cart towards her.

He was dropping off her favorite sweet, Calizi squares, a small chocolate pastry with a coconut filling and lemon topping. Although the treat was simple, to bake the delight properly took skill.

"Nana…" He began to say before correcting himself. Tradition was to be honored.

"Naiyan, you must eat even if it is only a nibble now and then…" He paused to hold back certain emotions.

Naiyan had lost weight and, from the dark circles under her eyes, had lost sleep as well. Her cheeks, once full, were now hollow, and her eyes held no sparkle for life. The traces of beauty remained, hidden behind anguish.

He had been present when she was born; his wife Chachan and Anel delivered her. From that moment, he loved her as if she was his very own. His heart ached, Naiyan no longer held the joy of life in her grasp.

Iver watched the woman stare at the pastry tray.

Patience.

He knew she would eat in her own time. However, he needed answers as to what really happened the morning his dear friend Anel was killed as did the Assembly of Seniors, but now his only role was in supporting Naiyan.

"Besides, I do not want to be the one to tell my wife that the Calizi went untouched." His attempt at wit was light, but his words about giving an explanation to his wife ran to her stomach.

Naiyan sat with her legs crossed, thumbing the gold clasp between her fingers before rocking forward. She stretched and placed the jewelry in the sack at her waist.

Her light cerulean dress unfolded as she walked toward Iver. Her braided hair fell down her back until she moved it all to one side. Her skin was ashy and needed olive oil and honey.

"If your sisters see you like this, I'm afraid you'll never hear the end of it." Iver hugged her and pointed to her container of moisturizer.

"Funny, but you're very right." The tightening feeling in her stomach brought her attention back to the silver tray. The cramps first caused by crying and now hunger made her appreciate having family. Besides she really did not want to be giving excuses to Chachan.

"Thank you, Master Iver, for everything." Naiyan pulled one of the three wooden chairs away from the table and sat. She offered him a chair. He declined.

She slid up to one of two square tables, reached out, and selected a piece of baked sweetness. Holding it in her hands, she bowed her head and closed her eyes.

"Thank you."

Two simple words offered to the Creator. The first kind words spoken in prayer since Anel had died. Naiyan's affinity for pastries and chocolate delights were legendary, and before she knew it, she had devoured three.

She caught herself grinning as she ate with a mouthful of pastry.

He returned her smile but wondered if she would ever be able to remember the events at the lake the morning her mother was killed. She had been found unconscious at the side of Anel Improvi by those first to arrive on scene. It had taken two days for her to come out of her sleep, and when she woke, she had only the recollection of her mother's final words.

Seniors gathered in the assembly chamber, debating what happened, and demanded that answers be found. *Was this an attack on Ledoma or a singular person? Who could wield such powers and go unnoticed*? Each question asked led to even more questions. The only person who could answer some of the questions posed was Naiyan, and she was still grieving.

Iver along with the general of their armed force were tasked to ensure the safety of all the communities surrounding the lake five miles in each direction. Local groups banded together to protect their farms and other property outside of the weathered city by adding citizen patrols.

'*All of that was for show, small measures for a large problem.*' Iver let go of the thought as he stared at Naiyan, wondering how she had not been killed.

Naiyan reached for a small linen cloth to wipe the bits of chocolate from her fingers before she spoke up.

"Mother would've given me two tongues had I eaten these as fast as I have." She smiled awkwardly. The taste of the baked sweet also helped her realize that she needed more than just a dessert.

"Your mother knew exceptions were always factored into the equation. That's what made Anel great at settling disputes between children and nations." Iver shuffled his feet as he walked to open the wooden shutters.

"Excuse me one moment." He pivoted towards the door as if he were departing.

"I'd like to keep those closed if you don't..."

He ignored her words before he opened the hinged front door. In the small entrance of the doorway, the entirety of his wife's doing was waiting.

Peppered beef and seasoned fowl, spiral noodles with a rich tomato sauce, rice, wild potatoes, and bread and a tray all to itself of more sweets all on a carrying cart.

"Master Iver, I will not be able to eat all of this..."

"Naiyan Amitsa, I am so glad you are ready to eat because you had two choices: eat with or without my help."

Chachan Balent burst into the room followed by several others. Her voice was raspy and her entrance a commanding one. She wore a long linen skirt with deep green stitching as a symbol of her magic. Fair-skinned with small freckles. Her eyes were shaped like large green ovals and her face held onto a semblance of youth; even now in her most full frame many younger women envied her. Her overall demeanor was cheerful; however, the strength in her will nearly matched Anel Improvi.

The five children she bore were boys with one exception, who was of the closest in age to Naiyan. Imani Balent was bed ridden from a disease that weakened the joints and made every movement painful.

Naiyan had spent two hours with Imani nearly every evening for the past seven years in the Balent home. Naiyan found a way to genuinely smile when she heard her friend Imani's voice,

"Be glad Father entered first. Mother was going to barge in and then force food into your mouth. You are well now?" Imani's linen skirt covered her leggings, and she adorned no footwear since she had to be carried from place to place as her old roll-chair needed fixed.

Naiyan understood that this subtle question was her way of saying 'you are not alone'.

"I am well sister." Naiyan walked to her bed and propped a few pillows on the bed for Imani's comfort. Her large bed supported all three of them on the many nights they slept over. They took extra precaution to make sure Imani was comfortable. Naiyan pulled a makeshift personal tray for Imani to use when it was time to eat should she be unable to at the table.

"I see she made all of you brand new fashionable attire."

Naiyan laughed along with Ransa, who accompanied them. Her head was cleanly shaven; it was her way of remembering her mother before she died giving birth. She wore her hair in the same fashion.

Iver's eyes turned to the door. He was first to hear the latch on the door being jiggled before it was pulled open. A deep baritone voice bellowed into the room before his presence was made.

"There is enough food to feed the armed guard." Ziri, their eldest son, looked around the room while rubbing his belly as he entered.

"There is enough food to feed our family." Chachan interjected before taking Naiyan by the hand.

"You are my charge now, and the first thing we have to do is get some meat on these frail arms; at least Ransa has some muscles." Chachan kissed Naiyan on the forehead and rubbed her shoulders as a sign of support..

No words were spoken as the nine people moved to the tables that had been joined to form a sitting area.

"My dear, will you lead us in prayer?" Chachan motioned, but her husband relinquished the prayer in this moment to their eldest son.

"Ziri, you will bless our meal."

This had been the first time Naiyan had seen him in over two months, and once when drunk, he told her he hoped to be her husband one day.

Standing a little above six feet tall, he had broad shoulders and his mother's green eyes. He wasn't as burly as his father, but he could handle himself. Zuni, the second oldest male, had his father's disposition and physical traits. The final two, Milo and Milos were the youngest of the children. Soon to be leaving adolescence, they gravitated towards fun and games, often the jokers of the bunch. Both were extremely intelligent and charming. These two traits kept them out of serious trouble throughout the years besides being the children of Iver and Chachan.

Ziri blessed the meal, asking the Creator for understanding and guidance.

"To the Highest; into your universe we submit our fears and anguish. We seek your peace in the places you have kept secret until the time of revelation. Naiyan knows, as do we, that you have not forsaken her because this is not your promise. For the hands that prepared the feast, we thank you. For the grounds in which this nourishment was grown and developed the nutrients so that we may glorify your light, we thank you. We thank you for the gift of Anel Improvi for the wisdom that she shared, the firmness of her beliefs and the love that she encompassed each of us with, yet specifically for Naiyan Amitsa. We submit to the love that you have surrounded us in, now and forever."

When he concluded, he shocked everyone present with the next four words expressed.

"I love you, Naiyan." His voice was full of conviction and without hesitation, his eyes locked on hers.

Naiyan didn't turn away from him as he looked into her eyes.

Iver stared at his wife, unsure what to say.

The twins smiled and told Naiyan that they loved her too, unknowingly breaking the odd moment.

When Ziri concluded, Chachan put a small amount of each type of food on two plates for Naiyan.

"Thank you, and I love each of you. Now let's eat." Naiyan dug into her plates of food, not caring how fast she was eating.

"Slow down, child, and don't make yourself sick." Chachan spoke softly, and Naiyan began to chew her food instead of hogging it down.

"I expect it will take just as long to get some meat back on these bones of yours that it has taken to make you thin. So, I'll be staying to make sure you are on your way to being fit again. Plus, I need some exercise, so we can work through all fifty movements of 'haishu" daily."

Haishu had different names associated with it. The fighting form was initially perfected by the ancient gypsies, wandering folk who compiled many of the techniques the students learned.

The most basic forms taught blocking, punching, and kicking. While the more advanced, whom Anel had returned with from her stay up North, were closer to the true art form. Not only were hand and foot strike combinations taught but also certain techniques of ground fighting and submission holds. Weapon training was useful once the other techniques were honed.

"Elder, if it's okay with you, I'd like to participate." Ransa chewed her food and talked with her mouth open until Chachan sighed.

"If you were as quick to master 'haishu' as you are in chewing with your mouth open, child, you'd already pass into the healing stations… and those ragged clothes I saw you in a few days ago, burn them." Chachan waited for the Ransa to acknowledge her words before continuing.

“Of course, you will train with us; what we know will eventually be required again. The universe moves us closer to the next great battle. The Soachim had been erased for all eternity according to prophecy… well, according to Anel and Somerset,” Chachan finished, but the eyes at the table were drawn to the twins because Iver had just slapped one of the twin’s hands for reaching for more food without cleaning everything off his current plate.

Naiyan placed her hand over her mouth as she shook her head towards the twin. She finished chewing a portion of food before adding to the conversation.

“I’ve never met my aunt. My mother spoke highly of her. I guess the only difference is Aunt Somerset has auburn hair with two black streaks in it. My ma said it nearly killed her to watch her ride off on horseback. That’s kind of when I came into her life. She said that I helped fill the void. Now, I understand what this void is, and I hate it… I feel empty too. Every night, I—” Naiyan began to choke up before being interrupted.

“We know, sister, and we are here now and always. I’m going to be staying with you,” Imani called out from the comfort of the bed.

Naiyan did not respond immediately to Chachan. She would tread lightly.

“I promise to eat at least once a day, and I thank you for acknowledging that I have lost a few pounds.” She paused as Ransa began coughing loudly.

The cough was deliberate, the aspiring healer’s eyes wide open, conveying a message she hoped would be understood; Chachan wasn’t leaving this up for debate, the decision to ensure Naiyan’s recovery firm.

"And I am happy to be part of this family. Everyone's company will be welcomed." She received Ransa's point. Even though Naiyan had sought solitude, she accepted the support from those who loved her.

"I guess you do know better than to fight a battle you can't win, especially with the women in this family. You must be strong enough to take your own medicine." Imani was quick to add from the bed.

Iver Balent let out a quick chuckle. His wife, although recently busy with Assembly matters, always had a list of items she wanted complete. With her preoccupation of Naiyan and these other matters, he calculated what days he could fish or hunt, and what nights he would make his presence known in gambling rooms since he was going to be let "off his leash" as he put it.

"Dear husband of mine, if you think that now is your time to play, then you had better think again. You will do my chores as well as yours. You will be gone for over half of the week traveling to Ethi to protect the villagers' goods to market. When you return, I am giving you one extra night throughout the week for leisure, and that is all. There is still preparation for the First Master's dinner that I am responsible for, and with Anel, I am not on vacation, and neither are you."

"Why can't the usual channels, like the keepers make all the preparation for the First Master's dinner? They take care of everything else. We never get a chance to see you."

One of the twins pushed the other, urging him to stop talking.

"They get too much attention and power," he finished.

Imani was just as big on tradition as her parents and made the other twin explain why they were important. Everyone waited as he explained that the First Masters were the leaders of their respective elemental houses, a feat only the strongest in their magic would attempt at becoming elected.

"However, it isn't their power to wield magic that gives them this designation. It is also political maneuvering in order to get the most votes cast in their favor. A series of obstacles stand in their way besides any opponent challenging for the position. The first being a speech to the entire assembly on the merits of their position within the element they represent. The speech needs to detail accurate information and show that their actions match their ideas. For this reason, the majority of those seeking the position are the seniors close to one hundred years in age. Those who pass this portion of the process move forward into a test of pure strength and pitted against their remaining opponents. It is purely a show of force and endurance. Either being overwhelmed with pure magic or lasting longer than your opponent is a measurement required. Those who win this portion aren't always raised to First Master because in the end the casting of votes is the final challenge. The members of each House caste stones equal to one whole vote, while the other elemental Houses casted stones allot for only one third of a whole vote." He finished and went back to eating his food.

Imani wasn't done with her younger twin brothers. Being the second oldest child didn't keep her from assuming leadership between her siblings.

"And you, why were Aunt Anel and now mother important to the Fifth?"

The other twin had tried to remain silent. He shook his head back and forth, succumbing to his sister's question.

"The Four Masters plus one more makes the Fifth. The person assigned to the Fifth must be an elder unless voted in unanimously by each elemental house, like Aunt Anel was and... mother is currently." He hesitated to make sure he didn't offend his mother because she only received three of four votes, but that was all required as his mother was an elder. She nodded for him continue.

"So, the Fifth is all Four Masters plus one more, who is simply called the Fifth. They are the deciding vote should things be deadlocked on matters of importance between the other. Mother, although no Master, has more access to any and all information of each elemental house without hindrance because as the Fifth, she represents Ledoma at the highest level of politics."

Chachan nodded her approval to the younger twin boys as Naiyan wanted everyone to recall a most treasured memory of her mother. For the next hour, the group nibbled on food and talked while one moon made its appearance.

Naiyan was drawn to the sounds of Lake Ledoma through her window as she listened to the group's final bits of reminiscing. She was last to speak, and from the look in her eyes, she was exhausted. Everyone was, including Chachan.

Iver hugged Naiyan first then kissed his wife before departing the room to tend to "man's business" as he called it. When he walked out the door, Chachan told the twins to follow him home to keep him out of trouble.

Ziri watched with a smile on his face. He loved the way his parents got along. Even though it seemed they were always thinking about separate ideas, they could not be more in sync. He kissed Naiyan on the cheek and bid her good rest, telling her he would be back in a day or so.

"Wait a moment, Ziri. I will walk with you. I need to ask your advice." Zuni, the second born son, gulped down the last of his wine and bid farewell.

. . .

Ransa stretched and dumped the leftover food from the plates into separate containers and wiped the two tables.

Naiyan swept the floor for the small scraps from the table.

"Worry about that stuff later." Chachan removed the silver fastening from her hair and allowed her locks to flow unhindered down to her waist. Her work for the day was almost complete. She still had one final important challenge ahead for Naiyan, but Imani interrupted her thought.

"I'd like to go see Auntie tomorrow; there isn't a bunch of time left." Imani winced, moving her body slowly against the pillows on the bed.

Anel's body lay in stasis in a chamber in the temple. A tradition long passed was granted for her. Beloved by nearly everyone in Ledoma, she was their champion against the Nation of Carcero and any other land set on weakening Ledoma. One week remained before her body would be moved to the catacombs beneath the temple to be honored alongside only a handful of elders.

"Yeah, I guess that's a good idea. Thank you all again. It means the world to me having you here." Naiyan wiped her hand on a towel she had taken from Ransa's waist.

"What we need is rest. Tomorrow we'll throw out those things we do not need and start fresh… *all* of us." Chachan stroked her hair and draped it over her shoulder, pausing before addressing Naiyan.

"Where do you keep the extra linens? No one is going to freeze tonight. Snow and freezing rain are what the sky casters called for. Snow in late spring once again."

Ransa knew exactly where the extra covers were, so did Chachan. The blankets were through the only door that had not been opened in some while, the entrance to Anel's larger portion of their adjoined cottages.

Knowing Naiyan as they did, they knew it would take a gentle nudge for her to walk through that door. The small push Chachan had just provided was slight motivation. Now Naiyan only needed strong support.

"It's already getting chilly; I'll go with you to get them." Ransa understood the intention of Chachan.

Imani listened to everything, and she could see what was going on in this subtle approach.

Naiyan had to face everything head-on to completely conquer any fear or emotion she now possessed. It was done in such an expert way that they still left her an option.

She could not be inhospitable, so she had to retrieve them. The real question right now: Was she walking through the door with or without Ransa's assistance?

"You have planned this all along, haven't you?" Naiyan shook her head at Chachan and inhaled. Just like her mother, Chachan always had some additional angle to play. .

'*So, it comes down to this.*' Naiyan's stomach fluttered, and she could feel herself becoming lightheaded. She pushed through.

She was nervous, but her mother's words flashed in her mind.

'Fear is what you are willing to accept.'

Two choices remained and she took the option that best suited her and grabbed Ransa's hand.

"Well, let's go then." They approached the door that linked her space with her departed mother's. If she was taking this step into an emotional unknown, a step requiring her to push past the fear, or having the floodgates of pain open, she was not taking the chance of being overwhelmed alone.

CHAPTER FOUR
Questions

The latch seemed to hold in place for a second longer as Naiyan pushed the door open. The weight of the door was exactly the same, but it was a heavier push than she remembered. Ransa curled her fingers around her own, steadying her friend. The gesture was an acknowledgement to the moment.

'*Smells like her still*,' she thought. Visions of her mother bombarded her at the scent of the room.

Naiyan's chest didn't expand normally, the tightness across her body, slowed the draw in air as she took steps deeper into the front room. strange to be so hesitant in a place she had always known to be safe. Everything had its place and purpose. The most valued possession was a wooden carving of the First Mother holding her babies up to the Heavens on a single shelf above her sitting area.

'*Now is not the time.*' She pushed past each memory.

"Will you open the shutters please?" Naiyan asked as she walked towards the fireplace. Each night her mother had meditated in front of the hearth. She said that the flames were a way to focus the energy in her spirit and a bridge to other energies around the planet.

Ransa walked away believing that her friend needed space to square her emotions, but as she opened the shutters, she was startled by a question.

"Do you think unicorns or giants ever really existed?" Naiyan retrieved the gold clasp from her leather pouch and was now alternating it between her fingers again.

'If they exist in the mind then surely, they do.' She formed an answer to her own question before lighting an additional candle.

The night breeze caused her clothing to lift as the candle flame flickered before settling back. Ransa could see through her friend's shift, noticing that she had indeed lost a lot of weight.

"Where are the blankets?" Ransa rubbed her arms to warm them, wanting to avoid any subject that would spin them down the rabbit hole. This was uncharted territory, even for her. Healing of the body she was versed in, but this was different. Her friend didn't seem to have a firm grasp on the moment.

"If it exists in the mind, it has to exist somewhere… and energy can't be destroyed," Naiyan continued thinking out loud.

These small sayings had anchored inside Naiyan. Her understanding of such philosophy was still growing. Her departed mother believed knowledge was the best tool for life, and thus her home was full of literature from various lands. Whether the information came from teachings considered controversial or the small tidbits of books filtered down from the holy land, she kept the important manuscripts and shared most with those who could listen with an open mind. The mention of the new age was a hindrance to those in power, but she knew prophecy cared naught about the ambition of humans or their ignorance.

Ransa adjusted her blue drawstring midi skirt and slipped off her worn footing before walking into the formal area. She had learned various healing techniques in this very space by Anel. A quick study, Ransa used whatever means to cure, often putting her in conflict with Medici who healed using traditional means, but both Anel and Chachan had supported her, and for this reason alone, Ransa was better at identifying ailments than Medici, who had practiced healing for years.

"Just point me in the right direction, and I'll grab the woolens." Ransa was beginning to feel awkward not knowing where this conversation was headed. She would do her best to keep them on task, but she was on loose footing, and Chachan had entrusted her to support Naiyan with this endeavor.

Naiyan lit a second candle before handing it to Ransa and motioned for her friend to follow farther back into her mother's quarters. This wasn't the first time Ransa had been in Senior Improvi's personal space, but she was beginning to feel overwhelmed looking at the pieces of art spaced throughout.

The tapestries in the room were small but significant and vibrant in color. Four in total, one for each wall, were charts of the upper continent. The Land of Prophets containing the Pramum on its soil was the most impressive visual. The threads of the tapestry upon investigation were thin filaments made from the Tree of Life.

"Blankets are there." Naiyan spoke up and gained her attention.

A pile of quilted linens was stacked against the wall beneath a group of hanging tapestries.

"Come with me, Ransa. I simply have to know if…" Naiyan's voice trailed off as she walked into the back portion of her mother's quarters. Each step she took, she fought through emotions of loss. She reached back for her sister-friend's hand.

Ransa followed behind in wonderment at the scrolls and papers stacked neatly in between the bookcases. Volumes of leather-bound books, some scattered, lined shelves three feet wide. Everything was neatly governed by simple alignment like the universe. The stars were governed by the same force that presided over the sun.

'Order.'

"Mother said that there was an additional space behind the prayer room, and for all I know, what she died for could very well be behind these books…" Naiyan moved her eyes over the shelves, tracing each volume. A set of worn journals were out of place, and as she went to straighten them, she heard a few clicks before the bookcase swung inward, revealing two chairs placed opposite a simple wooden table. Placed on the table were two scribes.

"She had more secrets than any of the other seniors," Naiyan admitted to Ransa.

She lit candles spread throughout the space. Her mind, racing, couldn't comprehend why she was never told of this place. An older parchment caught her attention first. The document was wrapped in fresh vines, but the loosened seal contained a symbol she recognized, an infinity symbol with a circular cross intertwined with each other.

"That's a symbol from the Order of Petals." Ransa stared down at the engraving on a second set of parchments grouped opposite of where they stood.

"Are the rumors true? Was Anel initiated into the Order when she travelled abroad; she is one of three people on our continent with a *lifestick*?" Ransa's curiosity had taken over her tongue, and the questions flowed easily one after another.

Naiyan couldn't confirm or deny. She had no answer for her sister-friend.

Anel Improvi and her twin had left Ledoma as young teens to be taught in the ways of B'nobi. From there they spent three years under the tutelage of The Rose before another three years in the Capitol of Medellin. The States of Medellin was one of the only lands on the lower continent that stood in the way of Carcero seeking more control. It was here that they had first met Cruella Odward, now the Speaker of Carcero.

Not much was ever spoken of about Anel's time away when they returned, but many rumors circulated.

"What to do with these?" she motioned towards the table.

Naiyan studied both items.

Ransa walked to stand behind one of the cushioned chairs at the opposite end from Naiyan. She knew now was not the time to fail her friend, and having more support in this moment was necessary.

"If we don't get back soon, Chachan is going to come looking, and honestly, I have no energy to deal with her. Can we ..."

"Yes." Naiyan interjected, answering quickly, but her body had contradicted her words as she sat down at the old table.

Ransa followed Naiyan's lead and sat in the opposite chair. They were in this together.

"I told you I'd be with you, and I am. If Chachan grows impatient, I'll handle her..." She paused as Naiyan looked at her with brows raised, knowing her friends attempt would be futile. No one could *handle* the elder woman.

Naiyan refocused on the items on the wooded table.

"Well... what, what are these?" Ransa was curious but uncertain how to proceed.

It was a simple question that Naiyan didn't know how to answer. She didn't know how to feel. She was expectant as she stood up with one of the scribes in her hands. An emotion surfaced, not a sense of danger or panic, but she was anxious. Naiyan realized she had been holding her breath. She also knew reading each one would require more wisdom than either of them had. Naiyan handed Ransa half of the parchment and blew the candle out in the center of the wood table.

"I think we should grab the blankets and let Chachan decide what to make of these with us."

"Agreed," Ransa responded following her friend back through the hidden bookcase.

CHAPTER FIVE
Another Discovery

Imani watched the two young women she called sister walk through the door separating the two living quarters. What she had wished for wasn't self-indulgence; the silent prayers sent to her Goddess were to help relieve her sister of some of the pain and suffering. She knew that Naiyan skirted on the border of sorrow, and now she wanted to share in that burden as Naiyan had shared in hers.

As if on cue, her mother spoke.

"The Creator builds greatness, and Anel was a great friend as are those two." She turned to face her daughter.

There had been less moments like this between mother and daughter over the past few years. Whether it was Chachan assuming more responsibility as an elder or her daughter maturing and wanting more space, she was unsure; yet in this moment the bond between mother and daughter was apparent. Chachan embraced the closeness between them again.

"Yes, they are the best sisters." Imani readjusted on the bed, recognizing the tension in her joints. She was grateful the acute pain subsided at times.

Chachan gave her red wine from the last bottle not poured yet.

"What the… this is no good, Ma!" she exclaimed, pushing the cup away from her face. She squished her nose together in disapproval.

"It's supposed to be bitter. It's from Carcero. I thought we would try something different." Chachan responded by taking a sip. Her expression shifted to mirror her daughter's.

"You are absolutely correct. That is terrible." She shook her head, laughing while placing the cup back onto the table.

The night had set in. Chachan sat down in the black rocker chair next to the bed and stretched. She still had more business to attend to but would spend a few more hours with these three. She kept glancing at the adjoining door expectantly.

'*As long as I get some answers before the early session tomorrow, Anri will have no reason to seek votes to question Naiyan'*. Now that Anel had passed, Chachan only trusted her eyes and ears, along with one other's. She needed to have answers because her responsibility was to the safety of the people of Lake Ledoma and to keep Naiyan out of the council's crosshairs.

Looking at her daughter, she resolved to find the information needed to protect all of them. She also knew at first glance that Imani was about to say something of importance because she cleared her throat before addressing her mother.

"The remaining ashes are being studied, to make sure the nature of the problem we face is not born from dark western magic, but no one has really talked about... about the Soachim being destroyed. Elder Improvi could not have been the means of their end. Even in her fullness, she did not have the strength in combustible magic. Do you think that Naiyan could have?" Imani paused, hesitating to say the ideas that some people were thinking and even spreading rumors.

Naiyan had been weighed and measured by the elders to determine what magic, if any, she possessed after she turned twelve. Her gift was so minimal that she was not even chosen to study to become a Medici with Ransa.

Naiyan had been asked to recollect the events of the day, but Chachan told the general of the armed guard to cease all interrogation after Naiyan broke down in tears merely a day after awakening. The Medici were unable to determine why she had been unresponsive and why her memory had faltered. The military pressed her on the timeline of events from that dreadful morning. Each question pushed Naiyan into painful emotions and frustration. Even as she cried from distasteful questions, they kept urging her to reveal more. Those who had troublesome times with her mother insinuated that Anel created the Soachim and lost control of them. A fact she vehemently denied but in the end she was unable to remember anything except the final words her mother had spoken.

Now with her daughter asking her the question, she wasn't sure how to answer.

"Of that, I am not certain. But I am sure the event of that morning is mentioned in the Prophecy of Esroun." She walked into Naiyan's kitchen area, opened the spigot, allowing water to pour in from a small outside reservoir to fill the full-body wash basin.

Naiyan held no appreciation for modern belongings, so this faucet was the only "so-called" modern mechanism she allowed in her home.

As the outside water poured into the basin, Chachan used her secondary magic to heat it.

"You think you should check?" Imani asked, but before her mother answered her question, the door opened.

Both Naiyan and Ransa carried multiple linens, some of them sewn and stitched together in multiple designs.

"I've warmed the water in the tub. Strip down and get clean." Chachan pulled the heavier blankets from Ransa's arms to lay across the bottom of the bed.

"Well, strip down, child."

Naiyan began to remove her clothing, and as she unfastened her belt, each faded parchment fell to the floor to land at Chachan's feet.

"These were left behind for me, I didn't tell anyone during the interrogation because she left them for me. I do need your help." Naiyan bent at the knees to retrieve them before handing them to Chachan.

As the elder woman stared across at the younger woman, she could only wonder what other secrets Anel hadn't shared with her.

'*I earned your trust long ago...*' she thought, but she knew it wasn't a simple matter of trust for her departed friend. It was also protection.

"Get in the basin. These will not be opened or read without your presence. Ransa, help me with Imani, and when she's done with the basin, you strip down." She finished by putting the scribes on the table.

After each woman bathed and settled, Imani spoke first.

"If you need to view these separately, we understand." She was anticipating what each contained, but it was not her decision to make.

"Can we figure this out together?" Naiyan looked toward Chachan because wisdom in this moment was tantamount.

"It would be my honor. Light those candles; my eyes are not what they used to be." Chachan removed herself slowly from the bed to allow Imani to shift herself up onto the pillows without discomfort.

Uncertainty filled the room. The three young women would rely on Chachan; she would know how to read the lines and in-between the lines.

Naiyan slowly unfastened her first script, laid it flat across the table, and began to read out loud.

"This shall be recorded from the hand of a traveler in a land sparsely populated and unknown to his soul. The homeland of Uteri is greatly missed, yet I have submitted to the Creator's will and thus accept the result of my actions. As there are many rooms in the Creator's Mansion, there are also "rooms within rooms".

To the point I am lost... I am also found. Perhaps I have simply journeyed into another section of the Creator's garden. Regardless, I am divinely blessed and, therefore, warded against evil in as much or to the extent that it is recognizable. In these travels I have heard the song of the wind and known the treasures of the earth. The rhythms of life birthed in water have quenched the thirst of my soul while the tunes and melodies in the pits of fire dance with my spirit. I, like the garden in which the Great Tree grows, have been given the attribute of foresight.

With hindsight, clarity rumbles against perception, yet Prophecy does not hold this privilege. The face of the warrior watches like the mountains of the sky, and even though the seed is planted, the harvest remains unknown. Two moons separated by stars and distance with one sun joined in one purpose must stand in judgement by the eyes of the Creator. To know the madness of life is to understand the peace of death, yet the essence of chaos cannot penetrate the first element where perception is transcended by verses of reality. The heart must see what the eyes cannot. Neither the waters of faith nor the Tree of Life require hope. They require peace, for the time of chaos marks the beginning of the end. The Hordes of Sirini and the Dark Master must never prevail!

For generations, I have ignored the signs and visions that have dominated my every breath, yet they have become so vivid that I am no longer able to distinguish them between what is real and what is false. How I came about the other script is not as important as to why. I am a descendant of the original author and grave digger of a final resting place. Had I not also been given this "Gift of Foresight", I would not understand much... yet I have seen and smelled evil in the six beasts creeping through the mist... and my eyes have seen those yet to come. I do not have the empties, nor am I insane. I am still of right mind.

The age of chaos that has passed will come again just as "The Tree of Life" prepares... As each season fades, another appears, and the travelers of the universe will be judged under the Eye that sees all. My season is passing as is my reason for fighting the slight separation of my mind, and I do know that I will always be a vessel of the Creator's composition. In as such I have failed to attain the inner vision of the mind, so my thoughts are fragmented in their rate of vibration. The scroll contains a cipher, and prayerfully, someone with internal awareness will one day understand its complete meaning. Symbols and ideas can produce change, the only variation being the vibration of consciousness. Three must be weighed under the Creators' eyes. Three must be one, and one must be three. The path of spiritual consciousness lies deep in the vault."

There were multiple diagrams and symbols of the rays emanating from the sun spreading across the wholeness of the earth, the planes of life and death. The symbol signifying the entrance of the garden frequented this level where clearly it was meant to be recognizable in the realm of dreams.

The next diagram had three figures standing side by side, all three with their arms crossed and folded flat against their chest with smaller figures standing on staggered levels; one congregation had the outline of an ankh, the mark of probationary students like apprentice.

Neophytes, the second set, had the inscription of inner vision and mind, indicated as an infinity sign, only in a vertical position.

The final setting depicted scene had a procession moving through an archway into an unknown with the symbol of the Creator placed at the epoch of the arch, and on each opposite side of his room sat the figures of three sitting in a perfect circle.

The elder woman knew exactly what she held in her hand and its significance; it was the City of the Undead—the archway to both life and death.

Chachan rolled each parchment up and handed them back to Naiyan and then spoke quickly. "Blood of my blood and heart of my heart, nothing spoken in this room in this moment will escape or part." She sealed the weave. This spell was done for protection. It was complex in nature, requiring the elements of fire and earth to be woven precisely. She understood the risk of performing this forbidden weave. Using both elements inaccurately would kill her and those within this room.

The City of the Undead was not to be mentioned out loud, and now that she held this in her hand. It added weight to the Prophecy that Anel had mentioned to Chachan. Only these four women would be able to discuss this subject amongst themselves, and even if an inquisitor put them to the rack, they would never reveal its content.

Chachan wasn't immune to hearing her peers whispering of "The morning Sirini touched the Lake of Faith". Those who followed scripture were spreading their understanding out into Ledoma, not fearful of censorship from the seniors for speaking outside of their purview.

Midnight had passed hours ago, but Chachan knew the people she had to see before the morning session were still up. Four hours before dawn was like midday for both.

"We will discuss this later. For now, you all need rest. Ransa, I will cover your time tomorrow with the seniors; check in before evening with the keepers." Chachan rocked forward and kissed Imani on her forehead as she closed the door to Naiyan's room and walked outside. The amber and faded cobalt hues were still visible from the protection weave Anel had placed over their cottages. It would remain for years and keep out those negative energies that didn't belong. It was a small victory to know her magic still existed and it brought a semblance of peace to Chachan.

CHAPTER SIX

Night Shadows

Chachan was fond of the tall fescue grass under her feet as she walked on the edge of the worn yellow cobblestone. Each step of familiarity took her into memories of her youth with Anel.

Movement caught her eyes along the cottage tops, and by the time she narrowed in, whatever had been moving in the shadows was gone. She heard footsteps approaching her along with multiple voices.

The night patrol was making a circuit two by two, and she greeted them and kept moving. Chachan needed to make progress before the session in the next five hours. It was crucial to have something concrete to speak on, to move conversation away from interrogating Naiyan.

The farther Chachan moved away from the living commune, the more open space the wind had to circulate. Luckily the freezing rain and snow had not fallen as the sky casters earlier prediction, but it was brisk. The chill ran across her face; however, it was the sound of an approaching party that her ears were focused on. She had sensed the vibrations and frequency within the earth continue to spread across the terrain before the shadows came into view.

Traveling down the dirt road fading in and out of the moonlit sky was a small caravan of wagons, weathered cover tops barely clinging to the frames of their makeshift procession. About forty people were visible, and at the sides of horses pulling traveling compartments rode saddled worn men with cudgels and swords within their reach.

A pre-dawn arrival was surprising, but the emotion shifting in some of their eyes told her that their journey had been eventful. Bending down as if she had something caught in her footwear, she paid close attention to the procession where the men's clothing wasn't as battered and the horses didn't look worn.

The first rider sat atop a white Percheron. His salt and pepper beard was braided into two sections, but even in the dim light in these earliest hours, Chachan could see that his presence was commanding, and his approach seemed to indicate he was the one who lead. His voice confirmed it.

"Hey… you. Where are the senior quarters, more importantly, the Sanctuary?" The bass in his voice penetrated the air, and she sensed the low vibration in the ground beneath her feet through her magic.

Chachan understood the direct question. She also abhorred his rude tone as they were guests in her land.

Chachan would be patient, a much better way to gauge their intent.

"Is someone ill? We have Medici who will take care of—"

"Do not ask questions. Where do we find the seniors' quarters or the old Sanctuary?" He eyeballed Chachan while the other mounted soldiers slowed.

The patrol who had passed her by previously had returned but with a troop much larger than their original number. They walked toward the ensemble of caravans, looking intently on what was happening with their weapons accessible.

Chachan took that as an opportunity to take leave by pointing in the direction of the large number of persons approaching.

'I am not done with the rude one.' She glanced back as the man steadied his horse and dismounted.

She needed to check the progress being made with the remains of the Soachim, but most importantly, more background on history and a specific prophecy was required.

The northern library had been frequented more readily by both historian and magician wanting to decipher various prophecies after Anel was killed. When she entered and walked the oval center of knowledge, she was torn. She missed her friend.

In moments like this, she always had Anel to throw ideas back and forth with. Even the ones that made no sense at all would be considered until discarded. The proof that the new age was transitioning in laid in secret, being studied by Whal Stanjz. The elder alchemist was the best option with the amount of science in his background.

Chachan walked the aisles until she came upon the section where ancient prophecy and scripture were kept. It was older manuscripts she sought. They were not privileged to anyone but seniors.

"The First Gypsies and Land of the Giants" was dusty and the scribes associated with it weathered. They both had seen better days.

'*Today begins anew.*' She sat down and skimmed through the first few pages that showed the known lineages of the First Mother from which two great nations grew.

Chachan was exhausted, but she knew as the three younger women slept, now was the best time to find answers. She still needed to visit the alchemist but having some answers prior to the meeting would go a long way.

She memorized sections of each book, and once she read something, she was able to retrieve that information nearly word for word at a later time if she concentrated.

'*What the....*' Chachan thought she saw movement on a different floor above her. She watched intently before being startled from a sound in the opposite direction.

"Goosebumps," she muttered while slipping her moss green sandals off. Her magic was formidable and thus could determine if others were present through the vibration, even in the marble flooring.

Chachan moved to where she had heard the sound and was unsure of why an unbound manuscript had been left on the floor.

When she picked it up to return it to the shelf, she noticed it was flipped to a page with pictures while the language was old Uteri. Luckily, she was one of three people remaining in Ledoma who could decipher it, but as she went to close the book, her eyes were pulled back to a passage.

"*The three bearers will stand against darkness alone, but they all must be present at the moment of convergence, when both moons rise to mark a new era.*" She continued to read and was completely taken by surprise.

"*Naiyan Amitsa - Bearer of Harmony.*" Chachan read the name out loud. She was unsure how the name was now attributed to someone she loved. This was a name written before the time of Esroun. The other names and who they belonged to didn't matter. What mattered was the protection of Naiyan and what she had to do with any of it.

Chachan kept reading, and her eyes squinted, coming to a passage she had overlooked.

"*In secret, she bore children, and from these descendants, one of which will be a child who would later become Esroun the Great Mage.*"

Chachan was stuck on the word: *children*. Had Esroun had a sibling or siblings… '*Children*' was plural.

Chachan moved the book to the side of the table and reached for the second book of prophecy she had retrieved. The slate blue stone walls of the library held no warmth as the heat built up from the sun faded throughout the night. She fumbled through multiple pages before noticing one of the wall torches flickering, drawing her attention back to the shelves of books.

She felt as if she was not alone, but no one had entered. She hadn't ascertained a shift in the earth under her feet. Chachan shook off the feeling, attributing it to her tension being high with the recent events.

"*D'ianna traveled south to forge a new life, where she settled near the Lake of Faith. They lived a full life.*"

Chachan could not take her eyes from the line. The book over a thousand years old, it was not included as main literature to be studied. This remote characterization made it possible that Naiyan's father could indeed be a descendant of the First Mother.

"Which means so would Naiyan." Chachan let the words slip out and finally confirmed that she was not alone, seeing a free-flowing shadow moving along the wall.

She yawned, keeping her hands low as she weaved a spell to illuminate the room to hold the shadow in place. These apparitions had become more frequent, and now she was certain it was this spirit that had been following her since leaving Naiyan's cottage.

"Illuminate." She spoke the words quickly, leaving no escape for the shadow. The brilliance flashed like a bolt of lightning.

Chachan cast a second spell to influence talk.

"By the Power of the First Mother, I compel you to speak. Who do you serve?" Chachan had centered herself to respond quickly if she determined any false pretenses or if the shadow was an agent of the Dark Master.

"*I—I serve no one... yet?*" The voice was deep and spread throughout the chamber now, without a mouth, the vibrations of the stone walls reverberated as its mode of speech.

“I play no games with you. Are you friend or foe?” Chachan brought forth her magic and stood ready.

“*I must protect the daughter of Anel Improvi. There is more at stake than you are willing to accept.*”

Chachan understood it would speak in half-truths until pressed. Chachan knew that whatever words being spoken in this space were true for human and spirit alike.

“You have not answered my question. Are you friend or foe?’ Chachan pulled more energy from her surroundings into her core. The static electricity was rising as she searched for the currents of energy under her feet.

The shadow, stuck in space, answered, “*I am friend to those who are friend to Naiyan Amitsa. Bearer of Harmony.*”

“Give me your name if you don’t wish Naiyan any harm,” Chachan demanded.

The sound of a door opening made Chachan lose her concentration, the momentary lapse had giving the shadow time to escape.

Two guards entered the room with uncertainty on their face.

“Are you okay, elder? We heard voices.” The first guard entered with his hand on the pommel of his sword. The second guard looked around the chamber.

“I am alone. Did you allow anyone in?” She attempted not to be sarcastic, but their interruption cost her information.

The guards looked at each other before back tracking out of the space.

Chachan closed the books and returned them to their original places. She had two more bits of information to add to the equation; Esroun had a sibling, and his mother lived on the border of Ledoma. Secondly, a spirit was protecting Naiyan. As she walked out of the library to visit the elder alchemist, some things would begin coming into focus.

CHAPTER SEVEN

An Unpleasant Introduction

Ziri wasn't surprised he was the first to enter the sanctuary for morning salutations. He arrived two hours earlier than usual. Getting a start before many woke meant he could pray in peace before preparing for the festivities and the multitudes of people. The First Master's dinner would be the precursor to one of the large festivals that Ledoma hosted every ten years.

The city prepared for an influx of visitors. Areas had been set aside for those wanting to pitch tents and stay just outside the city while the inn keepers and those with additional sleeping quarters updated their rooms for those who wanted firm beds and hot meals. There would be enough coin to go around. Between boarding fees and the multiple gaming booths, some would make thirty percent of their annual income during this time.

'*She won't be helping this year…*' Naiyan filled his thoughts. They typically staffed the ball in the basket station but, now that he was a senior, that work assignment would be passed on to someone else.

He then thought back to Naiyan's appearance at dinner the previous night.

'*Thin, much thinner than I can remember.*' He knew that his mother would bring her back to health.

A voice startled him.

"You haven't even got started yet?" Cheney Joli walked into the sanctuary with a small knapsack in her hand. She laid it down before removing her sandals. Her ecru chemise and matching white gown trimmed in yellow indicated her magic. The indicator for each magician's primary power was not only shown in the color, but also in its richness. The deeper the hue, the stronger the magic. Magic in its most natural state was balance. No element of nature was greater than another, and it was all in how the spell-crafting was manipulated and the power within each magician.

"I thought I'd be first today, seeing that your time with family extended well into the night. How is she?" Although Cheney wasn't a close friend to Naiyan, she did have a slight bond with Elder Improvi.

Ziri wasn't sure how to answer her question.

"Honestly, who can say? We had a feast prepared, and she ate, but I had to leave earlier than I wanted. Elder Battelle has me making sure the delegates from Carcero have everything they need." Ziri motioned for Cheney to take a seat next to him.

"The keepers were already prepared. The list of necessities they sent in advance has cut down on any surprises, well most of them anyway," he finished.

"Pompous and pretentious if you ask me." Cheney crossed her legs after sitting. She placed her elbows on her knees and touched her index fingers to the thumbs in each hand.

"Well, no one did ask." Ziri laughed before assuming his position to sit in silence to begin their morning prayer. Each one had crossed into the Senior Assembly together with the last cycle. Ziri was well accustomed in the ways of magicians long before he became an initiate. Cheney was new to the entire system of education an initiate had to endure being sent from a small village. Ziri had been the first to befriend her, and it was why she would forever be grateful.

The ringing from the bell tower echoed into the sanctuary as they finished prayer. The formal day had begun, and for Ziri, it meant keeping a watchful eye on the keepers attending the delegates from Carcero.

Ziri slipped his soft-leathered shoes back on before stretching his arms.

"Less than twenty more days of chaperoning people who despise us." Ziri paused to acknowledge others entering the sanctuary to begin their morning prayers.

"They're takers. They only want to see how we can help them profit." Cheney added before a younger male keeper waved to get Ziri's attention.

“This ought to be good.” Ziri motioned the boy forward.

The young boy adjusted his pickle-colored breeches before clearing his throat.

“Senior Balent, Ambassador Janae has requested you personally. She said it’s of great importance.” He rubbed the side of his face vigorously. His teeth was clinched even though the corner of his mouth forced an awkward smile. He had an empty feeling in the pit of his stomach each time the ambassador requested him.

“Thank you.” Ziri understood how important the relationship with the Nation of Carcero was for Ledoma, but Ambassador Janae had already attempted to push his buttons.

“Hopefully she will be wearing clothing this time.” Cheney smirked at Ziri before he and the young boy walked away.

Cheney didn’t have it any easier. An elder was seeking the position of First Master, and she had chosen Cheney to prepare the speech she would give. If that wasn’t enough responsibility, she was also tasked with providing the new members being added to the list of seniors with their housing selection. Their choice was between the senior quarters or communal living as Anel and only a handful of others had chosen.

“It still amazes me that a small village child could grow into a budding woman.” Cheney didn’t need to guess that Elder Batelle had his mind on one thing, and it wasn’t prayer. She had dressed in extreme moderation as a neophyte, but after crossing into the Assembly, she allowed herself the freedom to express herself in her clothing.

"Good morning, elder, had I known you'd be staring at me like a—" Cheney was interrupted by two sanctuary attendants who sought Elder Batelle immediately as they entered the space.

"What's so pressing that it can't wait until after my morning salutations?" His voice was heavier than it needed to be, his self-importance at the forefront.

"There are travelers, I mean visitors… It's an entourage of…" Neither could form the words to say.

Elder Batelle shook his head and followed them outside only to be met with hundreds of Ledoma's guardsmen surrounding a caravan of people in tattered clothing but well-armed.

"Sir, you've been requested." General Merico Roner appeared at the elder's side. Elder Batelle did not allow Merico to finish before becoming boisterous, drawing attention to himself.

"By whom? I am the one who requests; and who thinks my presence so important before our morning prayer!" he shouted loudly.

The large powerfully built leader stepped forward from the group arriving earlier in the morning. His beard was knotted in two twists while his hands resting in front of him, palms open, indicated that they came in peace.

"We have traveled some distance to be here, and I agree prayer… faith, is what guides all of our days. Perhaps we can pray together and then allow us to speak in turn."

Elder Batelle couldn't understand how a caravan of travelers, seeking him out, had not been disarmed of their weapons or stationed far away from the sanctuary.

"Currently you are disobeying an order from a superior. General Roner, if you will." Elder Batelle pressed the group to relinquish their arms.

The breeze shifted as General Roner motioned for the guards closest to the burly man to secure his weapons.

Elder Batelle had reached into his magic, this time as intimidation.

"We have come in peace…" the burly man said again.

"Enough!" a woman's voice was heard through the window carriage before the door to it opened. An older woman emerged, just as worn down from their travels as the bearded man, but her commanding presence did not go unnoticed. Her netted facial veil allowed only glimpses behind the covering.

"Commander, at ease." She walked closer to speak directly with Elder Batelle.

"We are in need of food and rest after we pray with you," she said politely but with the intent that what she said would be followed.

Elder Batelle shook his head back in forth before he lost his patience.

"You are in need of… in need of…you need better manners when you require my help, and you need of a better servant than this one who dares to ask to pray with me. We have an important event and the festival I'm sure you've come to make money from three weeks hence. What you need is trivial. All your traveling companions are to disarm. Leave your horses and follow my men to be questioned before I…"

"You're a pompous ass, I see. First, the sanctuary does not belong to you; it belongs to the Creator, and unless I am mistaken, any person can praise the Highest in any sanctuary. Secondly, you have offended the very nature of magicians when you reached into your magic at my commander. There was no threat to anyone's safety…" She paused and put her hand up to stop Elder Batelle from interrupting her.

"Third, I see you need help in reacquainting yourself to the purpose and responsibility you have."

"Arrest them. Arrest them all!" Elder Batelle pointed at the entire group as a handful of seniors who had been inside the sanctuary were now walking outside.

"Elder Anri Batelle, you have failed as a senior of Ledoma. You can either step aside or join us for prayer." She spoke with such force it startled Elder Batelle, and his anger got the best of him. He reached for his magic, the second time he committed this offense.

The diminutive woman shook her head before her iridescent cloak shifted behind her and moved with such speed she had appeared by Anri's side quicker than the eye could blink. Her facial covering now lowered, her voice was clear for everyone to hear.

"You are not worthy." Her hands gripped the side of his body, closest to his ribcage. She pushed her fingers into various portions of his body to temporarily disable his ability to use his magic. Those bearing witness couldn't believe what had happened until after General Roner motioned his troop to advance, but a force held everyone in stasis as the woman elevated above the ground.

"I am Santal Culdris. You saw us as undesirables. The very ones magicians have been given a responsibility to care for. We will pray with you and afterwards, and we shall see how you earn the position to lead again. Has it all gone to shit since Elder Improvi's passing?" The force that held them in place relented. She took a prism styled trinket from her pocket and waved it across her face. The momentary illusion was now gone; it was the Matriarch of Medellin standing in their presence.

Elder Batelle was in shock. He never expected the Matriarch to make the trip and couldn't fathom why they were dressed like refugees. He had errored tremendously.

Santal Culdris was the Matriarch of Medellin. The spiritual guide to all formal magicians on the lower continent stood before the crowd. She stared at those gathered before motioning General Roner forward.

"Please help attend to those who need care. Commander Ghamrod will assist and be at your disposal." She motioned to the burly man who simply grunted.

The young messenger who retrieved Ziri earlier, came running through an older narrow path that had not been trimmed yet, unaware of the situation at hand. He ran straight into the back of the Matriarch's commander.

"Oh, uhm… I didn't see you. I mean, not until I couldn't stop. I'm sorry, sir." He tugged at his shirt, not certain what to do next.

"This young man has the manners that some adults, especially those making the decisions for such a historical land, have forgotten. Your name, little one?" the Matriarch asked as she bent down to face him eye to eye.

"It's Dart, ma'am."

"I bet you're pretty fast. Do you know Elder Antal and Elder Balent?" The Matriarch stood and reached into her waist band to pull from it a shiny coin.

"Yes, ma'am, I do."

"And do you know Elder Stanjz?" she followed up.

Dart's eyes attempted to remain on the face of the older woman, but the coin sparkled as the sun kept drawing his eyes back to it.

"Yes, ma'am," he answered anxiously.

"Can you find them for me and bring them to the sanctuary swiftly? Tell them that it's an emergency." She flipped the coin into the air. Dart snatched it before it hit the ground.

"Thank you." He smiled before taking off in the opposite direction he had emerged.

The area had now grown as those inside the sanctuary filed out into the open space, and a small group of those who came as emissaries from Carcero had made their way closer to where the commotion had built.

The older woman motioned two women from her entourage forward before turning to face the sanctuary.

"Young woman." The Matriarch pointed toward Cheney, who was stuck in between Elder Batelle and the seniors just exiting from morning prayer.

Cheney walked slowly past Elder Batelle who had not come up with any words after the Matriarch revealed herself. Cheney was hesitant to engage initially because Anri was the First Master of her house and didn't want to offend him.

"Yes, Mother." Cheney bowed slightly.

“That’s not necessary. I’d like you to show hospitality to my daughters. We will lodge in the old priests’ quarters; we don’t need much. I want you to oversee our stay. Will you do that for us?” The Matriarch reached for her hand.

“Yes, of course, Mother.” Cheney instinctively returned the grasp.

The Matriarch walked toward the remaining seniors and made introductions.

“I am Santal Culdris, and despite the rude greeting upon our arrival, we still come to honor Elder Improvi. I will meet with each of you after we are settled…” She paused and whispered something to Cheney, who in turn, whispered back.

“Senior Joli is our master keeper, and any requests will go through her.” She motioned for the young assembly member to accompany her towards the entrance of the sanctuary only to be followed by the rest of the traveling party she arrived with.

CHAPTER EIGHT

Creator's Glass

The sun was rising slowly as Chachan walked from the library and through the commoners' quarters. It had been roughly three hours that she spent researching in the library to help make sense of everything that happened. After reading the parchments Naiyan had returned with, Chachan was certain, there was much more to discover in relation to Anel's death; along with understanding prophecy.

Guards were missing from their normal stations, but she thought back to the large group of travelers entering the city late in the night and understood why they weren't posted. She thought about Iver leaving to accompany the shipment before she could see him off.

“Good morning, Elder Balent.” The voice nearly startled her. Two unfamiliar women walked by with welcoming smiles on their faces. The women were walking to the lake, followed by other familiar groups to start their day. The energy surrounding them was open and inviting, and perhaps it was why she greeted them with a blessing.

‘*Early arrivals for the festival.*’ She imagined.

“Good morning, may B’nobi shine bright upon your faces.” Chachan smiled and continued forward. She would get updates on the caravan and most importantly have a word with the rude man on horseback. For now, she needed to press forward for any clues or indication to who was responsible for the attack on Ledoma.

The remains of the Soachim were small bits of bone and ash, burned by something or someone who exhibited a powerful magic not known for close to a thousand years.

Whal Stanjz had discovered a combination of energies within the remains, something foreign to the lower continent and traced back to the conquerors of the West who occupied Uteri.

Now he attempted to discover how this source was cast into the spell but, more importantly, used to penetrate the blood of the beasts. All creatures made with ‘energies of life’ were balanced or destroyed by other energy. The Soachim could only be created by variations of fire and earth energy using dark spellcasting. Water should have countered the spell woven, but it failed. It was the element of fire, heat reaching temperatures of volcanic level proportion, that killed them.

Chachan, being patient, had waited extra days to ensure some progress had been made and knew now was the best time for a visit before the First Master’s dinner and the festival.

Whal Stanjz was a prudent man and seldom rushed with anything. Being deliberate revealed what others overlooked. His intellect often put him at odds with others as he thought himself superior. Two things were certain: His magic was strong, and secondly, now that Anel had passed, Chachan was only two of the remaining seniors he respected.

As Chachan disappeared from the main road to walk an old route, she thought about the entourage of travelers. She did recognize the sigil of the riders, but nothing about the men appeared to be authentic of the land they represented.

The land of Kefise was more than one hundred miles from Ledoma. Those born with magic lived within their borders, but none sought formal education or training.

These people lived very simple lives and worked extensively with their hands. She was unable to make out all the features, but what she did know was they were imposters. The people of Kefise shaved the hair of both man and woman once they reached the age of fifteen. Those arriving this morning had hair nearly the length of her daughter, and they wore multiple earrings in each ear. An accessory or a rank she was unsure, but she knew the seniors would gather necessary information while addressing their concerns.

As she approached Elder Stanjz home, she saw him standing in the window looking out smoking from a calabash pipe as if he had expected her arrival at that exact moment so early in the morning.

Chachan walked up the faded cobblestone walkway and started to knock, but the door swung open.

"Elder Balent, come in… Come in," he said audibly excited, closing the door behind him. Then he did two odd things Chachan had never known him to do. He did a small dance and then proceeded to hug her.

"I'm so glad… so glad you came… early," he said, tapping his index finger on the stem of his pipe.

"I've… I've… I've…" he kept saying before simply pointing to a container which had some of the ashes left behind.

"What is it?" Chachan walked toward one of his workstations. Two burners were lit with colored liquids in thin glass containers with heavy sweet-smelling smoke adding fragrance to the air. The mixture smelled like sweet citrus, but as she approached the lone table, an eerie feeling came over her. Spread out in a series of diagrams was the symbol of the Dark Master.

"What is this, Whal? This is blasphemy," she said, getting ready to take a cloth to wipe it on the floor. Chachan reached into her center out of reflex, making her magic accessible.

"Won't matter, Chachan… It's—it's not going to go away. It pulls back into one. I tried using a wet cloth first… but it wasn't enough, so I grabbed that bucket of water and doused the flames. This is what's left. If you touch it, it's nothing but ash. I can put-put it-it in a container…" He paused to walk towards a shelf where five containers held ash—containers with the symbol of the Creator marked in the glass.

"…but the ashes resurface." He finished by puffing on his pipe again.

Chachan ran her fingers through the symbol, and the ashes shifted, but when she took a small linen cloth to push the ashes away on to the floor, they remained fixed in the same exact spot.

"The Dark Master's grasp is reaching be-beyond Sirini..." Elder Stanjz paused to search his space for one of his canes. "It is such a changing world, world we're living in."

Chachan stared in disbelief; the foundation of her life, the core of her spirituality had come face to face with physical proof of the Dark Master's existence. Along with the old scripts and the tragic death of Elder Improvi, Chachan kept being peppered with strange energy causing the hairs on her arm to raise.

"That's an understatement, Whal. Goosebumps… just goosebumps." She stared at the ashes again while shaking her arms.

"Who else have you told thus far, Whal… who else knows?" she asked, keeping one eye on the symbol and the other watching the multiple containers with other ash in them.

"No one… No one. I don't think… think that the others will believe even as… as their eyes say. I've told no one. Perhaps after the festival, the elders can-can determine what to do next. I think it best to slowly give this information to our peers."

Chachan cut in.

"These came from the original gathering of the remains. How can so little produce so much more? Are there histories you've read with information about this, Whal? I can't recall. And secondly, how did you come about the Creator's Glass?" Every statement and every question had to have purpose; the people who arrived recently had a story, but until she had these two questions answered, she would remain there. Creator's Glass was forged as volcanic lava cooled. and the first magicians combined their power to remove impurities from the hardening magma. The remains became Creator's Glass, the only known material strong enough to hold dark energy. None had been seen in ages and Chachan needed him to be forthcoming.

"I've read about everything or close to it, but I couldn't recall anything written in the day, days of the shadow or even the Wars of Heaven…" He paused to empty his pipe.

"…but in an old… old book, I remembered a passage. Hold on… Hold on. It's right over here." Whal used a small amount of magic to remove a heavy stack of books, only to end up with a small leather-bound book to be suspended in the air before him.

"I hate using this so-called gift, but in my aged co-condition, it makes my days a lot less com-com-complex." He exhaled to release the book into his wrinkled hands.

"I purchased the containers passing through new-new settlements close to the border of Ilens. Once a great land, it consists of only hunters and farmers mixed with no ability to forge forward. Stuck in their ways of barter and exchange, I couldn't just give my coin away without getting something in return… inequities." Moving slowly toward a second wooden table, Whal wiped his brow of sweat. The energy he used with his secondary gift of air had exhausted him it seemed. Water was his primary magic, and only a few could best him. The deep blue trim around his glass frames was the only tone he wore for this status. Other Assembly members donned themselves in vermillion or scarlet to show their ability with fire, verdant or hues of green for earth magic.

Chachan followed behind, wary that more questions would arise.

"I thought the jars fancily cute, and a small child was happy when I gave her ma and da two silvers, but it would appear that the amount was insufficient. Each of them is authentic. Had the sellers known they could've bought an estate in Ilens. The Ancient Ones who made them cast a spell strong enough to contain the ashes and render them harmless." He fumbled for his pouch of tobacco in the pocket of his light-cotton trousers.

Whal had lost two elections to rise to First Master in landslides. He had bested both of his challengers in strength of magic, but he believed because he was deemed as an outcast even after nearly a century as a Senior and didn't have the personality of his challenger, and when the votes were cast, he received less than twenty percent.

This stuck with him. He knew that the path Ledoma had gone down had weakened their position in the world. History had a way of creating illusions, like the power Ledoma once held, but once the veil was pulled away, the outside world would see them as dysfunctional with no direction.

He was adamant against selling land to Carcero, a land that despised the very foundation of his being and anyone else with magic. If he had his way, he would take half of the Assembly of Ledoma and a quarter of its army to bring Carcero under their control, but instead, he bit his tongue until he had enough standing to do more than voice his opinion. Anri Batelle, his supposed friend, had secretly poisoned the water against him when he was voted as First Master.

Now Whal spent much of his time exploring lands in expeditions. He had never recovered after the woman he was engaged to, ended the relationship once he lost his second attempt to become First Master. Within six months after breaking his heart, she began dating Perci Rax, First Master of Fire.

Whal had never allowed himself to love again. A man with attractive features once was now revered for his intellect. With nearly ninety years of teaching behind him, he spent the last twenty traveling before isolating himself for periods of time.

He fixed his wired framed glasses across his long-pointed nose. He glanced at Chachan who stood by his side.

"Yes, it does seem insufficient..." Chachan pondered the true meaning behind his words. What did any of it truly mean?

"Whal, just how long have you had these containers, and when you say close to the border, how close did you go to the wilderness or close to its border?" Chachan asked curiously and cautiously.

He was not an innocent man, no matter how child-like and innocent his movement portrayed even at an old age. His life as a child was harder than most imagined.

Whal Stanjz was initially raised near Ilens, the same land he visited to obtain the Creator's Glass when those with greed governed and had no intent on helping build communities. Instead, they concentrated on wealth and the accumulation of power at the expense of others. Side deals brokered in darkness destroyed any resemblance of a unified land. Now it was the land Somerset Improvi resided in and managed as best as possible after leaving her sister decades ago. If he had traveled north and west of Ilens, he was lucky to have returned from the isolated wilderness of mountains and desert in one piece.

Whal, being the oldest of nine, was an additional earner for his younger siblings and was introduced to a life where being weak was fed upon by those stronger. Never a large man, he used his mental faculties to coordinate plans and schemes of theft. No blood was shed and, more importantly, no one ever caught. For this reason, he knew those who wished to be unknown. When his family moved to Ledoma because of his magic, he was torn. Although he kept on the path to become an enlightened historian along with being a leading alchemist, he still held onto a few of his criminal connections from his past.

He placed more tobacco in his pipe before turning pages of the book until he came to a passage.

"Dream's Breath… here it is… Here it is…" He paused to answer Chachan's initial question.

"Very, very near the border, Senior Balent. It was the land I was born and raised, and I can defend myself even at this age. Now, listen, no… No, you read it for yourself." He stepped away from the volume, allowing her to lay her eyes on the words.

Chachan had both answers provided, and as she read the first words written on the old parchment, her mind had formed new questions.

"The earth will split, and the people will divide. Symbols cast with spells will not be sufficient a power to keep the Gates of Sirini closed. Only the three can. Two will leave, but three shall return when all hope is lost. Battles will wage in the past, present, and now. The Three must be present before the last leaf falls. The Pramum must survive at all costs." Chachan bent down to re-read the passage again and then turned to face her older counterpart.

"Whal, what else are you not telling me?" She still held one hand on the book and awaited a reply.

He ran his hand across the edge of the wood table before extinguishing the flame from the glass burners.

The smell of citrus and his tabaco didn't mix well, and even though Chachan coughed from the fumes, her mind remained intent on an answer.

Whal deliberated his reply, and with one last toke on his pipe, he answered, "Chachan, I recall some of the best advice I ever received in my life from Sister Improvi. She said the best way to deal with a bear when you have no retreat is to remain quiet until they decide what they want of you… It appears that you are the bear today." He exhaled and moved away from the table before continuing.

"I traveled the border with an old friend set on expanding his reach. In those travels we met many, but some… some we saw but never met. You see, some of the people rarely left their homes when we arrived in some smaller lands. We only caught glimpses of shadows in some spaces and, mind you, not those of departed loved ones. Shadows and most certainly 'dark fades' but without power to fully manifest. Coming across two of the last villages, we heard only the cries of babies. No sign of them and no sign of life, just the whimpering sound of children hanging on the wind. What was stranger is that the next community were not expecting to see us emerge." He hesitated like he was going to keep something from Chachan, but with her steady gaze on him, he kept on.

"Villages we occupied for a night, during our travels, were full of rumors of what happened to the abandoned villages. You see, some of the men accompanying us sought the comfort of the local women. You know, most times it's the natural ability women possess that allows them to secure information, but a few of the men had enorm—" He paused again, realizing the size of a man's endowment held no weight in this moment.

"Some of the men came back with stories of gibberish or at least I had believed." He stopped and stared out his window. There was movement in the shrubs.

"Did you just see anyone?" His voice trailed off as he moved toward the second window.

Chachan walked towards the door, believing Elder Stanjz was trying to avoid any additional questions, but she caught movement outside too. She thought back to the shadow she encountered in the library and readied her magic.

As she opened the door, Whal used a different energy force to hold the eavesdropper in place than he did when looking for the book.

"Dart, you're going to have to announce yourself much faster than that." Whal shook his cane at the young boy playfully.

"Elders, they-they sent me to get you both!" Dart blurted out. "I got a nice shiny coin from the lady, too, but I've told you, and my job is done. But I can walk back with you if you want me to. She was nice." He had elation in his voice. Both elders saw the silver but didn't see any markings to indicate the land the currency came from. Silver was silver.

"Who is *she*?" Whal wasn't satisfied with this information. He wasn't going to be summoned by anyone, let alone by an unnamed elder.

"I don't know," Dart answered flatly.

"You know what? It does not matter. I think I'm ready for an argument this morning." Whal motioned them away from his door and challenged Dart to beat him back to the sanctuary.

Dart took off running, nearly tripping down the white pebble trail. Chachan walked with normalcy but Whal, with a sturdier cane in hand, was nearly on the heels of Dart, and they had put distance between her.

Whal had a questionable mind above all other things, so he could do nothing to slow his step. Chachan simply smiled as she walked. She was curious just as, if not more, than Whal, but Anel told her when they were young neophytes that "whether we run or walk, we'll get there just the same, and they'll still be there" when they were given tasks that couldn't be finished on time. Coming into the open areas, she noticed a few of the young children hushed and huddled watching with eyes of intrigue.

CHAPTER NINE
Better Clarity

Elder Batelle was carrying some of his belongings from his seniors' quarters, placing them under an enclosed tent with make-shift sleeping assortments. Walking behind him was his closest ally and another one of the leaders of their community.

'*What the hell is going on? Whoever is in there, I'll end this now. That Batelle is an idiot.*' Chachan saw them in the distance, but she continued forward until she heard the same voice from earlier in the morning attempting to hinder her progress.

"You haven't been requested to enter the sanctuary, so if you can take a seat…"

She ignored him and pressed forward.

He called out again, "Elder Balent, you have been requested, but you must wait. She said you would be most difficult. Had I known it was you this early morning, we could've bypassed all the unnecessary pleasantries we have all endured. Also, she apologizes in advance." He walked away to see that his men had their provisions instead of continuing his engagement with Chachan, risking any further tensions.

Chachan promised to wipe the smugness from him when she sought him out later, but now she would rectify this situation.

She pushed past the last few gathered around the temple, and the moment she stepped onto the walkway, all the wind was sucked from her stomach. She couldn't breathe and fell to one knee with her hand pressed to the ground to break her fall. She recognized it immediately.

"There are wards on the sanctuary. Who allowed this?" Chachan retreated after feeling the energy webbed around the walkway leading to the entrance. She could make out the auras of emerald green and sunglow reds, but the strands of azul were knotted unlike any other she had ever seen.

"You all are acting foolish… and childish… Senior Batelle… Anri!" Chachan called out, but Batelle looked at her with such pity that she felt betrayed.

"Anri, what is going on exactly? Someone is going to answer me!" Chachan yelled, losing her composure for the second time in one day.

"There is no need for agitation. You shall have all the information you need…" an unfamiliar voice came through. The reaction from Batelle and Bungle told Chachan this was the person responsible for everyone walking gingerly.

"Call it impatient, but you have acted like intruders, and who believes to be qualified to ward entrance to our sanctuary? Are you agents of…" Chachan paused. She would not say the name or make any more reference to the Dark Master, but she was sure the point was made.

"…only they would attempt a feat like this, and it seems you and your people have it mastered." She did not know who she addressed or what to expect. She didn't reach into her gift but stood ready.

Many seniors continued to transfer some of their belongings, and Anri Batelle stood off to the side. The arrogance that typically surrounded him had been erased as had his voice. He held his tongue, but his eyes along with the many others were watching the interaction between the two women.

"Well, your reputation seems to fit you well enough, and in fact, I had hoped it would, Chachan Ohi Balent. There's time now to address your concerns, and we'll see if it fits into the plan." The Matriarch wore the same netted head covering that she arrived in earlier. The small-framed woman had a bit of amusement in her voice as she approached Chachan. She touched her tiny hands together before shifting her fingers, opening the ward to allow Chachan access into the space.

"Come." The Matriarch turned and walked away.

Chachan, in all her stubbornness, followed without hesitation on the heels of this woman. She determined the energy of the ward returned as she crossed the threshold.

"I am not here to change your land." The Matriarch washed her hands in the small silver basin near the entrance of the sanctuary.

Keepers of Ledoma were seen moving with haste as they assisted in making all the rooms ready that were required by the Matriarch's arrival. People Chachan had never known were being situated as the preparation of each temporary living quarter was completed. As the Matriarch was handed a towel to dry her hands, she concluded before slipping her sandals off, "...yet we do offer help in these times of uncertainty."

'*Uncertainty?*' Chachan thought. The only precarious questions in the present moment were about who these people were and why the Assembly acquiesced their position in their own land. Chachan had met the Rose of the Garden once. This woman was not the spiritual leader the Tree of Life had chosen. The Rose had been exiled after the king had been murdered. This woman was not the Matriarch, and even if the Matriarch of Medellin had sent this liaison with the intent to help transition from Anel's leadership, she would not let the States of Medellin uproot the Assembly. Ledoma always maintained their autonomy.

"What makes you think we need help or will accept it? As far as my eyes have seen, those men and their garb are forged with illusion because clearly they are not from the lands represented. We know there are many territories who believe us hesitant to embrace all the change the world has seen over the past two centuries. We also know that many of those seek the treasures and minerals still believed hidden in the land beneath us." Chachan started weaving a small bit of energy for protection once she had passed through the sanctuaries entrance. From her viewpoint, these people had assumed authority in her land, and she would not tolerate it. She chose her next question.

"Who are you?" Chachan asked with more force than previous. This was the moment where civility had come to an end.

The Matriarch walked past Chachan, unaffected by the tone in the question, waiting to answer as she came to stand in front of the marble sculpture of the First Mother and her young babies.

"Do you think that they knew who they were or what their true purpose was? My name is Santal Culdris, and I am the Matriarch of Medellin, but what's in a title, Chachan? I am a woman, a mother such as yourself. A woman has many depths to her. You are G'LA, named as a much stronger magician than those that remain, but you keep even that hidden. What other unknown chasms do you think are within you, Chachan?" The Matriarch removed the head covering and shed the spell to reveal her identity.

Chachan stood amazed. The Matriarch had not traveled to Ledoma in over twenty years. Her surprise would not allow her to lose focus on what the words the elder woman continued to share.

"With times changing as such, you can hide no longer; no one can hide. The Soachim have touched the Lake. The information clearly has not reached your borders yet, but Kefise is no more, and villages to the west of it have been decimated. Their attacks seemed to have been coordinated, but we don't understand for what purpose yet. There were no survivors. We buried the dead, and the aftermath has affected some of my daughters. It appears the universe has led us to Lake Ledoma to honor my departed daughter and seek answers in what was left behind by the Soachim.

Chachan was not sure if she should have been angry or happy that Ledoma wasn't the only territory affected, but she was feeling even more unsettled knowing the Matriarch knew much more about her than expected. Chachan wondered if anyone had been informed that the Matriarch had left the capitol of Medellin?

"Do you have any more questions, Chachan Ohi Balent?"

Chachan understood the Matriarch's position in the world, especially after the Rose had been expelled and banned from the holy land, but her intrigue had not been satisfied. Her responsibility would always be to Ledoma and its citizens first.

"Why are you here really?" Chachan knew for the best answers a direct approach was best.

"Inquisition, searching… but most importantly to pay our respect to Anel Improvi," the Matriarch answered without pause.

"Forgive me in advance Matriarch, but that is still insufficient…" Chachan noticed the energy shift inside the sanctuary. She noticed the breeze across the nape of her neck as the sconces along the walls flickered. Had she been set up, pulled away from the others to cause her harm? She contemplated reaching for the energies within her, but she waited. She would not be the first to violate the code of G'la, especially in the sanctuary.

"Surely, I pose no threat to you, Matriarch, and we can't shed blood within these walls…"

The Matriarch hesitated before turning to face Chachan with a befuddled look. Upon realizing Chachan's concern, she remedied it.

"Oh, no, come forth." The Matriarch spoke firmly.

Chachan adjusted her eyes as several figures emerged, seemingly moving from the shadows of the candle flames into the space.

"These are my daughters." The older woman smiled slightly as they approached her and Chachan.

Whether the Matriarch meant it as an introduction or statement, Chachan was uncertain. She counted five women, and each wore the same full, sandy colored face and head covering. The only difference was seen on the separate color jewelry they wore to indicate their primary magic. Each woman took a position to flank the Matriarch. They were of varying ages and from different nations as seen in the features.

Chachan observed the eyes of them, penetrating her as if to expose her secrets, subtly being weighed without permission. She held firm, no one would intimidate her.

"She will do just fine." The voice of the Matriarch broke the stillness.

Chachan realized she was overmatched in not only power but more importantly information. She had asked for this revelation of sorts. Less than a full day ago she had prepared a feast, and now she pondered if she had just bitten off more than she could chew.

CHAPTER TEN

Giants Among Us

"What in the world?" Naiyan said, sitting up quickly. Both of her friends were still sleeping. She sat staring up at the ceiling thinking she had just woken from a nightmare, but she couldn't remember what it was.

Naiyan heard the striking of the bell, but it was not the sound of a bell she had heard her entire life. The sound was vastly different, and unless they had slept for an entire day, morning was still hours away. Instead of waking the other two, Naiyan rolled out of the bed, and the wood in the fireplace began to burn more intensely as she walked past its hearth.

She retrieved a teapot to heat water and walked back to the fireplace and placed the kettle onto the metal slat to boil.

Feint noises were heard inside of her mother's cottage. She started to wake her sister-friends but knew that nothing could penetrate her mother's wards even in death. They were safe.

Naiyan realized she had not taken her hand away from the kettle as the water heated, but it didn't scold her skin. She stared at her hand, attempting to figure out why there was no pain, but then she heard multiple voices coming from the other side of the adjoining door again.

Naiyan approached and opened the door slowly.

The landscape was not her mother's portion of their adjoined cottages. Instead, before her appeared a grand wilderness that rushed past her, as if she were soaring high above the sky. Slowly, she could begin to see the fullness of the land. There were buildings larger than her mind could imagine and Sequoias taller than even the Tower built in Carcero, which was a monument of gigantic proportion.

Naiyan sailed back and forth as if soaring on the currents of air drafting upward.

There were giants standing nearly three times her height walking and carrying bundles of items strapped across their backs.

In the next instance, Naiyan was no longer flying freely; she was staring out into groups congregated around an evening fire that danced with orange and blue flames. Her mind could not grasp whether she was dreaming or not. She looked around the space from within the flame and was humbled. Enormous mountains were the backdrop as a waterfall that seemed to never end flowed more brilliantly than the one at Lake Ledoma. The water more arctic than blue carried with it a force that channeled its energy into contraptions used to power their land. The face of the mountain was lit with an unknown source, and Naiyan viewed an assortment of stairs carved into the side of it.

A loud noise drew Naiyan's attention back to those congregated around the fire. Three women approached the fire as they spoke.

Besides the women being nearly three times her size, Naiyan thought them stunning. The three-quarter pants they wore were supported with leather straps. The tops looked to be made of goat leather accented in gold eyelets with single shoulder intertwined leather cords that connected in the back.

Naiyan focused on their words and was able to zero in on their conversation.

"All I know is that he doesn't believe anything of humankind, and he won't change his opinion. The only words contained in the Otainis Codex that matter is those written after our king returns with the Three."

Naiyan was mesmerized that she could make out the facial details of this woman. Her eyes were different; one blue-green iris contrasted against a black iris. She wore wristlets and anklets like the other two accompanying her, but hers weren't made of silver like theirs. Hers were made with gold and had jeweled adornments.

Another much younger woman approached the group and kissed each woman on their cheek.

"Taflin, sister, they have found another one. That makes three in the last ten years, and I just found out that it is true that the Queen of Uteri has somehow removed the Rose of the Garden."

The woman with the fancy jewelry shook her head negatively back and forth before responding.

"These so-called rulers of humankind will destroy themselves. When the truly gifted of their kind still lived, we knew harmony, but as the sibling moons cycle again, man will eventually destroy their fabrics of life for ambitious reasons. There is not much that can surprise me. We never expected the exodus to last this long, but since the pact was broken, only our true king can reseal the bond. I'm not a historian, but they've killed the king and ousted the Rose. Who could we possibly trust of their kind? I think…" Taflin choked on her next words to stare towards the bonfire.

Naiyan was staring back. She wasn't sure if she could be seen, so she stood still.

Taflin tilted her head to make sure she could trust her eyes. She squinted deeply as she moved slowly toward the fire again, but each time she waved.

Out of curiosity, Naiyan waved back again.

Those who had been with Taflin were now staring at each other, wondering why their warrior priestess was walking towards the large fire pit.

"Taflin, what are you doing? You said the fire was large enough already." Taflin put her hand up, signaling them to wait and be patient. She waved one last time at Naiyan.

In reflex Naiyan returned the gesture and reached out to take Taflin's hand, and without warning, the image pulled away, and the land before her faded into nothingness.

'*That was different than the others.*' Naiyan was brought back into the moment with her hand still holding onto the door handle.

'*Am I dreaming*?' She went to pinch herself and that's when she noticed movement along the wall.

'*A shadow*?' Her friends hadn't moved in the bed. Something else had caused the movement.

"Goosebumps," she muttered, and then her heart fell into her stomach as the dark obscurity moved from the wall to the floor and back to the wall. Her attempt to move was futile as her feet were cemented in place. Fear was an insufficient emotion.

Unable to move, she tried to scream, but her voice was lost.

The golden red flames in the hearth began to shine brighter, and Naiyan could feel tingling across her back as an unknown energy flowed around her.

As the shadow pushed across the wall, it slid down to the floor, transforming its height and body mass. It appeared to be in the silhouette of a person, but it had no substance as Naiyan looked through the transparency of the shape.

'*Why won't they wake up?*' she began panicking as the opaque body advanced forward. '*Leave... Leave... Leave...*"

But the form moved closer and spoke.

"Before the dawn, He is coming through the darkness."

The form shifted again but into a non-human form with horns being pushed through the head of the shadow and large claws beginning to extend from where arms once were.

Naiyan's eyes went wide, and the scream stuck in her throat bellowed out as a mouth formed from the facial area. A horde of snakes emerged from the mouth cavity and were headed toward Naiyan.

"Before the dawn, He is coming through the darkness for you, First Blood!"

An eruption of fire sparked, and from it, a second shadow emerged. This one's focus immediately was drawn on its counterpart. Instead of advancing on Naiyan, it emitted a beam of unfamiliar energy, directed at the dark shadow.

It all went black.

"Naiyan... Naiyan... it's okay. It's a dream, only a dream... Naiyan." Ransa was holding onto her, preventing Naiyan from falling off the bed.

Naiyan stared into her friend's eyes, trying to decipher what was real.

"It was a dream... but it was so real... so real." Naiyan, now secured, still held onto her friend for a brief while longer.

The languid flames in the fireplace still cast its shadow across a portion of the wall and floor. A set of shutters on each side of her main entry allowed traces of moonlight into her space.

Naiyan scanned the room again; she needed certainty that it was indeed just a dream.

Imani, now adjusted up in the bed, also searched for anything out of the ordinary. The door to Anel's portion was still closed. The additional blankets still laid on a chair by the wooden table. There was no sign of intrusion. A few faint voices could be heard coming from outside from what they ascertained was the nightly patrol.

"It really was just a dream." Imani hoped her words added a small bit of reassurance.

"Sit there. I'll get you another shift. This one's soaking wet. If you're getting sick, then all three of us will be. I can't afford to get sick right now." Ransa rolled out of the bed.

Naiyan pulled her yellow shift down across her shoulders to replace it with a white nightgown.

"Do you mind if I lay between you two? I'm so tired I've had these nightmares every night." Naiyan pulled the quilted blankets up to cover her body while situating herself next to Imani.

"I'll take the first watch. That's what my dad calls it, takin' a watch. So, you two get some rest. I'm usually up this time of night anyways, but first, will you get me a glass of water, please?" Imani mumbled softly with her eyes half-open.

Ransa excused herself and walked towards the small table with the pitcher of water on it. She remained attentive of Imani speaking to Naiyan.

"Ma says sometimes when we're tired the mind gets overwhelmed, and we begin to imagine things. You have had the weight of the world on your shoulders. You've always been stronger than me and that one over there." Imani nodded in the direction of Ransa returning with water.

"So, now I am considered as 'that one'." Ransa shook her head playfully.

"Get some sleep. I'm keeping watch." Imani passed the cup to Naiyan to finish off the liquid.

CHAPTER ELEVEN

Demons Breathe

Imani did keep watch as they slept. Her joints felt pressure but not quite as much as usual. Her tolerance for pain increased as she had grown in height over the past two years. Now the growth spurt had ceased, and she was grateful to feel less strain on her body. She learned different depths of meditation to help her cope with the tension.

The three women were connected like mind and body. She couldn't remember any meaningful day without them, and she loved these two because of their willingness to accept her completely, especially with her ailment.

She had more questions about the Soachim being in Ledoma. Her mother had also shared that the poison in Senior Improvi was unknown but had attributes from tainted energy from the West.

For her, history was the greatest tool to understand the present and what to expect in the future. So, as she had read to understand her physical ailment, she kept on and found new cultures; in her newly found knowledge, her belief in the Creator grew.

"Ransa," Imani whispered, hoping not to stir Naiyan.

"Sorry, I knew you weren't sleeping, but I've been thinking." She lowered her voice.

"Will you secure a few books from the library for me?" She hesitated as Naiyan stirred, making sure they didn't wake her before continuing.

"I need the Beast of Sirini and Demons Breathe."

Ransa couldn't make out what she was trying to say in the scarcely lit room. She motioned with her hand for Imani to repeat her request.

Imani shook her head in disbelief and overexaggerated the second time.

"The Beast of Sirini."

Ransa understood that and nodded affirmatively before watching Imani repeat the additional book.

"Demons Breathe…" Imani repeated by saying each word by syllable.

"The man breeze." Ransa couldn't read her lips in the dark and didn't understand it any more the second time around than she did the first.

Imani simply shook her head and repeated it again.

"Demons Breathe, Demons Breathe." Her attempt to not stir Naiyan failed.

"Demons Breathe," Naiyan answered as she rolled over in the bed. She repositioned her head and nestled in the pillows.

Ransa understood finally.

Ransa would "borrow" the books like she had before. The way she saw things, everyone needed help in life, and for her friend, books were a way to keep her mind occupied as she managed her daily discomfort. It had set Ransa back a year of study, but it was worth it. When she had been questioned about why she was 'stealing' books from the seniors' library in the past, she took the liberty to correct the record.

"I do not steal, senior. I believe that I am a healer already. I'm simply learning the craft. I have a sister, a friend who finds comfort in keeping her mind occupied by reading. As a healer I am to commit no offense or crime against any, and thus I have not. I borrowed a singular book that had not been checked out in over three years. I did it to help my sister-friend and will accept responsibility for my actions."

A few of the other seniors decided that although her actions were for a "greater good", she still had gone against the "common rule." Senior Batelle wanted to dismiss her from her studies completely, saying she was putting herself above "the standards set to follow", but Senior Improvi spoke out with reason.

"What offense has she committed, Anri? She's followed a path towards serving the greatest good with pureness in her heart. This is more than many of us have remembered. She will not be expelled… She will have additional time added with Whal and Chachan who will undoubtedly ensure she understands common rule and common sense, but punishment and penance are two separate things, and we as Senior Assembly must remember this."

Ransa was grateful for Senior Improvi's input on that day, but both Senior Stanjz and Balent pushed her twice as hard over the extended year; she learned more in the one year than she had in her previous three years of advance medicine. Her most important lessons weren't found in books but in her mind's eye. Chachan told her this was the place where the force of the Creator resided in man. Since then, she was able to think outside the box and realized that the differences in magic were only frequency variations.

She had magic in her, but she shied away from it, choosing instead to focus on understanding what medicines and salves worked for specific treatments. No one knew how strong her magic was; only small insubstantial signs of magic surfaced when testing. Only a portion of what she was capable of had ever come forth. Chachan and Whal used an ancient technique attempting to unblock the energy, but it nearly killed Ransa.

Chachan encouraged her to practice small techniques in private and to keep studying the history of the world because others had found ways to tap deeper into themselves to find the reason they too couldn't access their gift.

That was the beginning of her growth process.

Ransa rolled out of the bed slowly and placed a log into the hearth to keep a little warmth present. She had slept longer than intended, but it was rest she needed.

Imani had fallen asleep from keeping watch. They knew the toll it placed on her body, especially with her ailment and it wasn't her way to complain.

'*I have to get through these last few lessons and be able to test to join the Medici.*' Her time as an apprentice had already been extended. The politics of the Assembly trickled down to her station. There were some magicians in the Assembly who didn't care for her.

More ideas flowed as she watched the two closest people in her life sleep soundly. Recalling Anel's first time testing her for magic to the moments of the festival when Iver earned the title of Master by besting four men in various intense challenges. He earned the title that no one else had in over two centuries. His title carried weight throughout the lower continent.

Each moment of importance in her life the Balent's and Improvi's were present. The thought of the emotional bond relaxed her, along with the rocking. Soon after, she followed the same course Imani had when keeping watch. She fell back asleep and stayed that way until awakened by Ziri returning mid-morning.

CHAPTER TWELVE
Ego or Identity

Ledoma had changed overnight. The early arrival of Santal Culdris created stress amongst a few seniors, but it was simple dialogue with owners of goods and open pit grubbers that broke the tension with the citizens.

A collection of seniors waited expectantly for the return of Chachan and the Matriarch who had not been separated since their introduction. Elder FloAntal was also missing with the group.

FloAntal had status amongst the Assembly, but she typically kept to herself. Her voice was often balanced and measured in times of uncertainty like this. She had declined becoming First Master after her name had been submitted and was one of the few people besides Chachan that Anel had personal conversations with.

The Matriarch had strongly suggested that there were many new arrivals setting up base encampments near the lake who needed to feel welcomed. She went so far as to tell Anri, the elder who had been embarrassed in front of everyone, to choose ten of his companions to also pitch tents. She strongly advised him that it would help them remember what purpose they served. He had been berated in front of the council when the traveling group arrived at the sanctuary and had learned his lesson.

The amber sunlight shimmered as the morning progressed. The temperature was more warm than usual for this time of year, and even more, much cooler air permeated at night. Many bartered and exchanged services while others paid coin for the items on their lists. Children played as usual, not understanding the gravity surrounding their old city.

Two women wearing green sashes accompanied by another who donned a yellow one were at the waterfront, paying fishermen coin for their early haul. The men appeared ecstatic with the amount of money they received and thanked the women graciously in return. By all accounts it was still early. However, jovial energy permeated the space.

Anri snubbed his nose at guardsmen who were sharing small bits of their background with those from the Matriarch's entourage. Entertainers who had come from far and wide brought their skill as they arrived a couple of weeks early. They dressed in vibrant clown suits and chased children around as others juggled or performed some creative feat. It was a festive continuation of the day, but Anri couldn't feel the joy.

Unbridled horses walked along the bank of the smaller stream running off from the lake, having their fill as a small group of armed men sat and relaxed. Anri had no doubt that the men were keeping an eye on his movements. His mistake was grave in the treatment of the early arrivals, a very bad miscalculation. He would show everyone that he was worthy of his rank, especially the Matriarch.

He was lost in the thought of redemption and the reason why he hadn't heard the cries for help.

"Elder... Elder Batelle." A young woman carrying her only child on the back of a mule approached.

Her voice startled Anri.

"Excuse me, but he has gotten worse." She held worry in her eyes.

Anri, feeling important again, strutted across the sand, over the dusty mauve pebbles and grass, between several horses left freely about the space. He slapped one last straggling reddish-brown bay and approached the child.

He had briefly attended to the boy two days prior for a high fever and constipation, but as he saw the darkening in the child's lips, he recognized that this was more than a stomach ailment. From first glance it was a sign that the child had either been poisoned or somehow was possessed by an unclean spirit. If poison, he could use his talent to pull it out of the child's system. If the other, then he didn't possess the strength to save the boy. If the spirit was still using the life energy of the male child, he could contain it after the child's life expired.

"What has he been given? What has he ingested?" Anri asked as he pulled the child from the buckskin mule to lay him down onto the ground. He placed his head to the boy's chest and listened.

"What has he eaten today? Quick, woman!"

"He's only eaten mushroom soup, sulfur shelf mushroom soup," the mother answered.

Anri inhaled and allowed the air to flow through his body before directing it through the boy's nostrils. He was using this to navigate his airways to find what the poison was attacking.

He could feel the faintness of the child's heart but could not sense the path of the poison. He directed his gift to expand which pushed the boy's lungs upward. The pressure was building inside the boy's chest cavity, nearly close to the maximum the young child could withstand. Anri was repulsed by a jolt of dark energy pushing back against him.

"Elder… Elder!" the boy's mother yelled, seeing the pain on the contorted face of her child. The boy's eyes rolled backwards until only the whites of them showed an increase in the child's fear as he clawed at Anri's arm.

His mother advanced towards Anri, more fearful of her son dying than the repercussion of attacking an elder.

"Don't interrupt me!" He bound the mother with air, restricting her movement.

…

"Hey… hey, Mani." Ziri whispered into Imani's ear to wake her slowly. As she stirred, he knelt to keep her from adjusting her body.

"I have to take Ransa. They're looking for her right now...."

Imani nodded.

Ziri fixed his eyes on Ransa.

"Hey, hey, Rags." He kicked the bottom of the rocker chair.

"What do you want, zit face?" She opened her eyes to look at him. If he was going to call her by a nickname, she'd do the same.

"I'll be there in another hour or so. I wasn't due till midday, and I've got everything prepared; they really don't need me, and your mother is covering my time." She adjusted to get more comfortable. If the city wasn't on fire, the seniors would wait if it was the last bit of defiance she could muster.

"There are those who have requested your immediate arrival to the sanctuary. Promptly." His hand extended to help her rise. He motioned with a nod of his head towards the others.

"Let them sleep. I'll check back on them later. But we have to go." His eyes showed more urgency than she would like.

Ransa folded the quilted blanket she used and placed it evenly in the rocker chair before following him out the door. She wasn't going to leave others to take care of her mess regardless of the request to come immediately.

It was much later in the morning, and the energy was different. The fog had already lifted from the small brooks, and as she walked barefoot with her footwear in hand behind Ziri, she thought about the revelations from last night and how Chachan had sealed their tongues from speaking about Naiyan and the information in the parchments.

"Z, can you slow down? They'll all be there when we arrive, and you can blame our tardiness on me. It's not too much more that they can do to me. Trust me, I know." She attempted to gain his attention, but he pressed forward, moving at a jogger's pace.

Ziri sidestepped two women carrying wicker baskets full of miniature energy stones. These were small beads forged with a small amount of magic's energy to help with small tasks like boiling water or cleaning items.

Unfortunately, Ransa wasn't as fleet of foot and tumbled into one of the women, knocking the basket out of her hands.

Ransa slowed to help pick the small crystal stones up when a young mother bumped into her pulling her child on a mule across its back.

The woman's attention was on locating a Medici to help.

Ziri ignored the woman's request and was only set on completing his task. He grabbed Ransa by her hand and nudged her forward again. The area was gleaming with new arrivals for the festival, and the energy was lively.

She saw a few carts selling fruits and legumes, not to be outdone by carts of cold cream and toppings.

Pigeons walked the edges of the worn dirt path, searching for crumbs left behind from vendors or those eating as they shopped. It was the same streets with the same sounds, but then she saw another face she hadn't seen before followed by yet another. The assortment of new faces intrigued her, and from the energy in the market, people were earning larger coin than usual. The closer they got to the sanctuary, the busier it became. She saw dozens of horses around the bank of the water in the distance.

"Who are they?" she asked, but he didn't respond.

Ziri walked with purpose, and as expected, Ransa was right behind him.

She was nearly jogging to keep pace, but when they neared the brook, she stopped in mid-step. She saw new caravans and horses. Soldiers that were not part of the armed guard were moving towards her and Ziri in three separate patrols.

Ransa saw Elder Batelle by the water's edge, but she could sense something was wrong and that the elder was overwhelmed. The mother was being held with his magic against her will and that his course of treatment wasn't adequate.

Without his permission, Ransa pulled energy from the surrounding environment to counteract the pressure Batelle had used when expanding the young boy's lungs.

Elder Batelle did not vocally object, but his eyes told Ransa that she had overstepped her bounds even though he knew he was in over his head at this point. For now, they would do what was necessary to ensure the healing of the boy, but afterward, Ransa would be kicked out of the program for Medici, and no one could stop him. She had not been welcomed by Anri, and she knew it, but for now all that mattered was the recovery of this young child.

"You don't have time for that; you don't have time for much right now. She is expecting you, and we have to go!" Ziri said, agitated.

"There is always time to heal. This boy is my priority, so focus on what you have to, but stay out of my way." Ransa gave Ziri an ice-cold stare and dove in. She had offended two seniors in less than thirty seconds.

Anri was still attempting to expand air inside of the boy, but Ransa saw the damage that was taking effect on the internal organs.

“Elder, please, you have to pull back,” she said casually without regard to his rank and stature.

Anri ignored her request and pushed farther. He was extremely close to the revelation of poison and thwarting the dark energy even if it maimed the boy. This would be the beginning of his redemption with the Matriarch.

The patrols that had recently passed had now turned to watch the two, attempting to care for the child. Ziri pinched his lips together but knew what was going on in this moment was out of his control.

Ransa shuffled her body to prop the dark-haired boy into her lap as she sat down. She not only was locating the source of malfeasance in the male child, but she had to block the overabundance of magic that Elder Batelle utilized.

“Elder Batelle, you must stop now; you are causing more harm than help. Please let me.” Ransa could make out the surge of energy in the binding they had attempted. Instead of relinquishing pressure, he was forcing additional energies to counter Ransa, and in the process, he upset the delicate balance from their previous binding.

Ransa was being ignored, but she also knew the child was not going to survive without direct intervention on her part. She knew if she redirected Anri’s flow, it would give the child respite and perhaps a way for the healing power in her magic to soothe the boy’s pain. The water would serve a second purpose as well.

It was true that air could move more freely inside of the boy, but water could penetrate the blood without the additional pressure, and this is where Ransa believed the problem lay.

Anri's eyes bulging out in anger didn't stop Ransa. She had manipulated his flows and interjected her own. She sensed the mist entering the blood stream, and she guided her gift to find the energy holding the poison inside of the young boy.

'*There it is.*'

Now she had to transition it out somehow and quick because the dark energy was growing resistant to the course she was following.

"Elder, I need you to draw the air out as I release my hold; it will cause vomiting, and once the dark matter is expelled, I will use the water from the brook to end it." Ransa was becoming winded, but she would not release her binding.

"If he's gonna live, you must follow my lead." This time the younger woman commanded the elder. She knew her life as a healer had ended, and even worse, she would receive admonishing for speaking out of turn, but that mattered a distant second to the life of this young child.

Anri followed her lead and released the pressure of air once she released his flow back to him. As the boy coughed, Ransa saw the bundle of darkness hovering around his lips, a demon seedling attempting to take root inside the child.

Ransa acted quickly as a ball of water formed and forced the dark matter inside of it. She had to pull more energy from the brook before binding her weave.

Anri, seeing the dark energy, added a different binding to Ransa's weave to add more firmness to it. He would take it to the sanctuary himself.

The young boy coughed and struggled to sit upright, but from the liveliness in his eyes, his ordeal had passed.

"Thank you… Thank you so much!" the boy's mother called out, rushing past the elder to replace Ransa, allowing her son to lean back into her arms. Ransa was proud to have helped save this boy's life. This was the first time she had encountered dark energy. She was able to sense the taint in the bundle partially devoid of light. Ransa had no doubt it would have killed the young boy and thus was grateful she was strong enough to bind it with Elder Batelle's assistance.

"*You*… you are done! Your name will be stricken from the books! None will come to your rescue this time. You've always been a nobody! Do you hear me? A *nobody*!" The older man was winded, but his emotions were sharpened by his tongue and cursed the younger woman.

Ziri watched from a close distance. He wasn't going to interrupt, and he did not have status to speak against Elder Batelle in the open. A mounted soldier moved closer towards them to see what the commotion was about.

"No… no, no, we just saved him. You were killing him. You had to know that you were causing more harm than healing; you were breaking one of the five laws. I mean he was close to death, elder. I meant no offense." Ransa's attempt at apologizing only antagonized the situation.

"Almost killed him, is that what you just accused me of, you, insignificant twat?" he snarled and then wove restraints of air across the younger woman's chest. His embarrassment from earlier in the morning drove his anger.

Ransa attempted to submit her will in the moment, now that her reason for interjecting had passed. She saw it as a positive outcome, but she was on the receiving end of an attack.

"You attempt to order me about, and you're nothing but a filthy trite. I almost broke one of the tenants of healing. Is that what you just said?" His words escalated and spread across the market and surrounding inlay of water.

The energy he summoned earlier in helping the boy was minimal in comparison to the binding he utilized to squeeze the air from her body. Ransa was barely drawing breath and suffocating from the pressure against her rib cage.

He overlooked the fact that indeed he had broken one of the five tenants by harming the child and restraining the mother. Two more offenses in the same day.

None of that mattered. He would break her in two without a second thought.

Ransa clawed at her neck as his magic tightened. *'Small quick breaths.'* The lesson Anel Improvi had taught her about survival skills against those who used their magic as an offense was helping her.

"Don't…" The words, barely heard, passed through her lips as she became faint. The mounted soldiers moved closer to try and separate the two, but Elder Batelle saw this as an attack and used the sand around the water's edge to hold the horse's legs in place. This was an additional offense. He simply didn't care.

"I am an elder and master of my house. You will be punished today."

Ransa fought the pain as her ribs beginning to break. Others looked on in shock and yelled.

Ziri was trying to break the barrier and failing miserably. Each step he took to get close enough added to the feeling his skin was peeling.

Ransa started seeing small bursts of lights in her eyes, knowing she was close to passing out or being killed. She concentrated the last bit of energy she could to form tentacles from the nearby water that latched onto the older man by his wrists before pulling him backwards into a waist high portion of the brook.

The soldiers stood between the two parties as the three women made eye contact with Ransa. She wasn't sure from their expression what would happen next.

One appeared to wink at Ransa before turning her attention to Anri who had turned beet red.

"Come here, you, little fuckin' cu—"

"*Silence*!"

The three women spoke in unison while they lifted Anri from the brook and into the air, held together by invisible bonds, which also cut his connection to his magic.

"Mother will be highly upset at him, don't you think?" one of the women asked the others.

"Yes, yes, Mother will be… *highly* upset." They turned and walked away with Elder Batelle gliding in the air with the energy of their magic.

When they passed Ransa a second time, they shook their heads in disapproval.

Ransa understood why they were disheartened. She committed an offense against an elder and had no right to interrupt his treatment of the boy. There would be no coming back from that offense even if he had attacked her first and was in the process of killing a young boy. She was not Medici.

Anri's eyes were bulging out, scarlet red with intensity. He scowled toward Ransa. Even in his bound state, he forced out words.

"You are going to pay for everything, you little shit. You are nothing, and you assaulted me. You have broken the tenants of healing, and I will make sure you never see the light…" Suddenly he gasped and passed out.

"We said silence!" The two women with green sashes smiled at the third woman in their party, who simply looked back at Ransa and spoke with amusement.

"You think that's bad; *you* were expected to have arrived over an hour ago." The three women who arrived with the Matriarch moved forward with Anri still secured tightly.

Ziri grabbed Ransa by the arm and pulled her toward the sanctuary with no other words spoken. He would not relinquish his grip even as they cut through a crowd that had formed near the temples.

"Excuse me, excuse us. Sorry, sorry…" They pushed past more selling carts leading to a small shortcut through shrubs and bristles, but Ziri pressed forward.

Ransa was still overwhelmed from exuding an amount of energy in saving the young boys life, but even more so knowing she had overstepped once again.

'*I was stronger than the elder...*' The thought abruptly ended as they came out of the thicket near the sanctuary entrance.

Ransa wasn't sure what she was witnessing initially. She was familiar with the faces of each person standing attentively with their eyes straight forward. These faces were usually adorned with lavish assortment of superiority and smug attitudes, but now they seemed… humbled.

The seniors under their third cycle were being addressed by a short salt-and-pepper haired woman wearing all white. She instantly knew that the woman before her was the Matriarch of Medellin.

"Young woman, when we call for your assistance, that means everything you are doing must cease!" FloAntal appeared at their side. She motioned Ransa toward a set of bald women with their arms folded in front of them. They did not look happy.

Their clothing, vibrant colors, were indicative of their magic. Ransa surmised the degree of richness, also indicative of their power or status as it had always been a true descriptive. Reds and shades of yellow along with bluish and greenish hues.

"Rainbows," Ransa whispered.

The Matriarch glanced at Ransa and returned her attention to the seniors of Ledoma.

The women led her inside of the sanctuary, into portions she had never been allowed. Ransa became anxious with her palms sweating. She bit her bottom lip to make sure she was still breathing and dug her thumb into her index finger. Walking into the lower level of the assembly hall, she was faint. Her feet were heavy and uncertain, but it was pure will that propelled her forward.

Suddenly, appearing behind her, were other women in various garment designs, each garnering some form of color to indicate which magic they possessed. She knew they were not from Ledoma or any surrounding territories. Filtering around the lower section where the First Master's occupied, they came to stand opposite of Ransa.

Ransa wasn't certain if she would be passing out as her rites of passage was before her. As the three bald women nudged her forward, she placed one foot in front of the other and onto the dark stone tiling.

Marbled columns held an interior area in which the smaller platform was situated. The columns held rainbow specks of colors in each, seemingly creating an energy source. Connecting each of the pillars were dark threads of what looked to be vines held together by interlocking weaves.

CHAPTER THIRTEEN

Challenging Tradition

Ransa was overwhelmed as the Matriarch appeared flanked by Chachan and FloAntal. She had been so in awe of having the strongest magicians in her presence that everything else had been diminished in size.

She stared at the Matriarch and the two women she had known for her entire life.

However, it was another younger woman who came forward to speak. There was no uncertainty in her walk, and those in attendance remained attentive.

"Mother, if I may." The young woman waited for approval to proceed. Her amber bracelets with a pearl setting on each wrist were recognizable as the sign of being a shaman—one who also used spirits and deeper magic in the practice of healing.

Ransa stood motionless, quiet, while staring at the young woman. It was the girl at the brook, near the water's edge earlier during the confrontation with Elder Batelle. She was dressed differently. Ransa found it odd that someone appearing not much older than she had already acquired the knowledge to become more than just a common practitioner of medicine.

The Matriarch nodded her approval as the crop haircut woman walked towards Ransa.

The perspiration trickled down the side of Ransa's head. What she felt wasn't quite panic but close to it. If she had a mirror, she would surmise that her face had also reddened, but she held firm.

The young woman stood face to face with Ransa before walking around her body. She looked out to those present and exhaled. All eyes were fixed on her.

"Just this day I have learned that not only have the 'great traditions' of Lake Ledoma been lost on many of the seniors, but I have also seen ignorance of our basic understanding; that curing illness is strictly left to those with proper credentials. The one who is called Anri Batelle has such credentials as an elder." Her hazel color eyes turned back to stare at Ransa. She paused, moving closer towards one of the columns. Something strange happened when she did; where her hand was placed on the column, a brilliant yellow color traced her fingertips along with green and red trim.

"The one who stands before us does not have credentials and interrupted the work we have been accepted to do."

Her heartbeat quickened and she pinched her fingers to calm. What she had thought was her rites of passage had turned into something more life changing.

"Is this true, Ransa G'esh, that you have done that which is stated?' The Matriarch moved forward to stand close to the younger woman. She reached out to touch Ransa slightly on her shoulder awaiting an answer.

"Yes, Mother, I did. The young child was suffering and was being killed." One lesson she had learned extensively from Anel and Chachan was to answer questions straight forwardly.

The Matriarch turned and walked back towards Flo and Chachan before ordering everyone to sit down except the young shaman and Ransa.

"Erri, is it true that the young boy was being killed?" the Matriarch redirected her question.

"It is true mother, and I would not have been able to prevent the death; the one before us used what was at her disposal at the expense of breaking tradition," Erri finished without emotion.

Ransa wanted to run out of the room, but the three bald women, now recognized as Diviners, had not moved from their original position. She wanted to say something but knew it wasn't appropriate. Yet.

"We have traditions for a reason, young lady. Some are outdated, but some are in place to ensure the safety of us all. Practitioners spend decades learning methods to use for healing. Shamans, like Erri, are rare. Even in the garden, under the tutelage of the Rose, very seldom do those of her age acquire the necessary skills to cure illness using her gift. It is dangerous." The Matriarch motioned for Ransa towards the dais and to stand on the platform.

"When Arjunai, Rose of the Garden, tasked me with keeping tradition, it was not taken lightly. The night that King Hasinho was murdered, I was there. That same night the Tree of Life shielded those unborn children from a great evil that threatens us even now, I was there. The Rose taught me what would be needed to ensure the knowledge was passed forward." She paused as she stood to walk the perimeter of the stage.

Her skin seemed to illuminate as she traveled. Ransa was unsure if it was her lightheadedness creating the small sparks of light she was seeing follow behind the Matriarch. When the elder woman touched the columns, as Erri had, her hands shimmered with hues of deep red and yellow. Small traces of blue flashed, but the brilliance of the intensified colors amazed everyone in attendance.

"These are unusual times we find ourselves in. The darkness continues to spread, and in our fight, tradition is not to be easily forgotten. Ransa, I have no indication that you are prepared to realize the potential you have. It takes years of training to interrupt another's remedy and replace it with your own. In fairness, I take no offense to your previous actions but tradition." She hesitated to stare directly at Ransa.

"Not only tradition but rules are in place to help keep a semblance of order. There is a price for everything," she said flatly before ordering Erri forward.

"Erri nearly died doing what you performed *after* she became a shaman. With all her understanding and magic, she was unable to save the life of the patient or the other traditional healer. Erri spent over three months recuperating, but you stand here without harm." The Matriarch stared at Ransa deeper than before, piercing to the soul, but Ransa would not shy away.

'*Meet power with force.*' Anel's voice rang in her head.

"Do you know what this room really is, what this stage and these arches are used for?" It was a rhetorical question.

It was no secret that 'rooms of reflection' had been built by the First and Second Order to measure what magic, if any, a person had. But this marble flooring was different; it had inscription from the Age of the Beginning.

"I have learned that none in recent history have had the privilege of being tested within this room of reflection, but yours will be conducted by me. You will be weighed and measured, here and now. If you pass this process, you are welcomed into the sisterhood of those present. You will continue to learn from who I designate. Every land must grow new traditions, and should you survive this undertaking, the weight that we carry between us will also be yours to share." The Matriarch finished without saying what would happen if she failed, but Ransa held no doubt of what would happen if she failed.

Ransa looked towards Chachan, and for the first time since her arrival, she saw concern on the older woman's face.

CHAPTER FOURTEEN

Who is Worthy?

"We have before us, one seeking entrance," Chachan called out as there was no need to wait.

On cue, everyone stood in a circular pattern to surround the stage while only Santal Culdris, and Ransa stationed themselves inside the columns now flowing with rainbow colors from the magic of those present.

Reaching their arms towards the heavens, each woman replied in unison.

"If she is worthy, Great Mother, allow her to pass; if she is not, allow your light to reveal 'her' truth." When they finished, they grasped hands and waited.

The Matriarch extended her hands outwards in the direction of the columns. The energy she was drawing in was substantial as she directed it towards the dark marble floor. As the light penetrated, symbols were revealed in multitude of colors moving towards the platform on which Ransa stood nervously.

This level of testing was for those who already were practitioners, less than one percent of those attempting to become a shaman passed this seldom used Rites of Passage.

"I believe in you!" Erri yelled out, and then everything outside of the columns faded to black. Ransa and only the Matriarch remained.

"For what purpose have you arrived?"

"I am here to serve the greatest good, Mother." Ransa understood that the Matriarch was inducting her into this order meant there was no room for error. It also meant that she would be weighed by a woman the Rose picked to lead the Order of Petals after she was exiled.

Ransa discerned the tingles in her feet first followed by a burning in her lower back, symptoms of the Ilenian flu. The remedy was simple—rest and orange-peel oil rubbed on the feet.

'*Good.*' The voice sounded in her head. It wasn't her but that of Santal Culdris. "She can read my mind?" Ransa's anxiousness took on new heights.

'*Concentrate, child!*' The sternness came through with the thought. It was not a request but an order to be obeyed. For the next three hours, she was tested and probed. It was more than simple combinations of medicine inside of the space the two occupied. The scenery changed with each remedy found. Initially, Ransa diagnosed cures for each ailment the Matriarch demanded.

What followed was a mixture of testing scenarios as the Matriarch manipulated the magic granted to her inside this chamber for each simulation.

The first three patients were simple, but as each remedy was found, the next series of patients forced Ransa to use her untrained gift to remedy each symptom she faced. Forbidden by even basic practitioners, using the gift in treatment, was saved for only people like Erri who had the power of the ancient ones. Not only was deep understanding of medicine a prerequisite, the power used had to create a harmonious connection or the treatment could kill both patient and practitioner.

This was no easy task for Ransa because she had never been formally trained in these techniques. Anel Improvi had taught her how to free her gift instead of fighting it. Chachan had made her sit in silence to find balance within, but Ransa had never been tested by either in this fashion.

Ransa noticed the tingling sensation increase from her feet upwards towards her torso. The vibration steadied through her whole body as memories from her childhood surfaced—painful memories that she had long forgotten. A picture of her mother and father flashed in her mind. Her mother had died due to complications delivering her second child. Ransa was only four years old when it happened. Neither her mother nor baby sister survived. It drove her father insane enough that he took his own life two years after the loss. Ransa was first to find him dead.

Ransa could feel the wetness on her cheeks as the next series of testing began and as the Matriarch spoke to her about releasing pain and guilt. Ransa fought each of these emotions. Pain from watching her mother die. Guilt for not seeing that her father needed help even at her young age. Ransa was bombarded with another memory. One that she had buried so deep that she had long forgotten about. She was naked, in the memory. A faceless man was chastising her for being disobedient. He stripped her naked and thrust his sexual deviances upon her. She smelled the scent of lavender.

She remembered being forced to ingest a liquid after. Realizing she had been drugged with a potion that affected memory, she understood what had happened to her and a third emotion surfaced. Anger.

"Calm your thoughts." The Matriarch's voice came through her emotions.

The Matriarch held substantial power within this enclosed area as a conduit used to excise memories such as the two from Ransa's past. In a sense, she was reliving the younger woman's memories along with her too.

The Matriarch needed to measure more than her knowledge and gift. She needed to know the heart of a person she had in front of her, and the Matriarch learned this young woman had more raw potential than Erri but was still mending from emotional turmoil from her early life. If left unchecked, they could steer her down a different path.

Unaware that her final test was about the pure power of her gift and nothing to do with medicinal purpose, Ransa waited while the Matriarch lifted her arms again towards the columns to draw energy into herself before releasing it in increments towards her. The vines connecting each pillar began to pulsate along with each column. The small speckles of colors were vibrant, like balls of light dancing. The spaces in between the columns were shimmering a reflection, and as Ransa peered into them, she released her magic reaching towards the light energy from the pillars. The colors in the columns turned ocean blue, and another column turned emerald, green. When Ransa looked deeper into the shimmering spaces, she saw something coming forth. The Tree of Life stood before her, as solid and real as those in the assembly hall. As quickly as the vision surfaced, it was gone and the shimmering along with it. Ransa was dazed momentarily.

The columns had returned to white, and the symbols on the dark marble flooring had ceased, but laying atop, was a dark wooden rod. The Matriarch used her gift to bring the staff into her grasp. She turned and walked away, leaving Ransa standing on the platform. The other women who had been present at the beginning of her testing departed along with her, with the exception of the three bald women.

Ransa was discouraged, especially after noticing FloAntal had not stayed behind at least to watch.

'I just don't get it; I just know this is my purpose.' She was discouraged. She was exhausted of energy but more so saddened that she had sacrificed so much in her studies to not be able to do what she knew in her soul was the purpose she had been created for. As she walked from the platform, the three women who had originally stood behind her reappeared and motioned her to leave by the exit the Matriarch had gone.

"Into the elder's space?" Ransa couldn't think straight. The embarrassment of failing, coupled with the aggression she knew she would face from Elder Batelle, was overwhelming. She had memories in her head that she was not fond of, but more importantly, she remembered being violated as a young adolescent.

In the end Ransa believed she would have to begin a new life elsewhere.

'He is going to strip me of all of my rights,' she thought as she pushed through the wooden doors the Matriarch had exited. Her hesitation was understandable as each side of her path was lined with the women who had departed first. The Matriarch stood at the opposite end of where she entered the room. Chachan was second in line from the Matriarch, and Flo stood next to Erri who couldn't contain the smile on her face.

"You have been found to be worthy." The Matriarch ushered Ransa forward.

As she walked the narrow aisle, tears flowed from her eyes. She realized that not only had she become a healer but a shaman like Erri. She knelt before the silver-haired woman while all those present surrounded her.

"We are bonded in time to protect those the Creator has made our charge. Our sistership was born in the shadow of the Tree of Life. You are a part of the garden and bound by oath to heal, protect, and when necessary, defend the light from the darkness. By tradition, you are now Shaman Ransa Ansar, daughter of Santal Culdris and inducted into the Order of the Petals. I will announce your status in time." She finished as the wooden staff extended from the older woman for Ransa to grip the other end. It turned brilliant white momentarily. Ransa was amazed to see an aura of green and blue tracing her fingertips much richer than she had ever imagined. The Matriarch took the rod back before telling those gathered to resume their places where they had stood when Ransa originally entered. As Ransa walked towards the back of the room to take her place in line, a few women blocked her.

"Your place is here." A woman older than the Matriarch moved down, motioning for Ransa to take her place next to Flo opposite Erri.

They all took hands as the Matriarch retrieved a long spindle of what appeared to be an untangled vine. She walked the length of the room, handing each woman a portion to hold. When she finished, she channeled energy between the long root to secure the bond these women now shared.

CHAPTER FIFTEEN

A Wife's Request

Small pebbles that had not already been driven into the dirt by previous travelers could not escape the three wagons filled with goods making its way to the grandest market. These assortments of products from the villages outside of Ledoma were part of the currency families needed to survive. Each wagon was pulled by two horses flanked by one rider on each side. Paid guardsmen were secured when previous shipments were seized by armed bandits.

The goods were high quality and the only reason they could be sold in the Grand Market of Ethi.

Ethi had its own place in history. It contained the oldest and wealthiest finance house on the southern continent, lending currency to only those with the highest credentials. Often, this bank was the difference between wars being won and battles being lost.

Iver found himself accompanying this caravan of sorts as a favor to his wife. Now as he sat next to his former commander, Bengor Gret, who drove the lead wagon, he wasn't sure why Chachan had given him this task at dinner with Naiyan.

"I think our wives wanted to get rid of us." Iver sat back against the wagon seat with a piece of straw between his lips. The long, winding trail was pitched, so each step the horses made needed to be measured. He was just as run down as the road they traveled after only getting two hours of sleep after the dinner with Naiyan two nights ago.

"Peni has been trying to get me to take small jobs that keep me active. Now I'm delivering goods with you, and this assorted bunch." The older man pulled on his thick white beard. Nearly eighty years older than Iver, Bengor was still physically capable. Many believed he should still be the Commander of the armed forces, but those closest to him understood that no one was immune to the politics in the land of Ledoma.

"No, old friend, you miss making a difference in the bigger picture. I once thought about taking a leadership position, advising the smaller nations and lands on our continent..." One of the horse's ears perked up. This group had left a few hours before sunrise on the day prior when the sky had been dulled out by clouds. After a brief night layover, they set out before dawn on the second leg of their journey; now the sun had risen, indicating noon was approaching, and the wind carried with it a slight musty scent.

Iver observed the approaching men from the vibration he sensed from their horse's gait. He could only surmise these were bandits responsible for the stolen shipment two months prior.

Bengor and Iver had seen the twenty-person group off in the distance when they passed them nearly an hour ago. Their first day traveling had been uneventful, and now it appeared the small band had circled back around to take ownership of the goods and products being taken to Ethi.

"No one dies today," Iver said loud enough for the older man to hear and acknowledge.

Bengor wasn't quick to anger, but he abhorred anyone being preyed upon. The last shipment had been stolen and the reason why they had been added to the delivery group. All of the group casually dressed as civilians, making them appear an easy target but were trained guardsman.

"Agreed, no one *needs* to die today." Bengor pulled on his white beard while holding onto the reins of their wagon with the other.

Iver left it at that. The former commander had never learned how to take orders. He hoped his strong suggestion would be taken at least at minimum.

Bengor kept the pace of the wagon steady and motioned for those riding on each side of the two wagons not to initiate an altercation by mere hand movements. They would not be the ones to escalate a physical confrontation.

Two of the riders from the trailing group galloped ahead of their wagon to bring them to a halt.

Bengor inhaled slowly to speak, but instead one of the bandits beat him to it.

“Old man, we seem to have lost a few of our belongings, and these wagons look exactly like they are carrying a few of those valuables. How about you hop down, so no one has to die today.” His voice traveled through the facial covering hiding everything but his eyes. One of the bandits held a canteen of water up above his head while the leader moved his hands in a circular motion. A stream of water floated across the space and then back into the container.

Iver understood the threat just given. The bandits had magic and weren’t hesitant to use it.

Bengor exhaled and shook his head in disagreement.

“You know just before you overtook us, my old friend said the same thing. I, for the most part agreed, with him…” Bengor shook his head.

In that moment, those who had traveled from Ledoma understood their former commander still held firm to tradition. Anyone using magic as an offense had to be held accountable.

Unfortunately for these would be robbers, Bengor, for nearly one-hundred and fifty years, had been the executor of such accountability.

“We could let you leave, and we can all be on our way, but I believe less capable travelers would be at your mercy, so…” Bengor hesitated again and focused his attention on the man holding the canteen. He moved his fingers slightly and used magic on the remaining liquid to explode the container. The leader of the bandits tried to take hold of the remaining liquid, but Bengor forced it into the dirt road by using his secondary air magic to make it dissipate.

"Please dismount your horses, and we will escort you to the authorities within the city," Bengor finished. He experienced the excitement of conflict he had missed for so long.

The guardsmen from Ledoma kept their horses steady as the other bandits moved theirs closer. They had failed to see what happened at the front of the lead wagon. They continued to aggressively surround the remaining carriers.

Iver moved quickly from the wagon and secured a long staff from the side of the carriage. He wasn't sure of the skill level of the group he now faced, but he understood that confrontation was unavoidable.

"We have no problem leaving you maimed to take what belongs to us, but we'd rather not. We simply want what's inside the carrier wagons." A younger voice was heard from somewhere near the rear. His voice also sounded like he did not want any part of a physical conflict.

"Shut your mouth! You should be grateful we even let you ride with us after the last time. If it wasn't for your brother!" The burly man holding the canteen of water spoke out before removing his sword strapped across his back. He looked at his partner who had just used magic and nodded.

Iver took that movement as an actual threat. He pointed the long staff at the man with sword drawn. The masked bandit believed he had an upper hand because he was still in his saddle and Iver on foot. He kicked his bay and tried to run Iver down. Iver used the long staff to strike him in the shoulder, dislodging him with quick precision.

The next few minutes seemed chaotic, but in the end, the bandits were broken and subdued. Half of them had taken off after realizing they were on the losing end of this altercation, leaving the other half to be taken into custody.

"We will hand them over once we reach Ethi," Bengor advised.

Iver understood that the authorities in Ethi would be fair according to their laws. Some more harsh than others, but it was one of the reasons the large market did well; those arriving to barter and sell would be treated as equals.

It had taken less than an hour to reach the gate of Ethi after the confrontation. The gate was an enormous monstrosity to itself. Many believed that giants helped build the city along with magicians as a symbol of their bond to each other. Others were not as certain because Giants had not been seen in over five thousand years. The magnificence of Ethi was only accessible by large bridges spanning two-hundred meters wide and another five-hundred meters long to gain entrance.

Magicians had carved out two waterways for the city that seemed never ending. In doing so, many of the canals spread throughout the city could be navigated by small boats. The canals were lined with grand adornment. Some were lavish floral arrangements or ancient artwork displayed depending on the district.

The ancient magicians also left behind wards that still tested strong. Magic was allowed, but only by those given permission by either being a senior of Ledoma or Medellin, or learned on the northern continent.

Those that came from the other lands were quarantined to ensure they brought no disease into their city. Often, the Medici of Ethi performed the checks and determined who had to be separated and how long their quarantine lasted.

Ethi held no expense in making sure their city was the reflection of what it had always been. The financial capital of the lower continent. The quarantine quarters were separated by those with financial means and those without. Those with excessive coin were waited on hand and foot while being sequestered in fancy suites. Those without money shared rooms, often smaller than eight by ten feet, in groups of four to six people.

The regents of Ethi were fair, elected by their citizens. Magicians and non-magicians could be elected; the only caveat was your familial heritage needed to be rooted in Ethi since the city was constructed. At one time Ethi had seven regents, and now that number was down to five.

After passing the first large silver gates, a man of stature had his back to the group approaching from Ledoma. He was barking orders at two men and a woman. One of the men met Iver's eyes and shook his head to acknowledge.

The man talking turned and saw Bengor first and shook his head positively. The smile was genuine. The gold pendant on his breastplate indicated the rank of general in Ethi's prime guardian military.

"Commander Bengor Fitz, I haven't seen you, well, since your statue was revealed last year." The man took long strides and hugged Bengor.

"Don't rub it in, Peni, actually..." Bengor paused as he was kissed on both cheeks.

"Well, you know your sister tries to keep me busy," Bengor finished. He always received the same camaraderie seeing his brother-in-law.

“And you…” The brother-in law shook his head up and down before pointing at Iver to acknowledge him. He embraced Iver by grasping his shoulders.

“Master Iver, don’t tell me you pissed your wife off somehow, and she has you chasing behind this old fart as usual.” He greeted Iver, gripping him by the elbow as Iver returned the gesture.

“It’s good seeing you too, Mose, but if we can get these goods to their consignment while you take these idiots who tried to rob us…” Iver separated to retrieve the magician of the group to bring him to Mose.

“This uncivilized person violated the tenets, and please drop the *master*,” he finished, shaking his head from side to side. Iver didn’t regret earning the title but it was an unnecessary acknowledgment to bear daily.

Mose motioned a group of his soldiers to jail them to await questioning.

“That’s the fifth one in less than three months. They are getting more aggressive. We have not had five amateurs in the past two years. Not to worry though, once they’re found guilty publicly and dismembered, that should be a huge deterrent to the untrained still committing violations of magic… I mean, that is, if they’re found guilty.” He disapproved as vehemently as Bengor did to those preying on others.

Iver didn’t like the idea of people losing limbs or body parts, but the alternate punishment had been death. Those who violated the tenets a second time would be executed by guillotine.

Mose pulled Iver and Bengor closer to him as the other soldiers from Ledoma moved forward across the oversized bridge to drop off the goods and receive payment for the funds not being transferred into an account.

"I have to speak with the regents this evening, but after, we are going to make up for lost time..." He hesitated as he was approached by another woman. She stood nearly as tall as the men, and as she walked, her muscles flexed with each stride.

"You wanted to see me, general?" she asked. Her hair, completely silver, indicated she was from an original family settled in Ethi or was strong in magic, perhaps both.

"I do. The gravity dam, we may need to reinforce a portion of the wall beneath it. You and two from your squad should be enough. I'll need an update before the meeting with the regents." When he finished, she nodded before making eye contact with Iver.

"You two haven't been here an hour yet, and your names are moving with the streets. If it isn't Commander Bengor and Master Balent." She acknowledged them. They all had history.

Iver smiled and nodded.

Mose and Bengor chuckled simultaneously.

"Everyone has jokes, I see..." He took her by the elbow in greeting each other. Although he had won the title over two decades ago, he was still the only one to achieve that designation in over five hundred years.

"The only master I want to be in the next hour is an expert in ale and gambling. My wife had to know I'd indulge in both activities upon arrival. She must be rewarding me for all the extra I've been doing." Iver shook his head up and down with a wry smile across his face.

Mose bid Iver and Bengor goodbye until after he met with the regents of Ethi. The three men had seen the fair share of battle together over the years. Many were skirmishes between bordering towns. The larger cities often squabbled over imaginary boundaries or over natural resources in an area, but there was one mission the three of them undertook that tested their metal they seldom spoke on.

Ethi was considerably different than any other city. The poor areas had more wealth than those of middle class in other large cities. The wealthiest were the descendants of those who had founded the city, held together by their history and a most formidable armed guard.

Bengor had a known affinity for joining the extra adult activities taking place in any city he traveled.

"Ale houses have women. Ale and women with special talents are never a good mix, my friend, for those in committed marriages." Iver slapped Bengor on his back as they followed the same trail their men had taken the goods. He hoped his elder compatriot would take his advice.

CHAPTER SIXTEEN

Winning and Losing

The streets of Ethi were large although not as large as the bridges crossed to enter. Walled off from most of the world, it was nearly as large as Ledoma but without formal elemental houses. Some with magic were sent to either Ledoma or Medellin to study. Those with adequate funding often went to Medellin and the other less fortunate to Ledoma only to return to Ethi once their studies were complete.

The streets were kept immaculately clean as the keepers of Ethi held their station with honor like those from Ledoma.

It didn't take long for the business to be conducted and concluded. After all the prices for consignment had already been established, the merchandise would be sold and funds transferred into accounts of those sending goods from Ledoma.

Iver and the rest of the men, with the exception of Bengor, had found themselves in Ethi's entertainment district. The usual ale and gambling houses were being frequented by others visiting or doing business in the old city. For all intents and purposes, it was a place many with wealth traveled for leisure.

The long semi-circle bar was full, but patrons tried to position themselves between those already seated. Peace was kept as security guards made their presence known and occasionally threw out those who drank too much. These establishments weren't local taverns that smelled unsavory. They were clean and aesthetically pleasing to the eye. The women and men attendants were varied, but besides serving beverages and food, each one was available for personal consumption as well.

These gambling quarters had a variety of people. Some citizens of Ethi, and others like Iver, were just passing through. There were another twenty or more tables, along with a few rooms set in private for gamblers with an affinity for high waged games. Each of these rooms had a list of those waiting to play.

Iver was primed to gamble. It was his vice, but he never gambled more than he could chance. He had seen the results of many others losing their life savings sitting at a gambling table or betting booth. As Iver sat across from the other players who had folded this large pot, he figured out only one person had small odds of winning the hand other than himself. It was the same opponent who had bankrupted the others who had sat down. His confidence had not faded over the night, and it showed when he addressed Iver.

"You probably want to lay your cards down this round, or you stand to lose a considerable amount of coin." The man was very thin but wore garments that showed his wealth. He was flanked by two women and one large man; he spoke with an air of superiority.

Iver wasn't sure if they were his personal attendants or security, but he was nearly certain the hand he held was unbeatable. So, he listened to the man exercise his ego.

"You folks from Lake Ledoma haven't fared well tonight, and is it any question why?"

One of his two women interrupted to hand him a fresh mug of amber ale.

"Why is that?" the other woman in his party asked to feed his ego.

"There's been no growth in that land in over five hundred years. The Assembly of Seniors are down to less than half of what their numbers were in those same five hundred years…" He paused to take another look at his cards. His disposition was nearly identical to when he had won large hands prior, putting a vast majority of previous participants out their money.

Iver balanced the man and his words, along with how the man had played all evening. Everyone had a tell, and it had taken Iver longer than three hours to figure it out.

"So, in keeping with Ledoma's five hundred years of mediocrity, that's what I'll raise this pot to. I know you people from Ledoma like donating your coin to others. Carcero won't be the only ones getting your money." He slid nearly all of his money across the table.

Iver knew by sheer odds he had a commanding hand, but the additional digs from the man about Ledoma made him feel more anxious than certain. Then Iver added another factor to the equation.

'He didn't push all in.' Iver made quick calculations based on his opponents play over the past three hours Iver had stayed away from playing him heads up, but now it was only the two of them remaining at the table.

"You are more likely right than not about certain customs of Lake Ledoma. We have been more peacemakers over the previous years but trust and believe we are always up for your type of challenge." Iver pushed all of his coin into the center of the table and waited for the thin man to follow suit with his remaining monies.

The eyes shifted to their table from others who were engaged in their own gambling of sorts. The wager was larger than any other placed. Iver had come prepared with winnings he earned in Ledoma to take advantage of a situation such as this. He had learned there was always a bigger fish in the ocean, and right now he was the shark.

The two women and man escorting the thin man looked at each other. Iver read the small discomfort and tapped on the table.

"How long must I wait to add my hard-earned money from Ledoma into your pocket since all we do is give it away?" Iver tapped on the table a second time.

Without recourse from being challenged, the thin man pushed all of his money into the table to match Iver. The silence in the room was a small buildup of murmurs waiting to reveal what each hand-held.

The thin man smiled and turned his cards indicating he had a very strong hand. His hesitancy showed that he wasn't sure he was in a dominant position, and as Iver flipped each of his cards individually, the expression on his opponent's face along with his entourage said it all.

Iver had won an enormous amount of money.

The thin man excused himself from the table, and as he walked away, Jaega approached Iver.

"Master Iver," she called out and, in doing so, caused more eyes to be drawn to the table.

Iver shook his head, grabbed his money, and pushed away from the table.

"Iver is sufficient from this moment on if that's okay with you, Jaega." He held a bit of disappointment in his tone.

"Yes, yes, of course, Elder Balent," Jaega replied without hesitation.

Iver shook his head in disbelief at his old acquaintance and then followed her out the door and into the streets of Ethi.

The evening lighting sources rivaled that of Ledoma. As clearly as one could see in the day, the main corridors were lit nearly the same. The establishments in these main pathways stayed open much later than others.

"A friend of departed Elder Improvi would like to share information to pass to your wife." Jaega slapped Iver on his back to make it seem like casual conversation.

Iver was confused but that quickly passed. Now that his wife had assumed the position of the Fifth, she would have access to those in high places.

'*So, that's why she wanted me on this trip.*' Iver simply walked side by side with Jaega. If she had any other pertinent information, she would have proffered it. Since she hadn't, Iver surmised he would have to wait a tad bit longer to see who summoned him.

Iver did wonder if he should be including his old commander, who was having dinner with Mose and his family, but as Jaega took remote access streets to underground tunnels that seemed to span the same pathways as the water canals, he was certain the information was solely for his ears.

Ethi was an old city built when nations of humans along with magicians, giants, and other creations of the light lived harmoniously together. Less than a dozen founding families remained, and only five seats were occupied by regents. Even with the façade of wealth, peace, and prosperity, Ethi was plagued by the usual system of politics and prejudices of the world.

Jaega walked assuredly. She was a descendant of a founding family, but she chose to become a prime guardian, believing it would keep her the farthest away from politics. Now as she stepped down the final few stairs into the isolated meeting space, she understood escaping the politics of Ethi was not avoidable.

Iver followed closely behind, feeling for vibrations in the earth to understand his surroundings. When Jaega reached the bottom of the stairs, he was able to sense a person standing in the dark before a torch was lit.

"Iver Balent, I know meetings deep in the night, in underground tunnels, can seem inconspicuous, so rest assuredly this is definitely one of those secret gatherings." A baritone voice was heard before the frame of a man emerged. His hair, barely stubble, was white as snow.

"You wonder why you have been requested? To be blunt, we have a problem. The bank has received monies for land north of Ledoma and south of Ilens but west of both. Does it have anything to do with why the Matriarch of Medellin has left the border of their States? Who can say? However, with the negotiating between Ledoma and Carcero, it is imperative that the Fifth knows. I can do nothing to stop the vote in acknowledging the owner of said land all the rights of a sovereign nation. I only have two of the five votes my fellow regents will cast. I don't want to say it's a conspiracy within our great city, but there's something of a conspiracy in Ethi. Our clandestine network still travels in whispers, but this information must be delivered in absolute trust." He paused as if contemplating delivering the last bit of information

"We have reason to believe the unsavory elements from the wilderness are amassing an army, and the *whoever* is buying the land, their benefactor," he finished.

Iver nearly staggered hearing the last bit. He knew the words carried weight, especially when they came from the second oldest regent.

'*Why wasn't the Assembly of Seniors given this information?*' Iver knew if the regent speculated an army had been built, then it was nearly certain. If so, Ledoma needed to gather as much information as quickly as possible since many of its citizens had homes near the wilderness and not much in defense.

"Was Elder Improvi aware of this?" Iver finished his questioning. Being the Fifth had so many roles associated with it. Was passing of clandestine information one of them? If Anel knew this, was it the reason why she had been targeted?

“She knew of the massive amount of land being pursued at the time because it was imperative to share the information when the first items of consideration were sent from Carcero to Ledoma for additional land provision. This is all I can share. Please make sure the Fifth knows what was just shared.” The older man turned and walked back into the shadows.

Jaega turned and walked the way they had entered. Iver followed behind with his mind racing. But an answer resurfaced a second time as he circulated his thoughts about everything since leaving Ledoma two mornings ago.

‘This is why she sent me with Bengor.’

CHAPTER SEVENTEEN
Friends or Foes

The seniors of Ledoma, who had set up tents three days ago, were strongly advised by the Matriarch to reacquaint themselves with those whose very lives they were chosen to help govern.

Anri had been allowed to leave even after hearing the multiple infractions levied against him from eyewitness accounts of his attack against another. He was, however, told not to appear at the First Master's dinner. His name would remain on the ballot for leadership, but his presence was not required.

"Who is she to tell us…" Whal began to say out loud, but Anri knew nothing good would come out of it.

"Just don't say it; don't even think it. She knew things before she even asked the question. The *lifesticks* they carry, I fear do more than enhance their powers." Anri tried to walk with his head high, but the heaviness of having his ego broken prevented him from seeing three of the soldiers from Medellin approaching.

"Watch where you're going," Anri said before knowing who they were being directed at. He pulled energy into him to use his magic, out of reflex, but Whal interrupted this altercation to prevent an escalation.

"Excuse us, it's been—been an overwhelming week to say the least I'm sure for all-all of us." He pulled Anri away from the soldiers who had yet to take their hands from the pommel of their swords.

Whal pushed Anri along the way.

"You need to be smart, and not just smart, but wise. These aren't merchants and ocean faring people from the sugar isles of Carcero or those easily manipulated. Right now, we need allies for when they leave our city. If you break another code, what do you think she will do to you?" Whal smiled at a few familiar faces that seemed happy Anri wasn't his usual narcissistic self.

"I guess we will be seeing a lot of each other more often now," a shop owner sweeping in front of his small business called out. He had a strand of straw pierced between his lips. The slight upturn crease of his lips and his smug facial expression showed a bit of satisfaction.

"Ha, you think…" Whal noticed the vibration under his feet and staggered as he made out additional resistance in his step. Anri was drawing energy in again.

"Yes, you will be seeing more, more of us, and we-we are definitely going to be helping you out. I remember coming into your family shop when we arrived long ago. Your mother made clothing with crafted skill." Whal paid the man a compliment to deescalate the moment. It seemed to work.

"Elder, it's not necessary. the Creator blesses us with more than enough," The middle-aged man replied as he swept the last bit of dust back onto the trail.

Anri was simply indifferent.

"Where are we going anyway?" Anri turned away from the shop owner before Whal caught up to him.

"I still have the two room cabin my family shared when we first came to Ledoma. It may need a quick overhaul, but between us, it should take less than thirty minutes. Once we are done securing our temporary arrangement here, my next step is to retrieve items more valuable than those *lifesticks* they carry."

"Do whatever you have to do. I'll need time to clear my brain." Anri rubbed his hand across his forehead, approaching the door. Whal released the magic used to prevent intrusion.

The latch to the entrance had rusted, so Anri used focused bits of air to push away most of the old iron. The door pushed open and dust particles circulated, mixing with the bits of sun rays peeking through the slats of the window coverings.

Inside, the two-room cottage had been kept neat although no one had occupied its space consistently for nearly a decade. Small footprints could be seen on the dusty floor from the rodents that found their way in.

“Six persons occupied these two rooms. My ma and da broke their backs toiling in the old fields to barely provide enough for me and my three siblings while I studied to become… whatever it is that we have become.” Whal exhaled as he walked to one of the support beams and traced his fingers across his name inscribed from when his family moved from Ilens to Ledoma.

“I remember the day my da allowed me to do this.” Anri laid his hand flat against the support and fashioned a small smile across his face.

“I had just come back from hunting. I outfoxed all the others and landed a healthy boar.

Anri moved toward one of two sets of three chairs stacked against the wall. He used his magic to separate two chairs for them to sit.

Whal bent down and removed a small wooden floor plank. He reached into the hole and fiddled around until he located what he needed.

He pulled into his gift and moved his fingers ever so slightly. The manipulation of air forced dirt through the hole. As it flowed out slowly, a skeleton key emerged. Whal grabbed it and held it out in front of Anri.

“If you will.”

Anri forced pressure against the key with air to strip away the last bits of dirt that Whal hadn’t.

“Why do you have that?” Anri’s eyes widened.

“Don’t be so naïve, Whal. You know why I have this. While you’ve been *playing* at First Master, I’ve been making sure that our city remains our city. I have found many things hidden beneath the portions of the old sanctuary. Now that the Matriarch and her daughters have arrived, I need to get a few items to protect us. We have more control than you think. Anel's death has afforded us great opportunity." Whal tucked the key into a pouch under his new white wardrobe.

"Those items you speak of are forbidden, trapped in spells woven by those whose powers were greater than any of us remaining now that Anel is gone."

"Anri, you can't be so far up your ass that you can't see past your ego. There is at least one. You were always first to be done when we were neophytes, but you were always the last to see the big picture. Chachan is a problem and FloAntal as well. FloAntal may not know how powerful she is, and we don't need to take any chances." Whal looked his old comrade squarely in the face.

"When I return, I will need you to decide if you are with me and Ledoma, or if you will shrink in the face of responsibility and history."

Anri listened to his counterpart as they straightened the space. It wasn't nearly as bad for being unused, but as Anri rearranged the few pieces of furniture, he had no idea what items Whal sought that could be more valuable than the very branches given by the Pramum. The Tree of Life was energy and intelligence. Those of the Order of Petals, when chosen, understood the Pramum was also the link between the spiritual world and the material world.

"I was wrong from the moment the group greeted me," Anri said flatly. He was coming to terms that everything he received from the Matriarch was warranted.

Whal bit his tongue. Right or wrong was not the point now.

Whal saw an opportunity for a power play and was going to take it. He had in his possession the ingredient to reanimate the Soachim to do his bidding. He could duplicate enough for two, perhaps three.

'*Three will be enough to take out her security force, and then I will negotiate their departure.*' Whal's thoughts led him to one of his major concerns in how many of the citizens of Ledoma would be casualties once the pendulum swung his way.

"We can take back our city and make sure every other nation understands we intend to retake our standing in the world. I will not allow our home to fall like Uteri has. I won't attempt to keep you from leaving. If you are here when I return, then I welcome you by my side and will share my plan completely with you. If you are not, I hold you in the same regard as I do now; just don't get in my way." Whal nodded and exited the two-room cottage.

...

Anri walked over to the support where Whal had scribbled his name. He wondered what the story behind it was. He remembered the seniors before him had spoken of ancient secrets laying in spaces buried deep under the oldest ruins. Some were artifacts used several millennium ago and others as recent as when Esroun walked the land during the last battle.

Anri knew about these forbidden rooms, the rumors at least. He had never stepped foot into one.

"Books of spells written before Esroun. Potions of life and death. Simply damn rumors," Anri mumbled, yet he knew if Whal had been so forthcoming, perhaps it was more than rumor.

"*What is he thinking*?" Anri shook his head defiantly. He had more pressing issues than some vague idea.

The thought faded as a knock on the front entrance of the two-room cottage drew his attention.

He walked to the door and opened it, standing across from two faces he had just become familiar with the morning he insulted those from Medellin.

"Elder Batelle, you have been requested along with Elder Stanjz to speak with the Matriarch this evening. Please be prompt." Two of the younger assistants to the entourage extended him an invitation on parchment. They turned and walked away without waiting for a reply.

Anri looked at the invite and then slammed the door in front of them. The door hinges, already weakened, came off track.

Anri spent the next hour fixing it before realizing he needed to be making his own decisions. Still uncertain of Whal's outlandish plan, he hoped it would not be the end of his old comrade still attempting to have greatness attached to his name.

CHAPTER EIGHTEEN

Plan For Success

Whal took old routes that had him circle deep into the wooded area surrounding an entrance over a half-century old. In his travels he procured many oddities that others thought held little value, but when he saw the skeleton key over twenty years ago, he understood its worth right away.

For the past two decades, he studied some of the items hidden in the secret chambers under the sanctuary. At times finding himself fighting for his life when objects, he was certain how to use but turned out to be something different.

He flashed back to the night a *shade* broke his leg. Whal barely escaped with his life. Since that moment, he studied every object with critical care. It was here that he found the first thought on returning Ledoma to glory. The one thing that he was certain of, with the reanimation potion, he would be untouchable.

'*Even the Matriarch with her daughters will be no match against my ambition now. I'll just need to keep her daughters occupied during the ceremony. There can be no Order without a Matriarch.*' Whal accepted the energy in the earth beneath his feet. He wove a spell to pull open the hidden entrance. He closed it behind him and shimmied down the small dirt decline.

It was dark and cold. He had grown accustomed to this feeling over the years; even now the space was not welcoming.

Whal lit the candle he had brought; he didn't necessarily need the candle. He knew every inch of this forbidden room. He extended the candle to light others. Shelves of items circled him while stacks of other contraptions were situated on the floor.

'*I will make them understand how great we once were and will soon to be again.*' He exhaled softly and moved towards a small table with two vials of a coal black liquid encased in glass.

Whal took the key from his waist pouch and slid it into the lock. He watched as the key turned by itself. The clicking sound of each sight rotation, sounded like the hands of a clock; however, it was the rainbow colors of the ancient elders and their residual power traveling the seams of the encased glass.

Whal marveled at the magic that some had been bestowed upon them in the past. He, himself, was a very strong magician, but the gifted ones, were named G'la,

As the key turned faster, the glass began to shimmer, and the bright light increased as the colors diminished. At the conclusion of the cycle, the glass case opened.

'*Ledoma will rise again.*' Whal secured the vials and slipped them into a different pouch. He looked around the room to find other items that could be used in the quick battle that he would wage against the Matriarch.

'*By the time I'm done, I will be both savior to some and demon to others.*' Whal didn't concern himself with either title. His goal now was to get Anri on board to use as the face of the rebellion, and if he didn't join his cause, he would make sure his old friend became the perfect scapegoat. Whal knew the secret ambition of power Anri had since they crossed the soil over seven decades ago. His hope was that the Matriarch embarrassing him edged him closer to the ledge, and Ransa besting him in front of everyone had pushed him over it.

Whal took the remainder of the day and continued to bask in the fact that the poor, lowly skinny kid that cried when he left Ilens was set to become the Principal Senior in Ledoma, a title not held in over eight-hundred years.

CHAPTER NINETEEN

A Road Trip

The last bit of moonlight made the bodies gathering their belongings appear as mere silhouettes. General Roner attached his saddle to his horse and watched Iver approach on his Percheron.

"Like a thief in the night," Merico said loud enough for his voice to carry. Merico had taken over leadership of Ledoma's armed forces over three decades ago. Taller than most men, he was sinewy but more on the lean side. Iver and he had known each other for nearly their entire lives.

"More like a thief in the morning." Iver dismounted and looked around. It had been over a week since he returned from Ethi. He had offered the information to Chachan shared with him, and now within that same week, the network of information had received messages of slavers running through remote territories in their land.

The armed forces stationed had been pulled back to protect the larger communities surrounding the capitol city after the Soachim attacked Lake Ledoma. The thieves of humans, and other criminals, took advantage of this departure of military presence.

"Trivoli and Patin are a half-day's ride apart. The lieutenant general still has another month in Ilens before returning. I am taking thirty-five men to accompany us. My subordinates have their orders for the next two days. Your wife cannot be too happy about this." Merico bent down to kiss the ground. A good luck ritual he had learned from his da. He saw a small group walking towards the area he and Iver occupied that caused him pause.

"Well, she's the one who sent me to Ethi, and I can make the choice to travel with you right now. She will get over it." Iver's voice faded as a small group was seen moving their way.

As they came closer, the shadows revealed a few from Medellin, including their leader.

"It seems we have received the same information… Slavers?" Commander Ghamrod got straight to the point. Slavers were outlawed on the southern continent, but the business of free labor had always been profitable, so there were those who still pushed the profession.

"We have it covered, commander. Perhaps it's best for you and your…" He paused to count the four men and one woman accompanying Ghamrod.

"Five, stay and keep Santal Culdris and her daughters safe. We know the land and the people where we are headed; we don't need your assistance." Merico had paid respect to him when they arrived, but any business related to Ledoma would be handled by him and his men.

"General, I respect your position, and often I've taken the same one. We are not here to get in the way. I'd like to travel with you as there is strength in numbers. Anyways, you have no providence over me or those I lead." He met Merico's eyes head on.

The momentary silence was awkward, and Iver realized neither man would bend. He excused himself and Merico for a moment to speak.

"It's only five of them with their own provisions, and to be honest, I'd rather have him with us than against us. We are allies; this isn't a pissing contest." Iver hoped his words would break through to a man who was nearly as stubborn as his wife. They turned back to face the other party.

"Commander, we leave shortly." Merico gently pulled on the reigns of his horse and walked away, leaving Iver with Ghamrod and his men.

"So, out of curiosity, did you really only intend to seek out slavers with only five people? They typically travel in squads of forty to fifty men. Kinda brazen, don't you think?" Iver didn't mince words.

"Only if we died," Ghamrod replied with slight sarcasm.

Both men smiled.

A whistling sound traveled across the area. Those who would be leaving on this expedition mounted their horses and followed in line as they headed out of the city.

The pace they kept was moderate, and they stopped once in the first three hours to let the horses drink from one of the streams they followed to Patin. This city was a large exporter of rice and barley, and its location, one hundred miles from the southern border of Ilens, was often used by travelers needing rest. There was another few hours before they would arrive.

Much of it had been a quiet ride. The hooves of the horses kept an irregular cadence as each landed separately. It was an hour outside of Patin that Iver began talking about the problems his children were putting him through.

Several of the other men laughed as they could relate; being provider and protector was an 'always' thing.

"Thank B'nobi, I don't have that concern." The only woman in the group had said her first words since leaving Lake Ledoma.

The path they followed close to the rivers narrowed as a group of hills came into view. The traveling road widened slightly as they made their way up the terrain. Staggered slopes created an incline difficult to navigate, but after another mile, the ground flattened out.

A man was pulling a brown and white spotted mule behind him with parcels of rice inside of a basket mounted on the back of the animal.

Startled as they approached, he nearly jumped a foot into the air.

"Scared the living shit outta me." He regained control of his delivery and mule.

"Forgive us, we are here to see your master of arms." Iver spoke out, drawing the man's attention.

The man looked closer at the group arriving on the path.

"The Sigil of Ledoma… of course, of course. We weren't sure when we'd receive the protection promised, from the taxes we pay to you bunch." He looked towards Ghamrod, the Matriarch's protector, before continuing.

"The master of arms is putting someone to question in the prison dungeon. Just look for the crowd, gathered around like vultures. Welcome to Patin." He turned and walked away with mule behind him.

A few carts were set up selling rice patties and cooked greens. The smell of grilled meats permeated the air on the widened business street.

"Gather the information you can and pay one extra copper for any of the goods you secure. I will accompany the general. Remember, we are guests." Ghamrod understood although they sought answers, hospitality was essential.

Merico relayed a similar order before they rode deeper into the interior where law and order was being issued. The entrance looked simple with two guards standing post, and upon seeing the general, they allowed entrance. Once inside, they could hear sounds clanging beneath them in the lower dungeon area. "General Roner, we did not expect to see you… Master Balent." A woman sat at a desk with stacks of papers in front of her. She was familiar with two of the three men standing in the space.

"Elder Yolan, we thought you were in Ilens with the lieutenant general." Merico was confused why the woman of letters had shortened her stay with his subordinate. She was to document their travels.

She sat back in her chair and then leaned back. Her frame was long and sinewy even at her age.

"Lieutenant General Mhere can be an ass. I knew that before the task was given. But he made detours that I was uncomfortable with. Being an elder, I do not fall under his command per se. So, I guess you've heard we have two slaver scouts being interrogated. Mostly lies so far, but I think they're ready to break."

Ghamrod looked around the building at the faces attempting to recognize who he was.

"Cevin Jahl is still the master of arms in Patin?" Ghamrod didn't see the need for small talk.

"He is, but the interrogation is being conducted by Lieutenant Ruvlin. Jahl took fifty riders with him to Trivoli after finding a substantial amount of Trivoli's coin on their persons when they were arrested. There have been no birds in the past two days sent from Trivoli. If none come today, I fear the worst." Yolan stood up and motioned for a guard to open an iron door which led to a circular stairwell leading down.

The sudden heat change could be perceived as they reached the bottom. The smell of dried blood and stench had built up over time. A hammering sound echoed throughout the dungeon, and that's the path the three men followed.

They passed large empty cells with iron bars with the remains of straw on the floor for what had once been bedding. Very few put to the question in these cells had ever seen the light of day again. The cells were all front facing in order for those captured to witness the pain of being interrogated; often it sped up information gathering for those not wishing to be put to the rack, strapped, or tortured to feel like one was being drowned.

"Where is the base of your operation?" A woman's voice was heard, followed by the sound of a hammer hitting iron. The ensuing scream was bone curdling, and hesitantly, Iver took the next few steps. He wasn't sure he wanted to see the punishment being served.

Ghamrod and Merico stood side by side and watched the lieutenant in charge, nail anchoring spikes into the lower extremities of their prisoner.

"I can take away all this pain with only a few more answers. This doesn't have to continue, but it's up to you. So, tell me, where have you taken the people to be sold?" She still had not observed the presence of the men. It was one of the two other soldiers standing guard who saw them first.

"General… we did not expect to see you with all the commotion in the city." Lieutenant Ruhvin walked out of the cell, leaving the man strapped on an old stone slab. It was fitted with a wood covering to help in securing the various spikes to his body.

"Keep him alive until I return." She led the men deeper into the dungeon where the second prisoner was being kept.

"Slavers have moved closer to Trivoli and have been abducting children and women to send to the other side of the mountain. This one gave up more information, and he's finally breaking. The plan was to secure enough workers and breeders and destroy the rest, leaving an empty group of villages. Tomorrow is the day ships are supposed to come upriver and dock west of Kefise. There they will take those trapped, into the wilderness. We haven't gotten the exact number of slavers, but his number is seventy-four, and the other is ninety-six. If either is the case, those who have traveled will be outnumbered nearly three to one. I sent an additional fifty-armed troop to support him, but they left only this morning."

Ghamrod was first to hear the commotion and scrambling of the guards stationed in the prison. A loud horn was blaring, and the speed in which Lieutenant Ruhvin had moved had not been expected.

"We are under attack!" She grabbed her sword and ran up the spiral staircase and out into the street where she saw a horde of slavers, all wearing black colored clothing with their faces hidden.

The slavers had made their way to Patin. It seemed the two prisoners were sacrificed to draw a portion of Patin's guards away and now by sheer number they thought they could simply overrun those remaining with this blitz attack.

The sporadic maneuvers kept those fighting back from gaining any formation of defense. The slavers seemed to number in the hundreds, many pulling the citizens away to be taken. Those not securing more bodies were cutting down and killing those in their way.

A woman carrying a child across her bosom was being chased by a man with a sword in one hand and a smaller dagger in the other. Ghamrod had already removed his cloak and pulled his sword first, striking down the man chasing the woman with child.

"Thank…" Her words were cut short as an arrow pierced her neck, instantly dropping her to the ground with her child staring down at his mother.

Iver had seen the direction the arrow had come from. He disappeared amongst the chaos while Merico identified the greatest current threat. Several men riding on horseback with torches were lighting the buildings on fire.

"You three!" Merico's voice carried to his men with bows across their backs.

"Stop them!"

Their attention immediately transferred to those within range. They notched arrows and fired. Three arrows set loose: Three bodies were now dead. Two of the flaming bundles, relinquished from their grips, burned in the street, but the other had rolled into a kiosk containing strong spirits. An ensuing boom shook the ground as the bottles of alcohol exploded with smaller flames being spurted outward in a circular direction.

Ghamrod and Merico did not slow from engaging any of the human traffickers. They cut through every advancing slaver with precision and power.

Lieutenant Ruhvin ran towards another group of people carrying torches. She couldn't understand how women were part of the slavers ranks, but they had chosen sides, and for that, they would die by her sword.

Iver had made his was around the tree line quickly. Being light on his feet was a trait he always had, but it was the magic he controlled that prevented the first archer from hearing his approach.

With stealth, Iver smothered the man's mouth as he drove his anelace into his back. Only muffled whimpers could be heard as the man took his last breath. Iver understood that there were more men hidden. He would repeat the same tactic, so as he scanned the area, he knew he needed to be methodical.

The slavers were realizing that they were outmatched as more than half of their numbers had been killed in what was supposed to be a show of force. Some attempted to flee, but with their disorganization, a larger number kept engaging in this skirmish.

The woman who was part of Ghamrod's five was thought to be easy prey. Two men and a woman advanced on her. Each person instantly regretted their miscalculations as she eviscerated the first two before throwing the woman to the ground and killing her with her own weapon. She watched Elder Yolan ushering the defenseless people into a safer area when she saw movement thirty yards away.

Two young boys had been surrounded as they were pushed back. One boy swung a mace too large for his control, but the threat of the weapon had slowed the men. The other boy held an old Morningstar and swung it just as wildly.

"No, stay back!" The boy with the mace had connected with the weapon. The flesh and blood of a heavyset slaver was sprayed across the bodies of those in the vicinity. The group of men had intended on kidnapping the two boys to increase their purse, but now they would see them killed.

"You little shits! You're not worth my brother's life. I'm going to rip you both in half." A younger man pushed through the others. Before he could raise his sword, he was engulfed in flames.

"You will never hurt anyone again!" Yolan Vane had no equal in combustible magic. In comparison to her peers, she stood above them in her respective gift. Diving into her magic, she redirected the flames from the buildings, controlling it with her magic by forming fireballs as attacks against the small horde of slavers.

"Find some place to hide," she commanded the two adolescent boys. As she turned to re-engage, an arrow flew past her head to land squarely in the face of a slaver she had not seen about to strike her.

"Master Iver, thank you." A quick short acknowledgement did not slow her from bringing death to those who were attempting to kidnap souls.

Iver kept letting arrows fly. Each arrow took one life; it was an equitable exchange.

Those who had come with Ghamrod were deep into the battle. A few had mounted their horses and were cutting down those enemy still on horseback.

The soldiers of Ledoma had killed nearly three times their numbers so far.

Merico and Ghamrod had stayed within fifteen feet of each other and pressed forward. That's when they saw a set of slave wagons being pulled away from the city. The screams were undeniable facts that some citizens of Patin were being abducted.

Ghamrod caught the reins of a thoroughbred a slaver had just been detached from. He swung upward onto the large brown horse with black mane and tail. He galloped behind to catch up to the wagons racing away.

Iver had joined his side in the pursuit. The two of them pushed their horses to close the distance.

Senior Yolan was still redirecting the flames away from the buildings to slow their burning as most of the threat had been stifled.

"Elder… Elder!" Merico called out to gain her attention.

"Can you stop those wagons?"

Elder Yolan turned and saw the slavers being pursued by a handful on horseback. In the next second, she embraced more of her magic, gained elevation, and moved with haste.

The wagons traveled with speed across the terrain. The heavy suspension kept the wagon from swaying back and forth or losing its balance. The wheels covered in metal hubs had strong spokes that helped these slat walled wagons barrel across the landscape.

Iver pushed the horse he rode. He was too far away to shift the earth beneath the wagons, but something would have to be done and soon. The stretch of land they approached was the beginning of a mountain pass. The slope began twenty feet above ground, would have a sudden incline, and there would be no room to maneuver for those in pursuit. He motioned for one of Ghamrod's men to follow him as he kicked the side of his horse to thrust him into a faster gallop. His plan was to attack the first wagons driver, remove him, and replace him with the men. With the first wagon slowed, the others would follow suit.

Yolan seemed to have something different in mind. She reached the first wagon and descended until she sat next to the wagoner. She used her magic to encase him into a self-contained fireball and kicked him from the wagon. Taking hold of the reins, she carefully brought the wagon to a halt.

After seeing the elder take control of the lead wagon, Iver and the soldier from Medellin climbed aboard the other two carriers and took charge of those with not a moment to spare with the wagons skidding to a halt.

Voices rang out as those taken were set free. Many began running back to the city to see if their loved ones had survived the onslaught.

Yolan, understanding the acute shock of what just happened, took flight and returned with them to see where more assistance was needed.

"Good work. We prevented an additional stain on humanity. We should have kept a presence here and none of this would've happened. This core of slavers have never been so bold to send their slavers to our lands, in such a large number." Iver watched family members finding each other after being let out of their recent cages.

"It seems like they don't care, and you are correct. There *should* be posts along these routes and villages, just like there is additional protection at the mountain pass near the sanctuary in Ledoma." Ghamrod had a measured response, but he saw the lack of preparation for basic defense had been part of the reason for this attack.

"Whatever 'should' be is insignificant. We must regroup quickly and get on the road to Trivoli. Who knows what Cevin Jahl and his men encountered? Ruhvin and Senior Yolan can see to the injured and restore calm." Merico mounted his horse and rode back to the city to gather the men and quick provisions. The others followed.

They had lost two men in the fighting, with another three injured, and they could not ride. Over one hundred slavers were killed. Unfortunately, one quarter of that many citizens had lost their lives. Death held no favorites.

Regrouped, the armed force from Ledoma was in route to see what was left of Trivoli and the troops from Patin who had rode out previously to help defend their closest allied city.

It was a three-hour ride that saw emotions contained between those who had just withstood an attack by hundreds. There were no signs of ambushes or skirmishes along the way. However, once they arrived, the city was barren. The buildings were intact, but the presence of life was minimal. Animals ran free, but there were no humans left to be found.

The men dismounted and looked around in sets of three.

Ghamrod and his men found the main temple. Priests, who had called this place home, had their throats cut and were laid one on top of the other to block the entrance of the temple.

"Commander." One of his soldiers had taken a closer look at one of the bodies. He pointed to a symbol burned into the hands of each of them.

"The shadow is rising." Ghamrod read the words out loud as Iver had returned with the news he had found no survivors.

"Where are Jahl and his men or the group that rode out after?" Iver asked no one in particular. He had an eerie feeling as if someone was watching the group but saw no movement.

"Slavers could not remove an entire village. We have found more dead, and half of those are…" Ghamrod nodded at the dead priests.

"There are several wagon trails leading west. We are two days away from the wilderness, and we don't have the numbers to pursue them into their stronghold. We ride back to Patin and send birds for more men." Merico had made his mind up to formulate a better plan.

"We will stay until we have some answers." Ghamrod looked at Merico who returned the stare.

"So be it. As you said this morning, we have no providence over you or your men." Merico ordered his men to make ready within the hour to be back to Patin before last light.

The soldiers from Medellin burned the dead bodies after looking them over extensively for any information or clues left behind. Merico and his soldiers had departed with an hour of sunlight remaining.

CHAPTER TWENTY
Remaining Behind

Iver stood in the middle of the street staring at the empty buildings. Ghamrod approached after speaking with the woman soldier he now knew as Shan and another middle-aged man named Quar.

"This is what you passed on your way to Ledoma from Medellin. I mean Kefise was... like this?" Iver asked. He had decided to stay behind with Ghamrod. There was no need for him to backtrack with the men from Ledoma to simply ride back in two days' time.

"Similar but not exact. In Kefise, the wind carried voices; it was dark magic." Ghamrod pointed to the sanctuary about thirty yards away. It was a good place to seek answers if there were any to be found. As they approached, the smell of the air changed. Although the priest's bodies had been removed, the stain was already set.

Death was a familiar scent, easily recognizable, but when the two men walked deeper into the Temple, an overwhelming stench permeated the air. They walked past a dining area until they came upon the sleeping quarters of the priests.

"Immaculate," Ghamrod said lowly, but the energy in the space did not feel clean.

Both Iver and Ghamrod kept their hands on the hilt of their swords. Iver was skeptical about using it, but he had his magic as a last resort. There could be wards placed throughout, but he was unsure.

A noise drew their attention back to where they had just passed. There was nothing.

"Goosebumps." Iver shook off his jitters.

They continued to search the temple and came upon a prayer room in a lower section of the building. It seemed to be the source of the ungodly odor. Ceremonial candles were still lit, and a person covered in blood knelt in front of the altar. The tension had risen considerably in both men as they could make out severed body parts situated near the person who still had their back to the two men.

"Are you friend or foe?" Ghamrod asked.

Iver distanced himself for a better range of defense if necessary.

"I am what my master intended me to be." A half-eaten body part fell to the floor from what used to belong to someone to lay next to a scimitar. The curve of the saber still had pieces of flesh on it and what appeared to be a piece of someone's ear.

Both men kept their composure. The body had been taken over by darkness at its time of death, and now a servant of evil had returned to walk upon the earth.

As it stood to face both men, they could see the transformation that was already taking place. The hollow dark eyes and pale skin could not be mistaken. The elongated fingers with black nails would be the only indication left of what it was after its complete transformation. Skin demons were aberrations. They had no soul and could only be brought into this world through submission of will. Whoever this person had been accepted evil into their spirit, and over time, it provided the pathway for their body to be taken over in death.

"You have no place in this world!" Ghamrod pulled a dark bottle from the inside of his cloak and released the liquid content over his blade and allowed Iver to do the same.

Iver knew instantly that it was blessed water and would help in killing the dark spirit.

"You will go back to the place you have come and never return again."

Ghamrod's words hung in the air. The skin demon pulled the curved sword from the floor and parried with Ghamrod briefly.

"Not bad for a human." The words echoed.

Iver had decided not to use his magic in the temple. He was unsure if any wards had been set in place, and if so, they could do him more harm than good. Instead, he switched levels to keep the skin demon off balance, but with each thrust and counter, they were met with resistance.

The blade was unlike any that Iver had encountered earlier. Each time curved metal connected, shades of blue sparked along the edges.

"That sword is from Uteri and does not belong with the likes of you!" Ghamrod attacked with a ferocity that Iver had not expected. Ghamrod parried with the demon, passing its guard to slice a deep cut into the knee.

Iver saw an opening and thrust his sword into the back of the same leg.

Shocked, the skin demon retreated swinging its sword wildly to create distance, but Iver kept on top of it, drawing the focus onto him.

Ghamrod's blade pierced the changeling at its shoulder as it turned to ward off Iver's advance. It wailed out loudly in the confined space, the high-pitched sound reverberating off the walls. Realizing death was coming, the dark spirit attacked. If it could minimize the threat down to one, it had a much better chance to survive.

Iver scrambled away, defending each advance, but he was running out of space to maneuver.

"You will take no souls in my presence!" Ghamrod called out to help Iver evade the attack, but he had miscalculated the amount of space behind him, and he staggered. The skin demon saw the opportunity and took it. It shifted all its weight on the one good leg, but Iver had dove into his magic to bind the feet. It was a chance that need to be taken.

Surprised, the skin demon hesitated to stare down at its feet bound by the force holding him in place before turning his attention to Iver.

"Magician!" The words were cursed when he spoke them, but this momentary lapse was all that was needed as Ghamrod thrust his sword into the neck of the demon and down through its shoulder.

Iver advanced immediately and swung his sword in a half-circular motion to slice through the lower extremities, ensuring its death.

The sounds of footsteps were heard making their way down the steps to the area they occupied.

Iver and Ghamrod made ready, but it was the rest of those who had stayed behind in Trivoli with them.

"We heard…" One of the men held his tongue upon seeing the skin demon taking its final breath returning to the shell of the human it had just inhabited.

"Secure one building, and we will hold there for the night and at dawn travel back to Ledoma. We have what is needed," Ghamrod said.

"What's needed?" Iver wasn't sure what his words meant and needed more clarity. Was there more to the five joining Merico's party than had been let on?

Ghamrod bent down and flipped the body of the skin demon onto its back.

"We encountered this on the way to Ledoma. Villages devoid of people and no traces of what happened. It was slavers we encountered in Patin, and this…" He paused to kick the dead body.

"When have slavers traveled in the hundreds? When have the seniors of Ledoma or any other magician across this land encountered a skin demon or Soachim? The slavers are on edge…

Why?" Shan, the woman in Ghamrod's party, finished her questions as she pushed through the men to see the dead body.

Iver still didn't have an answer to his question but thought it best not to push because it seemed her commander did not have any either in this moment.

They dragged the body of the demon up the stairs and out into the street. The stench remained even after death, and as Shan lit the body on fire, everyone covered their faces.

A separate fire was started in front of the building they had secured for the night.

Iver was one of the first to take watch. He sat outside of the small, secured building, picked primarily because it was easiest to defend. Iver had seen more in the last twenty-hours than he had in his last twenty-four years. Whatever was happening had created a vacuum in villages with entire populations missing. Nothing could have prepared him for the challenges just faced. He had a new appreciation for Ghamrod and those who followed him after fighting side by side. He recognized some of the movements were identical to *haishu,* but he had witnessed different combinations he was not familiar with.

A few hours passed, and Shan came to relieve him of his watch. Iver declined and kept her company for the next few hours.

She didn't speak much. Iver didn't take it personally. None of those with Ghamrod spoke much, but they were as good, if not better than he was in combat. For Iver, that was enough to get him through the night.

CHAPTER TWENTY-ONE

The Rod the Funnel

The morning brought sunshine, but the mood remained somber. The few hours on the road from Trivoli seemed longer in returning. When the group of six rode into the village, Merico and the soldiers from Ledoma had already departed. The seniors needed to be made aware that slavers had come more south than ever before, and more importantly over one-thousand people had been abducted.

Iver understood that the Assembly of Seniors would decree that a large number of soldiers were needed to return to the garrisons set up to protect the other large villages and what remained of Patin.

The smell of burnt wood was still in the air from the previous battle with flames. Many of those saved from the slaver wagons remained together, fearful their ordeal was not completely over.

"Many of them don't know what to do." Lieutenant Ruhvin approached the group as they dismounted. Her hair pulled back in a ponytail; it was apparent that she hadn't slept since the ordeal began.

"It's a lot to take in in such a short amount of time." Shan walked past the lieutenant and sought the farrier to replace one of the horseshoes on her bay.

"Some of them want to travel to Lake Ledoma, and a few with horses traveled early this morning. We have two of three slaver's wagons operational." The lieutenant pointed in their direction.

"Perhaps we shouldn't call them slaver's wagons. We can remove a few of the slats on each side and keep it more open. We will take as many of them back with us that we can, but we need to leave as soon as possible." Ghamrod then asked about the prisoner who had not been broken yesterday.

"He's still secured. I haven't had much time to reacquaint him with the rack."

"You will let us have a go at him?" He tugged on his beard.

"Of course." The lieutenant motioned for one of her subordinates to lead them to the dungeon.

Ghamrod retrieved the curved blade he had taken from the slain skin demon. He could only fathom how the blade had come into its possession over the past fifteen years as the queen of Uteri formed alliances with the invaders from the west. He was, however, certain that the prisoner still being questioned had much more answers. Was he simply an expendable low valued slaver or someone who accepted the task knowing that his family would never want coin again at the expense of his life?

Shan rubbed her hands together and followed behind her commander.

"Are you coming?" She looked back at Iver who was hesitant to follow. He had been consumed with more death in the past twenty-four hours than he had for the past sixty-years of his life.

"Of course." He gripped the pommel of his sword to release the tension he had been holding onto since he had killed the first archer yesterday.

The dungeon seemed more pungent than yesterday. The cells were filled with the slavers not killed in the attack. Some mortally injured while others held onto the anger of being held captive, not realizing the irony of their situation.

Several guards stood watch, and some still angered from the loss of loved ones were antagonizing those captured with the threat of a long death.

Silence ensued when Ghamrod's presence was made known.

He stared around the three large jail cells, scanning the faces of both men and women who valued humanity only based on currency.

"These two." Ghamrod would do whatever it took to get answers. From the healthy bodies of the two men, he surmised that they were higher on the totem pole.

The two men objected and fought back, to no avail.

"Her." He pointed to a woman sitting in the back corner of the second cell he approached.

She met Ghamrod's eyes and did not resist as they pulled her out.

The guards forced the other prisoners back with long staffs as the door was opened.

'*It would be easier with a lifestick.*' The thought was gone before it had come. Ghamrod took no pleasure in this type of inquisition, but it was necessary.

Ghamrod gave orders to bind both men. One would have the rack used against him while the other would be stretched with straps on his wrist and ankles. He made the woman choose which man to interrogate first.

Her hesitation was expected.

Ghamrod nodded at Shan who walked away from Iver still standing in the space between the cells and the chamber of interrogation. Irons were placed in a stone hearth to heat the metal. After retrieving the prod, Shan approached the man on the rack with the fire hot rod and waited.

"Choose which one will give us the truth, or you can tell us the truth right now." Ghamrod pressed her in a matter-of-fact tone. One action would lead to the next, and the commander didn't care how he got the information required.

The other jailed slavers were adamant that she keep her mouth closed while yelling obscenities at those doing the questioning.

"Eye contact between Ghamrod and Shan was all that passed before she took the hot iron rod and burned the feet of the man on the rack.

His screams were muffled slightly through the rag stuffed in his mouth.

She then moved to the man hanging and repeated the action.

The prisoner passed out from the pain.

Shan moved to the hearth and placed the iron rod back into the flames and waited.

The second prisoner came back around after five minutes. Those remaining behind bars had not been as boisterous, seeing the flesh of both men opened and burned to the bone.

"If I have to kill each and every last one of them to get the answer's I require… so be it." He motioned for Shan to repeat the same action as before.

Iver had not been prepared to see this side of the commander. His responsibility was to find answers and what other threats were to be considered.

As the screams dwindled, the man on the rack began to speak.

"I… I don't know much. The job, the job was to get as many souls across the border into the wilderness. We were to be paid handsomely, but that's it, I swear. Only those in charge had more information. I don't want to die. I just needed money for my family… to take care of my family, so we could escape the wilderness." He pleaded to be let go.

"Are any of those 'captains' present?" Ghamrod asked.

It took too long for a forthcoming answer, so Shan retrieved a bowl of salt and sprinkled the mineral into their wounds. The guards who were stationed near both men were even rattled while both bodies writhed in pain.

Ghamrod took no pleasure, but he would find the necessary information before traveling back to Lake Ledoma. He removed his rondel dagger, used for piercing chain, from his waist and approached the man hanging from the beam supporting his dangling body.

"May the light clean your soul." He ordered him to be lowered and dragged back to his cell with his flesh burned clean through. Ghamrod then pivoted to the man on the rack who had not shared any information.

"Do you have anything to say?" the commander asked and pulled the rag from his mouth.

"Please, please, I-I don't know anything." He begged for mercy.

Ghamrod nodded as if he understood, and in the blink of an eye, he pierced the man's chest cavity with his knife and held it in place for all the remaining prisoners to see. When he extracted the blade, the stream of blood covered it.

As the man coughed to breathe, greater amounts of blood were projected from his mouth.

Ghamrod waited until the last breath was taken before having him removed from the rack. The dead body was dragged in front of the cells and left.

Ghamrod returned to the cells and picked two more slavers to be questioned while the woman he had removed previously had remained in place.

Iver wasn't sure why the commander had not spent more time questioning the first two, but as the next participants to be tortured were strapped and tied down, each one began offering information without questions being asked.

The two men had revealed that there was still one left in charge and pointed to the woman taken out of the cell first.

Ghamrod had an idea that she was more than what she had let on to be. She had been given space on each side of the bench she had been sitting in the crowded cell, so he needed to drive a small wedge between those in charge and those following orders. The first two men were in fact guinea pigs for the remaining prisoners. Fear of being maimed and even more so death always moved the weak at heart.

"Each of you will stand trial by the light upon return to Lake Ledoma." Ghamrod walked out of the lower dungeon with the woman in tow.

Iver followed out of instinct. There was so much he had learned and witnessed in such a short amount of time.

'*Slavers and skin demons working together?*' The thought faded as soon as he walked back out into the street. The afternoon sun hit him first, followed by Yolan who smacked him on his head.

"You think your wife wanted you to risk your life?" She didn't bite her words. Chachan and Yolan were close, and she knew had Iver been injured or killed, Chachan would have been devastated.

"I had to…" Iver attempted to say but was cut off.

"No, you didn't have to Iver. Merico said to give you a message before they left this morning." She hesitated as irons were placed on the woman who had walked out with Ghamrod and Shan.

"There is only one of you."

"What?" Iver asked.

"There is only one of you. Now tell me what you found out." She was not leaving until he shared what happened in Trivoli and earlier in the dungeons.

The elder listened intently to Iver. Each detail was important to her. The volumes of information she had gathered during her travels away from Lake Ledoma was vast. She had run across much smaller groups of slavers who had been caught but nothing to this extreme. When Iver mentioned skin demon, she became even more attentive. Her entire life had been a quest for knowledge, and within the past day, she had learned much more.

"Skin demons? Are you sure?" It was more of a rhetorical question, but Iver missed that point.

"Yes, I am sure. I have never seen one face to face... Who the hell has? But Yolan, I know what I saw, what I killed. Why don't you come with me and listen to whatever answers they are finding now with..." He nodded in the direction of the building Ghamrod and his men now occupied.

Lieutenant Ruhvin was standing by the door when they walked in. She made eye contact and nodded to acknowledge their presence. Iver stayed situated by her side as Yolan walked the few extra steps to where the woman was sitting with her hands and feet bound.

Other than the restraints, she appeared to be uninjured.

"I have told you everything you need to know." She spoke lowly.

"We didn't ask that. We asked for everything that you know." Ghamrod nodded and watched as Shan pulled a bucket of water with a funnel shaped device attached.

Two of his other men lifted the woman up to lay her down with her back pressed firmly across the table. They secured her arms and legs with additional bindings.

"You can stand trial with everyone else if you just tell us where the staging area is." Ghamrod stood and took the funnel contraption from the bucket.

Iver could now see the fullness of the mouth opening device. Used properly, it would keep the mouth cavity open while water was poured down it to create the sensation of drowning.

"I didn't know demons were involved; I didn't I swear to you. I gave you everything…" She hesitated as Yolan walked to stand by her side at the table.

"You cannot hide from the light. Speak truth and be done with it."

Ghamrod didn't take his eyes from her, and he didn't like being interrupted.

The woman stared at the elder but shook her head no, defiant to give no more information.

"So be it." Yolan took the funnel from Ghamrod and placed it across the face of the female prisoner.

She used her magic to warm the water to just below the temperature for boiling.

"Can we get started?" She stared back at Ghamrod who then motioned for Shan to start pouring the water down the funnel into the woman's mouth.

It took nearly three hours to finally get all the information from her, but what she did provide caused pause. The Shadria, the invaders from the West, had sought an alliance with the wilderness people, and they declined.

It was said that the emissaries of Shadria sent to garner the alliance weren't too pleased and attempted to use magic against those in the wilderness. The emissaries were slaughtered and their bodies placed on pikes. They left one alive to return to tell the Shadrian nation there would be no negotiating, and it was best to keep their relationship separate. She advised that there is wild and strong magic in the wilderness, that other creatures beyond skin demons were under the control of a magician unlike she had ever seen before.

Ghamrod understood that the Matriarch needed to hear directly from this woman before the seniors could have her stand trial.

"We have what we need for now, so prepare them for travel. If we leave within the hour, we can arrive back to Ledoma before nightfall." Ghamrod walked out of the building. He needed to be alone to gather his thoughts.

Iver could sense the tension in everyone. The Shadria, who had formed an alliance with the Queen of Uteri, wanted to expand into the lower continent. This was always a known fact, but at least one magician had demons under their control. It was the greatest threat to all inhabiting the planet.

"Do you trust these people?" Yolan asked Iver as Shan and her companions walked her in shackles. She would remain separated from the other slavers who were being led out of the dungeon in chains, cuffed to each other.

"I do trust them to get to the bottom of this, but their motives may not be entirely in alignment with ours," Iver answered while walking away to join the group from Medellin.

CHAPTER TWENTY-TWO
Breakfast

Merico had already spoken to the seniors about the slavers and Trivoli devoid of any villagers, but they had more questions in which he had no answers.

It wasn't until the second group returned that more clarity was added.

Yolan was able to provide answers to the members of the Fifth when she returned with Iver and those from Medellin.

"Skin demon?" Isela Croft wanted to make sure that she had understood the words coming from Yolan's lips. Her skin like obsidian was flawless and her mind calculating, but the concern fell across her face.

"Yes, a skin demon. I believe the ones from Medellin secured the heart. More importantly we are unaware of the untamed magicians having the ability to summon demons. The attack on us that left Elder Improvi dead could very well be at the hands of these magicians. General Roner is good at conflict, but his vision is narrow. Weakening our position here by allocating ten thousand to the border of the wilderness is not ideal. A smaller scouting group, including one from each house, would be more mobile." Yolan exhaled. Although she had not participated much lately in Assembly matters, she was fully active now. Her voice carried weight not only because of the Fire Magic, but the knowledge she possessed from a lifelong ambition to information.

"And less suspicious. Is it true that prisoners were maimed and murdered? Capital punishment is the last resort." FloAntal was still wrapping her head around it all.

"Yes, but their deaths prevented countless more. I may not agree with everything that was done, but it was necessary." Yolan decided that she would answer any additional questions later. She had not slept in over three days, ensuring that all the refugees from Patin were safe and secure during the trip to Lake Ledoma. She excused herself and took the shortest route to her quarters.

It had been over six months since she had laid in her own bed. When she entered, she smelled the citrus scent her attendant used daily to clean her space. It always soothed her.

'*Home.*' She looked around her modest quarters, kicked her shoes off, and fell into her bed.

A knock on her door startled her awake. It had taken a moment to get her bearings.

She inhaled and exhaled to steady herself; it was her fault that she had not put the symbol to not disturb across her door.

"Good morning, elder. You are requested in the old sanctuary for breakfast." A keeper smiled as she delivered the message.

"Thank you." Yolan nodded her head in acknowledgement. She had no doubt that upon her return to Lake Ledoma that she would be in the audience of Santal Culdris. They weren't *friends* but were very familiar with each other.

Yolan watched the keeper walk away. She smelled the first fires of the day, saw the sun just peeking over the tree line, and realized that she had slept over ten hours. She bathed, dressed, and hid her most recent journals under a floorboard. She had accumulated so much information that it would take months to catalog, a skill she had learned studying in Medellin a long time ago.

'*This outta be interesting*.' She placed a ward on her home and headed to have the most important meal of the day. She was not disappointed; a healthy breakfast was waiting upon her arrival.

"Porridge, bread, and quail? It seems that some things don't change. I'm surprised there is no roasted chicken and some fancy eggs of some sort." Yolan trailed behind Jain into the Matriarch's makeshift quarters. The outer room was clean with plates and eating utensils placed accordingly at the square table.

"You still have the same unique skill of observation I see, Yoli."

Yolan had not heard that name in over sixty-years. It had once brought warmth to her ears, but now she wasn't sure what she was feeling. Yolan had been one of three who had traveled to Uteri for continued education in the Garden of Uteri; it was the epicenter of knowledge and only by invitation were they allowed entry. She was one of three granted permissions, alongside Anel and

Somerset Improvi. She hadn't expected to hear that name, and it created hesitation in her response.

"Thank you for joining me. I understand the last few days you've been busy. There are no injuries you have suffered?" the Matriarch asked with concern heard in her voice.

Yolan thought she had prepared for this day, and even with an hour's notice, she was still bombarded with strange emotions being in this room.

"I've been in more challenging situations but thank you for your concern Santal. I am sure you've been briefed by your commander and sorts, and I have just returned after a half year of traveling to document the changes occurring on the southern continent. Why am I here?" Yolan wasn't sure how she would feel about seeing the last person she had ever loved standing before her, but she would not let this become emotional on her part.

"For breakfast mainly, but I do have a few questions, if you wouldn't mind answering them while we eat." The Matriarch moved towards the table, but before they sat down, she walked to Yolan and embraced her.

Yolan was hesitant to return the hug, but even after the years had passed, the familiarity between them had not changed.

Jain cleared her throat as she poured water and orange juice for them both.

"If there is nothing else, I will take leave."

The Matriarch nodded to acknowledge her personal attendant as she motioned for Yolan to take a seat opposite of her.

The Matriarch made Yolan's plate mixing the porridge with the quail.

"If I can recall, this is how you eat your hot oats and milk. There's also honey and wild berries in it." The Matriarch was hesitant. She had not expected Yolan to be in Lake Ledoma during her stay, but here she was.

"My last intel was that you had traveled to Ilens to speak with Somerset Improvi while accompanying a small troop that was requested to help bring peace to some of their territory. How is she?" The Matriarch had built a strong relationship with Anel and Somerset during their studies in Uteri.

"She was devastated… is devastated. I wouldn't have truly believed that Soachim had killed Anel had your men not encountered a skin demon." Yolan took a spoonful of porridge and shook her head in approval.

"I felt her passing," the Matriarch expressed before adding butter to the bread she had sliced for herself.

"*Felt* her passing?" Yolan looked across the table perplexed… She didn't understand what that meant.

"Yes, and it was what drove me to come here. There is so much that has happened, but I won't go into too much detail because that's not why I asked you to have breakfast with me."

"Santal Culdris keeping secrets. Clearly nothing has changed." Yolan couldn't hold her disappointment. Secrets were what drove them apart, along with Arjunai forbidding them to pursue a romantic involvement. Yolan fought against the decision, but Santal, being a Petal, understood that duty to all was greater than the one. Yolan begged and pleaded, but in the end, the Order of the Petals had been chosen over love.

"Do you have to keep doing that? Everything has changed, and the world of G'la is my responsibility. The safety and security of citizens has been my charge for almost the past twenty years. Traveling beneath the earth, where over two hundred of the women I grew up with, girls I pushed in learning, were slaughtered as we were hunted leaving the Holy Land. Dealing with nations who wish to destroy simply because the Creator imbued us with gifts to use to help all living beings. Yes, much has changed, except one thing." Santal reached across the table, hoping Yolan would reach back.

She didn't, and instead, she took bread and dipped it into the hot breakfast bowl.

"You have more responsibility, but that is what you were created for, and it's what I was created for and so many others, but it's not the sole reason for our existence. Why could you never understand that?" Yolan's voice was revealing that she had become emotional, even as she consciously tried not to.

"I knew this was a mistake. If we have no business to discuss, I will have to take my leave." Yolan placed the spoon back into the bowl and stood up.

"Well, there is business to discuss. I just thought we could talk before…"

"Let's talk business. I can do business. I can't reminisce about you breaking my..." Yolan and the Matriarch eyes met. In that fraction of an instance, Yolan thought back to the first time they met when she was allowed to travel to the northern continent and study under the Rose of the Garden. The two didn't like each other. Yolan full of self-assurance, debated lessons taught by those with tenure, which included Santal. Over the course of three years, Yolan softened and embraced the amount of knowledge at her fingertips.

During that time, Santal had met Yolan's challenges head on, unlike a few other instructors who simply usurped their authority to quiet her. The two women gained mutual for each other while spending time outside of the learning circle. That time led to deeper understanding with intimacy, and they fell hard in love.

Yolan, now no longer a student, had passed into the Order of Petals along with Anel and her twin sister Somerset. The three were allowed to return to their homeland. Yolan wanted Santal to leave with her and start a life together. Santal agreed but had to get the blessing of The Rose. The Rose reminded Santal of the highest duty and offered that whatever decision was made, to stay or go had her blessing.

In the end the decision to serve The Creator outweighed their love.

The expression on the Matriarch's face seemed to mirror that of Yolan.

The moment passed as quickly as it had surfaced.

It was not the intent of breakfast, so after collecting herself, the Matriarch spoke about what she knew and would leave it in up to Yolan to share with the Assembly of Seniors.

"We have had reports of untrained but powerful magicians in the wilderness. There are confirmed reports that some relics of the Ancient Ones are in their possession. We have no clue what it is they have, but it can be certain that the Soachim and skin demon were their doing. Slavers have been working with them for a while, and the attack on Trivoli and Patin was just the latest. After troops were pulled from the garrisons, only a few hundred were left to defend against coordinated attacks. Kefise and Fuggna City have also been abandoned. I sent scouts west and will have a report sent soon. Many from your Assembly have lost their way, and they will need redirection to remember the oath they swore. Now, the business I need of you is helping Jain decipher the second part of the Codex of B'nobi."

The Matriarch seemed somber as she stared across the table.

Yolan had heard everything, relics created demons… the cities abandoned, but the only thing she had listened to was about deciphering the second part of the Codex.

"What about the first part? That would be the first place I started." Yolan wasn't fully comprehending because the scroll was a mixture of the first tongue and many other variations of the dialect. It also was a mathematical equation that utilized the position of the stars to reveal deeper content. Scholars across the entire planet had only speculated its true meaning.

"Yes, the second part… the first part has already been translated by Jain. You studied these dialects, and she understands the stars." The Matriarch reached for a glass and waited for her answer. They both understood that only three people on the lower continent had her skill in language. Somerset was in Ilens, and Anel had been killed.

"You could have started with that part, and yes, of course I will help. You have to tell me what the first part of the translation indicated." Yolan finished her porridge and second glass of juice.

"In essence, that the nations who are battling each other must band together because the true war is coming. That the Soachim touching Lake Ledoma broke the first seal. Our greatest weapon, or weapons, amount to three descendants of the First Mother; of which the bloodline has been lost." The Matriarch placed the glass back onto the table but didn't relinquish it.

Yolan closed her eyes momentarily. It was a lot to take in.

For the first time since she had walked in for breakfast, she truly saw Santal Culdris. A woman so full of determination and responsibility was showing weariness. A woman who had been tasked with such a monumental undertaking that anyone else would have failed. Now the States of Medellin were thriving, and the teachings of the garden had been continued. None of which would matter if the enemy could not be determined or if the Prophecy of Esroun was substantiated with the Codex of B'nobi.

"I will do everything I can to help Santal," Yolan finished as Jain walked back into the room. She was surprised to see that breakfast had not concluded.

"I can come back."

"No, no it's okay. I need to retrieve some books if we are to do what none other have." Yolan turned back to say goodbye to the Matriarch and realized that her hand was holding onto the woman she had once loved. She quickly removed her fingers and said her farewell, slightly embarrassed.

"She agreed to help?" Jain asked. It meant that Yolan would have to travel with the group until it was done, and Jain knew the history between the two women.

"For now." Those were the only two words offered in response as she stared at the door closing behind Yolan.

"The new refugees returned with Ghamrod are settled and making the best out of this situation. I expect there will be a time to adjust, and perhaps we should help reinforce that they are safe. I can have Myl and Jusie find out what their greatest needs are." Jain began cleaning the table as she spoke.

“No, have Kendra and Myl do that. Jusie is going to take a trip to the dungeons and speak with the prisoners they returned with. They don’t believe in capital punishment. Jusie will do everything short of it. I am surprised that Yolan took over the interrogation in Patin.”

There was a light rap on the door.

Jain opened it, and Erri, along with FloAntal, walked in.

“Good morning, Mother, we have some ideas about the celebration that we’d like to discuss with you.” FloAntal took a leftover piece of buttered bread and sat down.

Jain took the plate and left only the juice before walking out of the room.

“Well, let’s hear it.” The Matriarch had a full day ahead of her, and right now, she needed something to take her mind off Yolan.

CHAPTER TWENTY-THREE
A Family Discussion

Imani had stayed up for two nights, worrying about her father being away in Patin and Trivoli. Her mother had not slept, even as she made available the simple necessities for those who had not found proper housing. Pitched tents were stationed on land not used in decades. Chachan ensured that enough rice was distributed, along with bread. For now, it would have to suffice with such short notice of the hundreds that had returned in wagons.

Her father had returned when Chachan was dealing with negotiations that ran long into the night. When she wasn't occupied with that task, she was accompanying the Matriarch.

Chachan was greeted by her daughter upon arrival home after a long day.

"He's been home for a couple of hours. He passed out before eating. He seems tired." Imani had waited for her mother to return. She knew the emotional state she had really been in, hiding it the best she could by staying busy. Iver meant everything to her.

Chachan kissed her daughter on the forehead and rolled her into her room. She helped her onto her bed and placed the cover atop her.

"I am glad he's home too." Chachan closed the bedroom door behind her. She had intended to give her husband a piece of her mind for leaving without telling her, but it would wait. She crawled into bed and laid her head in the space between his arm and chest.

He was first to wake in the morning. He kissed her cheek, causing her to smile before her eyes opened. When she did meet his eyes, the smile was gone.

"Did you think I would have approved you gallivanting across the plains to chase slavers? Of course not. It's the reason why you didn't say a word... and then you don't even come back with General Roner. Instead, you stayed and put yourself in harm's way with a skin demon. Why would you do that? Please, please, tell me, dear husband. Why would you do that?"

Iver had thought about all the ways he could justify the lack of communication. She had a point, a very big point. But he knew had he not gone, he wouldn't have the few answers that he possessed. There were too many questions still left to be asked and answered.

"Why would I do that? Why *would* I do that? The same reason you sent me to Ethi, and yes, I'm fine, honey…" he said with slight sarcasm before continuing.

"Listen, it was supposed to be a quick scouting mission. That's why only thirty or so rode out. I understand. I'd be angry too, but can this wait until we eat whatever the kids are cooking?" Iver moved from the bed and out into the communal area without her reply. He was going to get yelled at either way, and he was hungry. He had barely eaten in two days traveling with the refugees.

"Iver, we are not done…" She attempted to say as he walked out of their room.

"Good morning, parents. We have prepared breakfast. Ma, for you, berries and honey bread. Da, you have rice cereal, and if these two don't burn the meat, leftover lamb and chicken we got fresh from the butcher." Imani had a smirk on her face as she told her younger twin brothers what to do.

"You three must've been raised right by two loving parents. Parents that make mistakes and forgive each other." Iver stared at his wife who had taken the seat next to him.

She squished her eyes together, causing her nose to wrinkle and her freckles appear more frequent.

"Don't ever do something so stupid again." She punched him in the shoulder with adequate force.

Imani advised the twins she would need their assistance in securing additional material and certain items required for a new design. She had already paid them each a copper for their assistance for the entire day.

She rolled herself into her room, retrieved a small pouch with a list and coin to pay for her merchandise.

"We will take care of the dishes. The little time you have this morning just enjoy it. I may have them take me to Naiyan's when we're done." She had her brothers push her out the door and down the small slope.

"She's more you than me," Iver said as he put butter on the honey bread.

"It's amazing how you think of that right now. You were in a small battle from what Merico has shared with the Assembly and not only that you helped kill an actual skin demon. The Matriarch wasn't certain, but she believes the abducted are not simply being taken for enslavement. She believes many are being sacrificed." Chachan grabbed a few berries from the bowl.

"Sacrificed, eaten…" He paused as Chachan coughed before continuing.

"Yes, the skin demon was eating the remains of several people. I know one thing: If I never come face to face with another dark creature, it will be too soon. Merico is allowing the prisoners to be interrogated by those from Medellin. I may not agree with their methods, but they worked. I am going to attend."

Chachan let her recent anger subside and updated her husband on the investigation of the remains left of the Soachim.

"The alchemists are studying whatever was brought back from the demon. Is it true that Yolan participated in the… investigation?" Chachan had always looked up to the older woman. Yolan had been one of her early mentors even though they had different magic. Perhaps because Chachan was nearly as powerful as she was in her gift, but whatever the real reason she revered her.

"Yes, it's true. If I'm being honest, she was good at it too."

A loud thud was heard before Zuni made his way into the communal area.

"I thought you were attending the questioning session this morning?" Zuni knew that if he wanted to attend the interrogation, his father needed to be with him. He waited for a response as he looked at them both.

"Fine, just remember our methods are not their methods." She watched Iver retrieve his boots as Zuni walked out to saddle their horses. The ride to the prison yard was adequate in time, and the trail often was unkept.

Iver returned tying the drawstring around the pants Imani had made for him.

"I am sorry." He properly apologized to his wife.

"I know." She accepted the apology and kissed him before he walked out of their home.

The strain of uncertainty still loomed over her. The Matriarch had been teaching her and FloAntal new techniques. She had to keep on top of the First Master's dinner plans in addition to making sure that the refugees had necessities. The Medici had triage stations to test for any sickness, and she had volunteered to assist.

CHAPTER TWENTY-FOUR

A Rose Still Blooms

No one knew who was being accepted into the service of the Matriarch. Some speculated that Chachan and FloAntal had assumed that status, even though they had already been tested and had years of age. Unlike the Order of the Petals, initiates came at an early age, typically before the age of bearing children.

The ceremonial pavilion had also not been used in decades, and it had taken the keepers over ninety days to prepare it. Now Petals could be seen mingling with citizens in the spacious grassy area. Some danced and sang. Others sat and listened to stories. A few keepers were still making final preparations in the space for the ceremony taking place in a little over a week.

'Naiyan better be there along with Imani,' Ransa thought as she watched the other women go about their tasks.

"Sister, will you lend me a hand? Chachan is tied up, and I need someone who knows where to locate an item, and that will be you." Erri walked the base of the pavilion and pulled Ransa by her hand without slowing her walk.

As they walked the streets of Ledoma, everything had changed in less than two weeks. The city seemed lighter, and commerce was picking up as Ledoma found many traveling from afar arriving to enjoy the festival and celebration of those passing into the Assembly. Others came to be in the presence of the Matriarch.

'It's amazing, everything that has gone on since leaving Naiyan's home in the early morning hours that day.' Ransa smiled at a few children who stared at her. She was wearing an off-white cotton shift with the deepest blue trim. It would take as much time for her, as it would for them, to accept that she was no longer an initiate to become a healer. She had ascended to a higher status and had no idea what it all meant.

FloAntal caught up to the younger women before they had gone too far. She had a container with liquid in it. She handed it to Ransa.

"Mother wants you to have this, and I think I'll join you two… but first." She paused at a booth with various sweets and paid for two caramel apples and one candy apple. She ensured Ransa drank the liquid now identified as 'tea'.

"Eat this." FloAntal handed them each a sweet after ensuring Ransa drank all of the tea.

"You are now a part of something bigger. Those who were your recent teachers will come to you for help. You wanted a title;

daughter of the Matriarch and I couldn't be prouder." FloAntal bit into the sweet delight, and that's when Whal emerged from an area uncommon to most.

"Whal, out of the dark and into the light." FloAntal wasn't sure what the older eccentric man was up to, but it seemed like he had not even taken notice to his surroundings.

"Ahh, elder…" Whal paused, slowly shifting his eyes to stare at Ransa who was taking a second bite of her candied apple.

"*She* has passed her rites of passage, great… just great. One more who has been expedited into our fold who has not been adequately tested. Wasn't *she* on another course to become a Medici? Is there any hesitation now in wondering why others see us as being conquerable?" Whal shook his head in disapproval.

"It seems you have been off doing something that I really don't want to hear or even care about. Much has changed in these days, and if you're not careful, what Anri suffered may also be your fate." FloAntal paused to nod her head to acknowledge a father carrying his young daughter on his shoulders. She waved and turned her attention back to Whal.

"The ceremony is a day before the festival, and you haven't been helping. I can only forewarn you that the Matriarch has asked about you. If you're quick enough, you may be able to object to your home being searched. Chachan shared with us about the meeting you had with her the morning they arrived from Medellin; you have Creator's Glass. Something that should have been disclosed and given to the Assembly, don't you agree?" FloAntal's eyebrows raised. She had taken offense to his insult about Ransa. She didn't care if he had been missing from the Seniors' Assembly a few days after those from the States of

Medellin had arrived. She had satisfaction seeing concern on his face as Whal's eyes widened.

"I-I will have words with all of you when this is over," he stated with fervor. It was a threat he planned to keep.

"What else will they find, Whal?" FloAntal put one arm around Ransa and the other around Erri before they continued forward with their apples being eaten heartily.

Whal shook his head in disgust once more at Ransa before he quickly made his way back to his quarters, moving his cane as fast as his legs would keep up. He wasn't sure if he had placed wards on his home when he left earlier and didn't want to have a violation where he laid his head.

"Thank you, elder. I mean sister. He and Anri have always had it out for me." Ransa was grateful FloAntal had been present. Even though she had passed, she still wasn't certain that she actually belonged.

The elder woman actually laughed loudly before responding.

"They should be worried about you. Your Rites were administered by the Matriarch; your raw magic puts you just short of myself. With training and control you will easily surpass me and be a force to reckon with. Do you understand that without advance training you became a healer that can mend energy? It's a wonder how you fell through the cracks." FloAntal couldn't make sense of it.

"It's been challenging to say the least. My family didn't have its roots in Lake Ledoma and not one of them ever had magic until me I don't think. If not for my life-sisters, I would have gone crazy by now." Ransa referred to Naiyan and Imani. She had seen them less since the morning the Matriarch arrived.

Ransa had a strange after-taste on her tongue and felt a little off, but she attributed it to the treat she had finished. She had still been unsure of their destination, so she simply kept pace with her two counterparts. The elder woman continued speaking.

"It is true that how and where we were raised has an impact on who we become, but when you are aware of who you are, there is no greater gift. What Mother has shared already I know to be true as you will understand the bond we now share as her daughters. If I am being honest, I am still unsure of a lot of things." FloAntal had made small pleasantries as they moved past more small shops with small groups congregating.

Ransa was lighter on her feet along with the traces of inebriation. She couldn't pinpoint what had transpired until she thought about the tea FloAntal had given.

She should have known the tea contained Ayahuasca after feeling the first effects in her body. She wanted to ask FloAntal why she was given it to drink, but a joyous energy penetrated the space. A few children were kicking a ball back and forth. Her attention was drawn back into the present, and it made her appreciate the moment she was having.

"Great day, elder… Yes, a great day." The children moved in the opposite direction, hoping not to have their fun halted.

Ransa was familiar with every portion of Ledoma, but she had concentrated on the candied apple. She had lost an idea as to where they had traveled especially after the psychedelic traits of the plant used kicked in. Realizing that their steps had brought them to a place she felt unworthy, she inhaled deeply.

'*I am not ready.*' Ransa had to calm her nerves as she started breathing a more rapidly. Her heart rate was increased and with each step she could feel her legs shaking.

This was the most sacred place in the city. The wards in this area prevented those without magic from entering. Those with magic could take the chance of either having a positive or negative effect on them, perhaps none.

The Ancient Ones had cast spells to protect the statue of the Sinai, the First Mother. Some believed it was a gateway, but over the past centuries, it was simply known as being forbidden.

"She hasn't appeared to anyone since the Days of Esroun. Clearly, today will not be the day." Ransa's attempt to downplay this moment did not erase that she never expected to ask for B'nobi to grant her a wish. The hallucinogenic traits of the plant were coursing through her body.

"Strip down." FloAntal began to help her undress. Erri took each garment and folded it neatly. Those coming before Sinai must come bear in mind, body, and spirit. Those who did not suffered unimaginably in silence as their inflictions were their burdens to carry alone.

Ransa attempted a smile, but she couldn't tell if it formed across her lips. She was not embarrassed in any sense of being naked, but there could be no preparation for whatever lay at the end of a path very few walked. As she walked away from Erri and the older woman, she wondered what the others had succumb to, the ones who had preceded her. She saw many of those who had passed their Rites of Passage looked over for this honor.

'*Is it an honor?*' She took one glance over her shoulder back at FloAntal and Erri as she rounded the small bend in the path. The answer to her question would be waiting at the end of this trail.

Ransa experienced the hardened dirt under her feet give way to smoother terrain the closer she got to the sitting image of the First Mother. For centuries it was kept off limit, not by those living in Ledoma, but by whatever energies powered the area. Whatever the person's magic was, a counter energy was used in greater consequence to deter anyone not deemed worthy.

The nervousness in each movement forward had her legs shaking with each step. She was tense. Slow and tentative because she didn't want to walk into an invisible barrier or something forming beneath her to hold her legs.

'*Or anything else that can hurt me.*' She realized that her thoughts were being amplified into sound.

"*Oh, shit…*" She put her hands over her mouth, still not truly understanding that it wasn't her voice that made the vocalizing.

She calmed herself by repeating a mantra taught to her by Anel and Chachan when she was made to sit in silence.

'*I honor the Creator within myself.*' These were the only thoughts that filled her mind continuing to walk. Almost everything was tuned out.

Then she saw the twelve-foot statue of Sinai. Made from ancient dark serpentine-type wood, it glistened as the sun beamed down.

'*May the Creator breathe life into your womb.*' The greeting was customary; she had learned this as she was able to form her first words.

She bent down and kissed the ground before sitting cross-legged and continued her mantra.

'*I honor the Creator within myself. I honor the Creator within myself.*' Each time, she could hear the echo of her thoughts like slight pushes of wind across her ear lobe.

Something was happening as she slipped into the void—the place where nothing existed, the space where all things were possible.

Still aware of her surroundings, Ransa saw a different perspective. Her body and spirit seemingly had come undone. She saw her body beneath sitting, but she was drawn back to the statue. It looked… different.

The terrain changed in an instant, and Ransa was no longer in Ledoma. Of this, she was sure.

Trees larger than she had ever seen spread across the horizon. Winged creatures, whose bodies were as thick as small single huts, soared freely.

Ransa was unable to comprehend. She had been separated from her body, and now… now she acknowledged another energy besides her own surrounding her and as if someone was holding her hand.

The landscape shifted again within what seemed to be a glimmer. She was in a home, a large tent, along with a woman. Her long silver hair was pulled to one side as she knelt in the center of the room.

'*Is she praying?*'

Like before her words echoed into the space without a sound from her lips.

The older woman's eyes opened and followed the course to Ransa's voice.

The woman, already on her knees, bowed even deeper before rising.

"B'Nobi, the days have been long since our last meeting."

She could make out the hand holding onto hers clearer now. She followed the hand up to the arm and could make out the face of what had once been just a blur.

'*She is beautiful.*' Ransa thought and once again her words permeated the area.

The silver-haired woman agreed before she retrieved her life-stick to extend it toward Ransa who realized that she gripped the hand of the Goddess B'nobi.

"You are welcomed into the Order of Petals. Tell the one you call Matriarch and only her that Bloodlines long lost are now revealed." The older woman shared the words, and in the blink of an eye, Ransa was back in her body, staring at the waterfall and statue of the First Mother.

FloAntal was standing by her side, and she had a curious look on her face but it passed as she spoke.

"Are you okay? It's been four hours, and you have a meeting with the Diviners. Do you want the Matriarch to have to tell you how…" FloAntal paused, her words stuck in her throat, realizing that the younger woman had not recognized her presence.

Ransa was still not certain of her experience. Had she daydreamed something that seemed so real? Where were the large trees, and who was the older woman more importantly? The description was that of Arjunai, Rose of the Garden, but she was dead or exiled.

'*Did the Goddess approach me? Was that other woman the Rose? I'm welcomed into the Order...'* Nothing seemed linear until she heard the question again from Erri who still held her clothing in her arms.

"Are you alright?"

Ransa could hear the concern in her voice.

"Yeah, yes, I'm okay. I think I fell deep into meditation, and we should probably get going. I am not keen on making the Diviner's wait on my behalf." Ransa took Erri's hand to help stand up.

"Did the First Mother speak to you?" FloAntal asked.

"She did not." Ransa's answer was truthful, and it was all she would be sharing until she could speak with the Matriarch.

She felt extremely famished and still some lingering effects of the psychedelic.

"I'm hungry. Can we stop and grab buttered bread and fruit really quick since we will be passing by a few carts?" Ransa sought the older woman's opinion and approval.

"Sister, you can do anything you want that doesn't upset Mother, that is. I'm not too sure about the Diviners though. They don't say much."

All three women stared at each other before laughing loudly because none of them had ever heard them speak.

"You haven't heard them speak either?" Ransa asked Erri as she slipped on the last of her garments. She couldn't stop laughing.

Erri's eyes squinted as if she were contemplating such a time before shaking her head back and forth no.

"Would you really want to hear what they have to say? They still scare me half to death in silence." Erri laughed with both women as FloAntal led them back into the small marketplace on the outskirt of the city before Ransa's meeting with the three bald women.

CHAPTER TWENTY-FIVE

Misdirection

Sets of keepers were dispersed to the quarter's that the delegation from Carcero were occupying. The events happening in Lake Ledoma had overwhelmed not only the seniors but also those who had come to negotiate terms for the land the seafaring nation required.

They had only arrived five days before the Matriarch had. The small postponement to the negotiations both nations agreed to participate in.

The three ambassadors had traveled with an entourage of servants for various tasks. Some for day-to-day undertakings, and others would be used as counsel when the terms of the land deal would reach an impasse.

The two male ambassadors were much older than the lone and much younger woman Ambassador Janae Fiah.

Keeble Jon and Cusi Tys were both from prominent families. The Tys family were large landowners while the Jon family had members, past and present, who had assumed the highest military honors. Once their families had pledged fealty to the now deceased speaker, and now that his daughter had moved into the same position, each family looked to gain more power.

Ambassador Janae Fiah was the cousin of the new speaker. She had an equal say in all matters that would be discussed, but both men believed because of their age and status, they would be able to dictate the direction of negotiating by minimizing her input.

Ambassador Fiah was warned of such tactics, so as she sat with Cusi Tys, watching the table being prepared for breakfast, she planted a seed of distrust between the two men. Weaving truth with falsehood was something she learned from her older cousin, who now sat in the highest position of power in Carcero.

A servant walked to their table with a keeper of Ledoma on his heels.

"Ambassadors, good morning. Will there be any additional requirements for the deliberations later this afternoon?" The teen's grey clothing was pristine. His nails clean, there was not a speck of anything to be seen on his person that was out of place. His strawberry blonde hair was neatly cut and trimmed. The keepers of the assembly performed their duty with as much honor as those in the active military.

"Where's the other one, the young senior? I hope I didn't scare him off. You know Ledoma folks shouldn't be so prude anyway. The human body has more magic in it than any G'la could wield."

Ambassador Tys took a sip from his cup of tea to hide the approval of his younger counterpart's words. He wasn't certain if it was a subtle insult or not. He hoped it had been taken that way.

"Janae, answer the question. It's directed toward you. You're the only one of us who has been… needy." Keeble Jon entered from a different door.

The all-white pant outfit he wore matched the groomed snow color of his beard. His long sleeve kaftan was trimmed in black stitching around the collar. His hair freshly tapered was a slight indication of how he paid close attention to detail.

"Ha, a good morning greeting before the jab would've been nice. Some of us want to explore the beauty of Ledoma. I can't help it if my urge to take in the city happens at odd hours of the night when old farts are fast asleep, no offense," Janae finished as Keeble sat down. One of the servants from Carcero placed a napkin across his lap before pouring him hot tea.

"We have no more requirements for the negotiation. Thank you." Janae stood from the table and walked the keeper out of the quarters, leaving the older men behind.

"We need to be on the same page. Do you think that was wise?" Cusi Tys was opposed to Keeble being part of this process. He seldom gave an inch in finding a common ground. The representatives who had selected Keeble believed now that Elder Improvi had passed, that he would find a way to maximize the opportunity because he was a brilliant strategist.

"We aren't here to make Janae happy or comfortable. This opportunity is once in a lifetime. With the Matriarch being tied up in their little prophecy 'thing', she has their entire assembly on edge. This is our advantage, and I won't let some wet behind the ears nepotism derail what our nation demands of us." Keeble reached for the plate of toast along with the violet syrup. He was done speaking on the matter.

Cusi excused himself and made his way back to his personal space. A moment of quiet was required before what would be a marathon of continued negotiations in the afternoon. The principal matters had been sent to Ledoma over three months ago, and with these deliberations being postponed, a conclusion was necessary before the ambassadors returned to their homeland.

"Will you need anything, sir?" An athletically built man stood at the entrance to his room.

"No, no, please and no interruptions until one hour before we begin." Cusi closed the door behind and walked to the small balcony off his suite. He looked past the small water fountain, towards the sanctuary. There were too many magicians for his liking.

Those in Ledoma accepted how those from Carcero chose to govern, but the states of Medellin were often at odds with the seafaring nation.

'*Have they brokered a deal with the states of Medellin*?' The question surfaced. The Matriarch being so far away from home had not been known prior to their departure. He wondered what else he didn't know, and it made him more aware that this was a delicate situation.

Both lands accused the other of using propaganda to drive their respected agendas. There had once been an exchange program for students of higher learning between the two lands. That agreement had ended abruptly after their last speaker died.

Cusi had been a part of the previous leader's closest counsel, but when the leader passed, those who had malcontent toward Cusi began to push him out of his assumed leadership role.

Cusi had no misconceptions about politics or some of the concessions he gave away in securing allies. He looked for opportunities to increase his power, and it was the one reason he had reached out to a few seniors of Ledoma prior to their arrival. Cusi understood that when it came down to basic human behavior, nearly everyone was susceptible to bribery—if the donation was adequate.

'*I won't be leaving anything left to chance.*' Cusi walked towards a smaller table to stare at the boundaries on his map should Carcero secure the all the land they wanted to purchase, and if not, what concessions would he be willing to make?

Jenae and Keeble would be at odds with each other. He knew that. She was of the ruling family and tolerated by others with great political ambition for this very reason. Keeble was a strict hardliner.

Cusi had been given inside information of what the seniors would barter for and had already calculated how to use the information to close the deal. Information he didn't share because his status within Carcero would rise with word of how he led his team.

Carcero would be in a much more secure place for the next hundreds of years.

Cusi understood that it made geographical and political sense for Ledoma to keep the areas surrounding their water sources, which ran to the ocean in the south. The old and battered worn down port that had blossomed once would take an enormous amount of coin and labor to make operational. Cusi planned for some of the monies being used to be taxed to offset the land they would lose out on if the deal went ahead. They would pay for the land, provide labor and a percent of their expenditures. This would even out by the amount paid by Ledoma until the port was fully operational.

Because the Carcerian businesses selected to be opened and stationed, he would propose that any tax to be collected by Ledoma be done every four months. He had petitioned for two of his family's businesses to be amongst those selected. He was uncertain just how everyone would fair now that Anel Improvi was gone. She had always been a fair negotiator, and up until the first meeting over a week ago, no one knew who the principle at the table was going to be, but when Chachan Balent was chosen as the Fifth, he believed her acceptable.

'As long as they can keep their word, I'll be okay.' Cusi thought about the meetings in secret he had and trusted that even if only a portion of what was promised came to fruition, his family would gain wealth and more power.

He removed his slippers and returned to his balcony to stare off in the distance at the waterfall pouring into Lake Ledoma. Cusi understood he still had an uphill trek. It would take a great deal of maneuvering the last items on the list of negotiations, but he was up for the challenge.

CHAPTER TWENTY-SIX

She Is Very Pretty

Janae walked with the keeper back to where all the preparations were being made for the First Master's celebration in just a few days' time. She had visited Ledoma when she was just a child. She didn't know the animosity against G'la at that age. With fond memories she never took a position that most of her people had. A free-spirited child with a gift for analytics, she could often see in between the lines and for this reason the last speaker, her uncle, had kept her by his side. Now, she had become the eyes and ears as her older cousin assumed the leadership role.

"Ambassador Fiah, is there something I can help you with?" one of those in a managing position asked, wondering why the ambassador was in the worker's stations.

Janae's eyebrows raised as she smiled. She had intended to visit the training grounds for those being learned in magic. That could wait, and for now, she wanted to appear unassuming.

"No, no. I actually needed to clear my mind. My two male counterparts, all they think about is negotiating and bartering. You know money, monies, coin. Me, well, I don't think so much in black and white as they do. I will not waste my time on the unknown… and to be honest with you, I had no idea where I was going. I literally talked his ear off." The ambassador nodded at the male keeper she had followed back from breakfast.

"Do you require anything, boss lady?" the male keeper asked. His shift had concluded nearly an hour prior.

"Thank you for listening to me babel." Janae offered and tossed him a silver before the older woman dismissed him.

"I've always heard about the honor the keepers take in their job. I wish we had this in my homeland. People always want more without appreciating what they have. What's that saying from Ilens…" She paused and looked out into space to recall the exact words.

"Oh, yes, that's right… Everyone smiles, but not all are genuine."

The lead keeper was unsure why this was the topic of discussion, but with respect, she listened.

Janae had done what she intended. Plant seeds. The keepers of Ledoma were not only responsible for the upkeep of the senior quarters and sanctuary. They were also the passers of information. The entire time they had been in Ledoma, Janae had given information that would make her appear more of an ally, that she was curios to learn more about the ways of G'la and that she had taken a liking to Ziri Balent.

"Ambassador, if you will excuse me." The managing keeper had maintained her smile but advised the ambassador that she would take leave to keep the workers on task.

"Yes, yes, of course. Forgive me."

Janae walked back out of the workers space and back into a portion of the city bustling with activity.

Each day that passed, more people had found their ways to Ledoma even with the knowledge that the Soachim had touched the city. The seniors ensured that they had taken extreme measures to ensure the safety of those coming for the events.

She wondered where the disdain had come from for those possessing magic. Sure, it could be used negatively, but she had never come to terms that something that the Creator had given a soul could be looked upon as evil. It was the way in which the talent was used that made the difference. Understanding was the key to overcoming fear, and she knew the people of Carcero were afraid of what they couldn't control.

Something ran up against her lower leg to draw her attention back into the present. She smiled as she looked down at a ball that children were kicking back and forth between them.

"Are you guys pretty good?" She placed her foot on top of the ball and moved it slightly away from a young girl who sought to retrieve it.

"I'm better than he is," a boy's voice called out as they waited for the return of their round kicking toy.

“Is that right, but can you do this?” Janae switched the ball back from foot to foot while the children attempted to get it back from her. She let a few get close before switching feet or putting a spin on the ball. The laughter of the entire group including the ambassador was contagious.

She left the group of children, and that’s when she saw Ziri walking with a young woman and pushing another in a roll-chair.

“Ziri…” she called out, but he didn’t hear her over the other voices, so she quickly caught up to the group after navigating the crowd in the street.

“Senior Ziri Balent.”

Naiyan was first to turn towards the voice. She didn’t recognize the face, but when Ziri’s body language shifted, she ascertained before he slowed that this was the ‘naked’ woman they had been told about.

Imani told Naiyan to turn her chair a little more, so she could lay eyes on who had flustered her brother in such a way.

“Ziri, I had hoped to have seen you before this morning. I will require your attention after we conclude our business with the Fifth.” She then introduced herself to Naiyan and Imani.

“I can see the family resemblance between you, and again, I offer my sincerest condolences for your loss. She was a great person, and a woman that many of us should aspire to be more like.” She shook the hands of both younger women and smiled again.

“Ambassador, we are at your call of course. I do, however, need to return to the sanctuary. The two newest seniors…” His hesitation was apparent as he let the words trail off his tongue.

There had only been two out of the ten neophytes who passed, along with Ransa. However, he wasn't sure what Ransa was quite yet. Once the events of the week concluded, he would seek Ransa out to ask her questions. For now, Ransa had been in the constant presence of those from Medellin. She looked wearier than she had before crossing the sands.

Janae injected into Ziri's sentence as his lack of resolution in finishing his statement was apparent.

"I understand there were a total of ten that tested… two out of ten, terrible odds." She stated it as a matter of fact. Imani countered.

"Agreed, terrible odds, but two is better than one…"

"And definitely better than zero." Naiyan finished her sister-friends sentence.

"This is true… This is true. It's been a pleasure meeting you both. I must prepare to make sure that we don't bump heads on trivial matters at the negotiating table." She winked at the three and touched Ziri's hand seductively and walked away.

"She's very pretty?" Imani acknowledged.

Naiyan wasn't sure why she didn't like the girl touching Ziri's hand. She had never been romantic with Ziri or anyone for that matter besides kissing the same boys as her friends when they played juvenile games.

This was just the second day Naiyan had been outside of her house since Chachan prepared the feast.

'*Two weeks.*' Naiyan exhaled. She had not seen or spoken to Ransa except once when she stole away from the Matriarch and the Petals to share with Imani and Naiyan that she had passed her testing, and she was gaining more control of an unimaginable amount of magic. Ransa saved the information of her being drugged and raped for a later time when there was no rushing involved, and she could express her truest emotions.

Imani glanced back over her shoulder at Naiyan before directing her next words towards her older brother.

"There were actually three who passed their rites. If I didn't know any better, I'd think you were jealous, " Imani called out to her brother.

"Jealous… what…"

"Yes, jelly jealous…" The Matriarch tested her inside of a room of reflection that no one knew about." Imani reached out for her brother's hand after seeing that he was indeed affected a little.

"Brother, I'm just joking."

"I know you are, but there is some truth in it. I don't know if I could test for four hours straight by the elders, let alone the Matriarch. I don't think anyone expected that," Ziri finished just as they arrived at the sanctuary.

"If you're going to Crater's Pond, I'll meet you there in a couple of hours. Once the negotiations start, I'll finally have a little time to enjoy." He kissed Imani and hugged Naiyan.

"Until the children return."

"Until the children return," they replied in unison, watching Ziri walk away.

CHAPTER TWENTY-SEVEN

Class Is in Session

The group from Medellin were departing in less than a week, after the second day of the festival. They had already been in Ledoma three weeks longer than intended. If they retraced the roads and communities that they had passed before, they would have an idea of what to expect. If they assumed the same route in coming, that route would take them six weeks to travel. If the entourage was to take the shortest distance between Lake Ledoma and Medellin, then they would travel close to the borders of kingdoms and states which at times had adversarial relations with those from the states of Medellin.

The regents and leaders of these communities respected the Matriarch's position, but they didn't always heed her advice. Would they be met with challenges like large groups of slavers or decimated communities? Even within the great states of Medellin, a few states pushed their ambition by wanting to increase taxation for their localities and redefining borders prior to the Matriarch leaving. Had any agreements been reached without her guidance? If so, she would tread carefully to maintain as much control over the direction of those agreements. She did not have absolute power, but she had allies who would back her.

The Matriarch stood next to a table with a single pitcher of water and three glasses. Looking out onto the faces of the two women that she had hand-selected to continue leading, she knew the legacy of Arjunai was a blessing and a curse. The Matriarch understood rebuilding the sistership would have perils, but it was necessary. The Order of Petals would not perish under her watch.

"We will go east and travel closest to Carcero. Send a few men ahead to secure a boat to take us the rest of the way home. Perhaps I'll pay a visit to Speaker Odward. I'm sure she still owes me a personal apology," Santal Cudris stated flatly.

The two other women looked at each other before FloAntal took a lean forward.

"Isn't that relationship between Carcero and the states of Medellin strained to say the least, Mother?" FloAntal asked moving from her seat to approach the older woman.

The Matriarch took her by the hand and reached out for Chachan to join them.

"Over the past twenty years, the emissaries traveling have come to broker deals and bargains to support them against invasion. Honestly, do you believe now is the best time to see how fragile that relationship between the two lands is?" FloAntal finished. She could feel the energy flowing between the trio. It was one of the techniques they had been taught since the elder woman's arrival. It opened the passageways for magic to flow with ease.

"If we were able to wait for the exact moment and time to handle *fragile* concerns then we'd probably have the world pass us by. I do agree there is enough strain on most relationships between six out of the ten larger nations. Although it is not the States of Medellin's business, your council is in negotiation with these same people who would see us killed for the magic we possess." The Matriarch's point was made. The elder woman kissed each woman's hand as a sign of appreciation.

Chachan held reservations still.

"I am positive your present location is already known with the information channel they use. We seek to strengthen a tedious agreement. The states of Medellin and Carcero's relationship has weakened to say the least. Gaining information is grand, but safety more essential," Chachan said. She didn't know all the details between Crummel Odward and Santal Culdris, but up until Speaker Odward, her father had cast his vote "nay" against creating the Nation of Three, so the two women were extremely close friends.

Decades after Santal and Yolan were over. Santal was sent from the Garden as an emissary to the southern continent. Santal spent a year in each major capitol city and, in doing so, developed a deep bond of friendship between herself and Crummel even when Carcero rejected magicians.

Chachan saw the slight movement of Ghamrod. His presence wasn't as offensive as when they first met. He sat in a lone chair nearest the door.

'He seems relaxed, if that's even possible,' she thought before the Matriarch added more to the conversation.

"For your concern about Carcero, I have only one, and this is it: Crummel Odward may be a lot of things, but disloyal is not one of them. Should I choose to speak with her to know if she's of the right mind or only a figurehead? But she is the only 'friend' I believe I have left."

"And if by chance she doesn't have her faculties, do you think anyone would wish you injury?" FloAntal attempted to ask when Ghamrod interrupted.

"Whether they wish her harm or not… no harm will come to her," he said firmly, leaning forward to stand up.

Chachan observed a strange energy emitting through the bond the Matriarch had created. It was admiration and sadness. Something she would not dwell on in this moment believing that some things were better left unsaid.

Ghamrod had not intended for his words to carry as much force as they had, so he lessened his tone as he continued with a completely different subject.

"Naiyan Amitsa has had someone speak on her behalf about traveling to Medellin when we leave. I've found knowledge of other cultures often lead to a better understanding of self."

Chachan shook her head in disbelief. She didn't believe that Naiyan would want to leave but realized so much had changed, and she couldn't be sure of much anything anymore. It still didn't prevent her from being slightly objectionable to the idea.

"She has lost her mother and survived an attack and then was thrown into discussions of prophecy when she is still learning the value of self. I doubt if Nana...." Chachan paused briefly to correct herself, but FloAntal interjected with a question.

"Are we certain Naiyan is ready for a life changing experience, especially when she's in the midst of one?"

Ghamrod moved to the table and poured a third cup of water.

"Who is every really ready for change?" the Matriarch answered the question with a question. Santal Culdris had intended to speak with Naiyan before they departed before the request. She owed it to her mother even in her death.

Anel Improvi had been passed into the Order of Petals decades ago, and it was the Matriarch's responsibility to ensure Naiyan had her feet on solid ground. She would seek questions to answers only Naiyan could provide. There was a powerful magician on the lower continent, G'la, who wielded power to bring the dark lord's creatures to life, and no one had any indication who it was.

"Change is necessary, but why do you think she is not prepared?" Ghamrod posed the question to FloAntal, but the Matriarch interrupted.

"Have any of you spoken to Naiyan... recently?" She touched the third glass of water and nodded in approval to her protector.

Chachan knew she had scarcely seen Naiyan over the past three weeks, but she had to believe her fine with Imani and Ransa keeping her company. Ransa's time was limited, but Chachan knew the three friends would never fail each other.

Still, no one was able to answer the simple question with affirmation.

"I'll go speak with her shortly. She's in the home of her mother still." It was a statement as opposed to a question. The Matriarch removed the shawl she wore and folded it, only to place it on the table opposite of the three glasses of water.

"I'd like to understand the reasons behind her thoughts before I decide to allow her departure with me. Her mind seems blocked from all the activity from the morning the beast of hell appeared at the lake. And the revelation of that morning may cause a shift in her spirit as those demons come back to haunt her mind." She rotated her neck and motioned to Ghamrod.

"Set privacy wards and keep watch till we are done," the Matriarch ordered as she retrieved a cup of water from the table.

Ghamrod tugged on his twisted beard and walked out of the room. When the door closed behind him, a noise ensued separate from the already present locking mechanism. The room was now sealed, and any magic expelled inside it would not seep out.

"There are forces, evil ones that crossed into the land of Kefise, Trivoli, and Patin. The threat could be from those within the wilderness. I cannot fight the battle alone, so I will teach you secrets of the Petals. The technique must be honed because there is at least one powerful enough to bring those things back to life. I only trust you and initially because you were the only ones Anel Improvi trusted." The Matriarch removed her shoes while taking a sip of water from the cup.

"Today I will be more deliberate." She placed the cup of water back onto the table and walked toward the fireplace. She opened her magic and lit the two logs in it. The Matriarch touched her index finger to her lips as if contemplating before placing another log into the hearth."

"I hope you two have embraced the lessons over these last few days I have pushed you through."

Chachan felt strange and from the expression on FloAntal's face, she did also.

"I can't breathe." Flo attempted to say as she grabbed at the necklace draped around her bosom.

Chachan was first to manipulate the flows of energy, diverting the force being ushered at her friend.

FloAntal fell to one knee. The attack was expected, but she had not been prepared. After regaining a sense of balance, FloAntal focused on the knots of energies being sent toward Chachan and used the energy of air that had been suffocating her to alter the pressure being applied against them.

The slight adjustment sent two chairs flying across the room to crash loudly against the wall, but as the wood splintered and bounced off the surroundings, the individual shattered pieces formed into a collective bundle before taking aim at Chachan.

Chachan pulled her magic upward to provide an earth barrier between herself and the projectile. She had countered the Matriarch's initial attack, and that's when she detected pressure to her neck and shoulders, forcing her down.

FloAntal saw the dirt beneath Chachan cracking, and although she couldn't recognize the combination of magic being used, she tried forcing the bundle of spinning wood away from her counterpart, but the air magic she wielded was slowly being used against her, constricting her body.

The Matriarch simply stared at both women expressionless as they each struggled to control their magic. It wasn't always possible to determine what threads were being used, but they could change the frequency. They were not passing this exercise.

Chachan created a variation in the flow of energies and moved them away from FloAntal.

FloAntal did the same for Chachan.

The Matriarch threw another log into the fire.

Chachan made out something different inside as she struggled, like it a thought emanating from FloAntal.

'Fire out… Fire out…' is what Chachan believe she had heard. Instead of trying to push the air binding back, Chachan invited the tiny strands toward her. The strain nearly overwhelmed her, but she held on.

FloAntal used her magic to suppress the splintered wood, now split into two.

'*Let go…*' Chachan heard in her mind again. There was no way she would let go and be injured or killed from the other bundle of splintered wood pressing forward.

'*Let go…*' She heard again, watching the ground beneath her feet give way.

'*Let go…*' Chachan heard, but this time the energy she had taken away from Flo was pouring into her, and she couldn't stop it and…

"Enough!" the Matriarch had expectations of success, but as she diminished the force of magic being used, the reality was expectations often brought disappointment.

"Why didn't you let her help you? You could have easily moved through that activity. I heard 'let go'…isn't that what you heard…isn't that what you thought, daughter? The Matriarch paused. "I heard fire out. You heard fire out!" The Matriarch raised her voice, and without warning the Matriarch lifted both women into the air.

"I've not begun to harness your true powers… Separately, you're strong… possibly as strong as the Ancient Ones, but in tandem, you can move mountains. So, you will learn!"

The wood that was sprawled on the floor was lifted once again, and then the bundle was split into four different sections, two for each woman to handle. Chachan had already used earth to block the wood and was attempting to repeat her same actions from before.

'*Let go….*' She heard again, and reluctantly she followed the command, and FloAntal's air magic nullified the wood spinning towards her.

The Matriarch used FloAntal's magic to bind them with strands of air while placing another log into the fireplace.

'*Fire out... Fire out.*' Chachan heard in her mind again. As Chachan was pinned against the mound of earth and struggled to get free, she identified FloAntal working the chains around her wrists.

'*Put the fire out!*' The mounds of earth exploded outward toward the Matriarch. Chachan saw the opportunity, and in that moment, fire and earth collided. The older woman used the element of fire to disintegrate the fist-sized earth balls hurling towards her.

Chachan took that split second to use the force of air to dispense the fire in the hearth, yet as soon as that was resolved, the Matriarch turned Chachan's thread of air against her to restrict her breathing. Flo was already taking the threads of energy dissipating from the fireplace and twisting that energy into a ball and hurling it to cut through the threads being woven to restrict Chachan's breathing.

Flo kept finding energy in bundles spread throughout the room to give Chachan time to regain her composure, but now the brunt of the Matriarch's attention was being directed towards FloAntal.

'*Help...*'

Chachan was standing and moving to FloAntal's aid.

'*Reverse the flows.*' Chachan formed a thought twisting the threads.

The Matriarch was concentrating much harder now as indicated by the intensity of flames that reignited in the fireplace.

'*Push back, Flo...*' Chachan thought, and soon after, the strands of air were moving away from them and a little closer to the Matriarch.

'*More earth, Chachan...*' FloAntal perceived the power in her counterpart rising as the ground beneath them began to shake and split.

The air strands FloAntal controlled were pushing forward.

The Matriarch was now moving her hands to control the various magics spread throughout the space. This exercise had turned into a whirlwind of chaos as the furniture was lifted high and pressed against the ceiling and back down to the floor, at times toward Flo and Chachan before inching closer to the Matriarch. Without warning, the fire had sparked again in the hearth.

'*Enough...*' was the final thought before the furniture was dropped back in place and the turmoil frequenting this room abruptly ended. The Matriarch ran her hand over her salt-and-pepper hair while Flo and Chachan fell backward onto the floor, exhausted.

"Much better but you two must trust implicitly. You are hearing the ideas and thoughts of each other while in the bond. A few more exercises will prepare you against two or three Class Ones… The more practice, the stronger both of you will become." The older woman placed another log into the hearth.

"With the expressions on your face you're wondering where all the energy went…" She paused again.

"Your mind knows the answer to that question. Retrace today's lesson in each moment, focus on the moments before each attack, and remember the first philosophy. Energy cannot be destroyed only take on different forms." She then used her magic to release the seal on the door.

Ghamrod stood firm with fierceness in his eyes, and both FloAntal and Chachan saw the silent exchange of looks between him and the Matriarch.

"I will take this opportunity now to speak with Naiyan Amitsa. There is no better time than the present," she finished.

Chachan was completely exhausted, and if she was still feeling the effects of FloAntal's connection, so was the other woman. She would force herself to accompany the Matriarch, so Naiyan wouldn't feel overwhelmed. She called out before the Matriarch departed.

"I'll go with you…." She slumped over again; she tried to mentally force her legs to support her body, to no avail.

"I'd enjoy the company, but for now, you need to gather yourselves. I'll have Ransa tend to your needs. She needs to become familiar in caring for Class One's such as yourselves. I'll have a few of your devoted keepers come scour and repair this room with a senior or two while you recover. It should teach them humility."

FloAntal and Chachan looked at each other before addressing the older woman.

"Excuse me, we've never been tested for that elevation, and in all truthfulness, no one has ever been tested for such a status, not since the Ancient Ones. We wouldn't have the knowledge to even do so or anyone considered worthy to even test…."

Chachan interrupted FloAntal.

"We mean that no one has been worthy or exerted the control needed to be tested, and besides that, we don't have the means to even utilize the chamber to test for such a distinction; we just learned of its true nature less than two months ago." Chachan mustered as much strength that she could to form her words.

The Matriarch stood still. She seemed puzzled with a questionable expression on her face before looking back towards the commander.

"I'll let them figure it out… Sometimes it is better that way." The Matriarch threw another log into the hearth. As Santal Culdris gathered her belongings, Ghamrod kept watching the two women still sitting as if he knew something that they should have.

"Commander!" the older woman called out and motioned for him to lead the way.

Chachan watched as Commander Ghamrod opened the door, and then she saw the half smirk on the Matriarch's face, but she couldn't understand the meaning of it. As much as she wanted to accompany them to Naiyan's home, she could barely make it to her feet.

"Who really knows of Naiyan Amitsa, Chachan?" FloAntal apparently knew what was concerning her friend. Chachan would protect Naiyan against anyone wishing her harm, and from the bond now shared, she knew it was not the Matriarch's intent.

"We should concentrate on what was meant by: *I'll let them figure it out…* It ought a be a strong revelation." FloAntal stood and walked gingerly towards the fireplace for heat. Her bones were chilled, and her teeth chattered against each other. As FloAntal approached the hearth, the fire was pushing out more warmth than expected. She rubbed her hands together.

"I feel that over here too." Chachan's curiosity forced the pain shooting down her legs, to the back portions in her mind, as she slowly moved toward her friend.

"I feel powerful remains of magic…" The answers were beginning to be brought to light.

"Why did she keep putting logs into the fire?" she finally asked.

FloAntal was looking into the fire and noticed that with the amount of heat extending into the room, and the logs should've been extinguished.

"Let's think this through. Each time she placed a log into the fireplace was right after we countered her magic." FloAntal looked on. What wasn't she able to understand?

"That log right there… All the logs have the element of fire, but do you see those small traces of air… and water?" FloAntal was perplexed. The simple small amount of magic added together created a sort of self-maintained energy.

"Energy can never be destroyed." Chachan stared intently at one of the logs, and through the strange bond, FloAntal became aware of which piece of burning wood the other senior was concentrating on. She noticed Chachan's magic moving again towards the one piece of wood that contained all three elements. They would have to work together if they were to succeed in separating the small filaments wrapped within the fire.

"Careful…" FloAntal thought while adding more energy to the force Chachan was using.

"The knot, we have to keep focusing on the knot."

Both women thought, and in that mere fraction of time, the one log they had concentrated on intensified before self-extinguishing.

"I think we are on the right path to discovery…" Chachan breathed heavily as both fell into each other for support.

"And what do we do about this?" Flo asked. Looking at their surroundings, she saw the ceiling and walls stained with soot. The wood was spread over the room sporadically.

"The Matriarch is big on following instructions." Chachan smiled at FloAntal. They were thinking the same thing.

"Anri," they both replied in unison.

The lesson had been learned.

CHAPTER TWENTY-EIGHT

YES...YES...YES

For the first time in over a month, Naiyan began to feel like herself again. Her taste buds were once again welcoming the spices she had grown to love. She had also willed herself to return to the spot she had last held her mother. It was now a memory to be drawn on in the future when she needed strength. She sat at the table, tracing her figures over the symbols in the scroll unable to understand how so many aspects of her life had been altered.

The small changes within herself became noticeable. Hot liquid didn't scold her. Where she had found the small fire magic within didn't bother her, it was such a minimal amount, but it was something. She could feel the different vibrations in the earth from those who were in her presence and able to distinguish people who were using magic.

Naiyan's challenge was to continue to learn every bit of information her mother had left behind.

'*I'll miss them dearly*,' she thought intimately as she packed. The excitement of a new beginning was equally balanced to the sorrow in her heart knowing she would be leaving behind those she loved.

She was unsure why Ziri's face had been imagined in her mind.

He had been like an older brother to her, protective and comedic. It was in one of his drunk and jovial moods years ago that he first told Naiyan that he was going to be her husband one day. When he sobered, he swore he had no recollection of saying those words, so when he said "I love you" at the family dinner about a month ago, Naiyan hadn't known what to believe.

'*I guess I'll miss him too.*' She exhaled, feeling a shift in her emotions. The thought was forced away.

Naiyan had made up her mind. If it wasn't the states of Medellin, then she would travel north and locate her aun. Would the familiar face be too much to bear, or would it be enough to make her feel whole again? Would Somerset even know who she was? Naiyan did not have an answer.

The house had taken on a different personality. It had changed for Naiyan the night of the life ceremony. She had hoped it was all a mistake, a dream of some sort. However, when each senior spoke of Anel Improvi, they used past tense words like "was and will be missed." For Naiyan, the realization slowly sank in, and it was when she heard "she leaves behind a daughter." It was absolute sorrow in knowing her mother was gone.

Eyeing the parchment and scroll laying on the round wooden table, Naiyan decided she should keep them more secured. She placed them both in a leather satchel and retuned them to her mother's secret study.

Naiyan only knew a few of the symbols, but she would be diligent in deciphering the contents of both. Although Chachan had seen a portion of the writings, she had not been able to translate much of it. Many were from languages of old tongues, and it would take time to decipher, but Naiyan vowed to learn each one.

She rubbed her hands together and concentrated on two of the candles burning. She imagined the flame igniting the others stationed nearest the two.

'*Voila.*' It was a sense of accomplishment learning small feats such as this. Achieving control over fire magic was one of the hardest to perform because it stemmed from emotion. Naiyan's feelings of being alone in the world had passed and now small steps were being made to understand her new normal.

The fragrance of the scented candles brought a sweet aroma, and with the shutters of the windows half open, Naiyan could see the first shift of the night guards' watch beginning.

Usually, a two to three men post was now double in numbers since the dark creatures had been found out. In addition to the stationary watch, several twelve-man patrols protected the city on horseback.

The Matriarch had helped make many decisions after speaking with FloAntal and Chachan on the first day of meeting them.

The land, the city that Naiyan had known, vaguely existed. The buildings and homes were the same. The ring of fire was located exactly in the middle of the senior quarters, but Ransa had passed her rites of passage and had new responsibilities. The time spent with her friends had dwindled. Naiyan barely saw Ransa after the Matriarch took a personal interest in her. Naiyan was proud that her sister was strong enough to stand the Trials of the Garden, given by the Matriarch. It was an honor and special designation.

Naiyan looked outside after hearing a variety of voices.

The unassuming posture of all the guards outside her home were now fully alert, and before Naiyan could move to get a better view, she heard the tapping on the door to the cottage.

"One moment." She wondered who it could be. She wasn't expecting anyone.

Naiyan heard a second knock much louder and forceful. It was a rude way to make your arrival known. Impatience bothered her—a trait her mother also possessed.

'*Now whoever it is can wait just one more bloody second.*' Naiyan concentrated on the candle in her hand. She closed her eyes and imagined what she wanted. When she opened her eyes, all the other candles in her room had simultaneously been lit.

'*Okay, let's see who this is.*'

She opened the door.

Her hand gripped the iron latch as she saw the Matriarch standing with hands resting by her side. Her facial expression looked controlled, but if Naiyan had to guess, it had an undertone of amusement in it.

Being taken completely off guard by this arrival, Naiyan shook, barely keeping hold of the candle in her hand.

'*Calm your nerves.*' She steadied herself.

"May we come in?" the Matriarch asked breaking the momentary silence.

"Yes… yes you may, Matriarch." The candle flickered in her hand for a second time.

"Thank you." The older woman walked towards the center of the room and looked around while waiting for the door to be secured.

"Have a seat, please." Ghamrod motioned Naiyan forward towards the table.

The Matriarch pulled a chair out for Naiyan to sit. Even though it wasn't the older woman's home, Naiyan sensed the apparent authority.

Naiyan placed her candle on the table, resting her hand on the small holder. Her mind was overwhelmed. Her eyes held fast on the small woman, but she was running through various questions in her mind.

'Is she here to try and get info that the seniors haven't gotten yet?'

The commander moved towards the door, shifting Naiyan's attention to him.

She looked back at the Matriarch who still trained her eyes on the younger woman.

Naiyan heard the latch lock in place and turned to see the commander standing, as if he was barring her exit.

'Are they preventing me from leaving my own home?'

The Matriarch sat across from Naiyan, and her slight movement forward shifted the attention back to the older woman who had now joined Naiyan in holding the single burning candle.

"Naiyan Amitsa, I have a few questions for you."

Naiyan's stomach felt empty, and the air was stuck in her throat. Anxiety prickled her skin as tension seized the back of her neck and shoulders. The blank stare expanded as her eyes widened, she could feel herself holding her breath.

"No... No... No... not those type of questions, young woman. I am positive that you have no union with the Dark Master."

Naiyan exhaled, and the flame nearly extinguished.

"Commander, you may have a seat. I think your stature is a tad overwhelming." She motioned him towards the adjoining door to Anel's quarters.

"Do you mind if he has a seat in the inner room? That way we can..." The Matriarch was unable to finish her question before Naiyan exploded.

"Yes, I do mind... It's my mother's room!" she yelled, rising to physically confront the oversized man.

The Matriarch cleared her throat, and Naiyan resolved her anger quickly after realizing she had overreacted.

"Yes, I do mind, Matriarch." Her tone had changed, but she held her ground, looking directly into the eyes of the Matriarch.

"That's good. Good you have a backbone." The older woman shook her head up and down. She made the commander sit near the fireplace.

Naiyan returned to the table, and the Matriarch asked to hold hands.

"I also understand you are wanting to travel outside of your home, and I once held your mother close like a sister. Is this your wish? To leave behind all that you have ever known?" she asked without emotion.

"Yes, it is."

"You are welcomed to come with us under three conditions. The first is simple: You will always obey my command while traveling." She hesitated to let Naiyan respond.

"I agree."

"Secondly, you will give me three years of being my attendant, and you will be responsible for my care. In exchange, you will be paid one silver per week in addition to any lessons I provide to you." The Matriarch waited for the second answer.

This time Naiyan didn't respond immediately. She needed to slow her thinking when coin was involved.

Three years of servitude for one silver per week was a considerable amount of coin, and in three years, it would make her moderately wealthy, but was that enough compensation to offset the tedious task of being someone's servant? Especially for the woman responsible for so many others.

'I'll get tutelage and eventually have access to books on history and prophecy and learn the secrets of the scrolls and scriptures I have.'

"I agree," she answered while unknowingly gripping the older woman's hand more tightly.

"And thirdly, once we leave Lake Ledoma, you will not engage in any practice of magic without permission from me, until I allow it or we reach the capital of Medellin," she finished clearly, changing the tone of the previous two provisions set forth.

'*No one knows I have any magic, so this won't be difficult.*' aiyan's eyes seem to lighten.

"Agreed on all three conditions."

Naiyan discovered her fingers tingled and then a faint burning in her feet.

'*Does she know I have magic*?' The tension rose in Naiyan, and the flame of each candle in the room extinguished except the one they still grasped.

A strange energy was moving within her, and as she met the Matriarch's eyes, the candle they still held onto went out while the others started burning again.

"I will hold you to all three conditions, Naiyan Amitsa. Your word and honor is important and lies within the flame we hold. Don't follow the course of deception that some of the seniors have participated in. We leave one week from today, on the second day of the festival."

The older woman stood slowly and touched Naiyan on the shoulder as the commander opened the door. When the door closed, she looked around at each candle still burning again. She wondered why she had gotten the burning in her feet and tingling in her fingers.

'*Two out of three promises will be sufficient and five days to prepare.*' She looked out the window at the guards who had become attentive again. It put a bittersweet smile across her face to know she'd be leaving. This would always be home, but the world awaited.

CHAPTER TWENTY-NINE
Agree to Disagree

Compared to the other portions of the city's architecture, the monetary building was simple in design. The delegation from Carcero sat across from the Fifth of which Chachan was now a part of.

Chachan despised meetings like this; high-level negotiations had never been her cup of tea. Any agreement that these two parties settled on would have ramifications for countless generations. She was relieved that her husband returned safe and sound days ago, but she was mentally worn. Chachan knew it would take an enormous amount of patience to last this day's negotiations.

As the pleasantries faded, Keeble brought up the next item on the agenda.

"We received the counter offer a few months ago. We have to say we were a little surprised to see how supportive your assembly was to make sure we understood the details to move forward. It will cost a substantial amount of coin and labor to return the Port of Ledoma to working condition, as you well know. We have labor that will work for fifty percent of this project's rate, we can pay that. If you provide labor for this venture, your coffers pay the difference."

Cusi listened. If there was one thing he respected his counterpart in, it was this.

Anri kept his breathing even. He didn't want to show any sign of emotion. This was by far the biggest agreement he had been a part of. The smaller purchases of land when citizens needed coin to pay off incurred debts was trivial compared to this.

Elder Isela Croft sat cross-legged in her chair. The white muslin trouser suit was stitched with intermittent colored threads of iceberg blue and canary yellows. Her rich black skin hid her age, but the wisdom in her eyes could not be mistaken.

"We could make our citizens very happy by accepting what appears to be such a generous offer. Families would be able to afford a much more comfortable life. Although, I admit we are really nothing but a bunch of ordinary folks when it all boils down. The concern in paying separate wages is heavy. This undertaking, should we reach an accord, will require a delicate dance between two very different cultures. The project rate should be applicable to all workers." FloAntal opened with their first counteroffer. Isela Croft saw the first bit of agitation from the delegation as Keeble ever so slightly tapped his index finger on the edge of the table.

"I am sure your treasury of coin has set limits on expenditures and have forecasted the time it takes for a return on investment. Our labor force will be grateful—I'm sure like yours—but we cannot exceed fifty percent of this project's rate. Keep in mind it is already ten percent more than their standard labor rate," Keeble responded as one of the economic advisors approached him from the rear and whispered something.

"Actually, it's twelve percent higher than their standard labor rate," he corrected the statistic.

"Eleven-point four percent to be exact, but who is counting?" Isela uncrossed her legs and sat forward before continuing.

"This third opening item should not take so much back and forth between us. We all know we have more pressing challenges ahead. For all labor costs, every worker gets paid seventy-five percent of this projects cost. Carcero pays thirty-seven-point five percent, and we match it. As my friend stated, we have cultural hurdles to overcome, and we will not make monies an additional one." Isela looked around at the three across the table who nodded their head to accept the terms.

"The next item for discussion is the ten-mile 'buffer zone' you've requested. Those lands contain valuable resources, water ways, and timber. Old mines still left untouched. The largest channel of water is navigated just north of the port. The old canal would need repaired as well. We have the technology to open an additional trade route. We must insist that the original map be honored." Cusi brought the next topic up for dialogue. He reached for the glass of water on the table in front of him. He wasn't nervous, simply thirsty.

"Insist is such a… strong… word." A deep baritone voice split the air.

Chachan met FloAntal's eyes before looking toward Perci Rax, First Master of Fire.

The air in the space shifted, and the tension could be felt as he continued.

"The Bagrah River is vast as it feeds from the mountains. There are multiple tributaries large enough for thousands of your people to harness from. We will open the canal in a time of our choosing, and we have our own means to make it ready. Of course, with the miles of land being adjusted just north of the port we understand both loss and gain. We offer a reduction of three percent from the monies to be paid, or we will offer you an additional five miles of coastline." Perci voted against this counteroffer before they had come to the bargaining table. Unfortunately for both he and FloAntal, Chachan cast the swing vote.

Cusi had not meant it as a form of aggression, but he had no doubt that Elder Rax had taken it that way. Keeble sat forward and stared across the table. They were completely blindsided. This land would've increased the gross national revenue by fifteen percent within the first five years, and it was one of the reasons they agreed to originally pay ten percent above their standard wage when Anel Improvi included it with the original counteroffer.

"I think perhaps a recess is required in this moment." Janae paused, making eye contact with everyone at the table, especially Chachan.

"It's a lot to process when one of the cornerstones of this transaction our business depends on is relegated to two unequal options. I'm sure pause is necessary for one hour hence," Janae finished, and without hesitation, she stood and exited the room with an advisor and attendant behind her.

Cusi and Keeble stood and followed behind their compatriot.

"That is what we agreed upon, Perci, but just because it was not in your favor, did you have to deliver the conditions with such animosity?" Isela scooted her chair away without waiting for Perci to answer. She left the room.

Anri laughed as he stood.

"Did you expect any different?" He walked through a door into a separate section of the building where he would wait the hour.

Perci inhaled deeply before making eye contact with Chachan and FloAntal who had moved closer to a window.

"Well, Anri does have a point." He moved in the same direction Anri had.

"I don't know how you and Anel could handle this, all of these years. Give me a simpler task than this and I'd willingly accept. I pray history will be kind to whatever happens these next few days." Chachan adjusted her shirt to drape across her shoulders. It had already been five hours of offer and counteroffer, and they still had quite a few more items of consideration to cover.

"Not me, it was all Elder Anel. She had more patience and a strange way of seeing the bigger picture. That's not to say Perci or the others didn't try to manipulate circumstances...." She paused as a keeper entered to clean portions of the negotiation room. She nodded to say thank you before the keeper left with two trays of cheese, breads, and various fruits to replenish.

"Keeble, he's always straight forward and to the point. Sometimes he will push the boundaries. Cusi is the one who plays the middle to ensure a mutual benefit, but the young woman, she's an oddity. I understand she greets certain guests in the nude,"

FloAntal concluded before excusing herself. With a small intercession, she wouldn't let the last bit of sunshine go to waste.

Chachan found a two-seat cushioned chair and sat down. So much had changed in such little time—the skin demon and Soachim, the delegation, the First Master's dinner and festival. She was being pulled in so many directions. In these minutes she missed her dear friend now more than ever.

Her family was shifting too. Both older boys were making their way up the ranks in their respected duties. The two youngest would soon be joining Zuni in the armed forces.

'*Imani.*' She smiled, thinking about her daughter.

Chachan had not spent much time with her daughter since the arrival of the Matriarch. Imani said she understood and would be fine with her two sister-friends. They seemed to understand her more than she could understand her own flesh and blood as of late.

'*But Ransa has new responsibilities and what of Naiyan and the burden she carries*?' The thought made her realize that what they were doing today with the delegation was ensuring that her family would know peace all the days of their lives.

The hour had passed, and the delegation of Carcero returned just a few minutes after the Fifth.

Both Cusi and Keeble took their seats, but it was Janae, now changed into clothing more comfortable, who had remained standing and dove back into the last topic before the interruption.

"As you know, we have offered much more than what we are getting in return. We could travel east and barter with the old gypsy folk, but that doesn't serve our nations' mutual interests. If…" She let the word hang.

"...if the Shadrians advance through the fog or if the rumors are correct that the wilderness folk are gaining power, Ledoma will be their first contact, which means we will be their second. The geographical location of the Bagrah River is essential in the development of the newly acquired territory. The tributaries you speak of that course from the mountains will not be enough in the long run. The canal, after completion, will allow a massive shift in trade and at least two of the five channels of water that the canal runs into are ours already." She touched each position on the map that she spoke upon.

"The reduction of three percent, as my compatriot shared earlier, is inadequate. Instead, we propose this." Janae then proceeded to shave the ten miles of buffer zone down to five miles each side of the Bagrah river. This would give Carcero access to several other water sources without interfering in Ledoma's water supply. Three-percent reduction along with an additional ten-square miles of coastline." The coastline had not been anything that the other male ambassadors had agreed upon, but both thought it a brilliant counter, leaving the elder's ample room to push back but also space to agree.

Chachan thought those were better terms; both nations had saved money on labor costs. The extended miles of coastline made no difference because the land was treacherous. The terrain rocky and the rogue waves more frequent, and that was before leading into the fog.

"The youngest of us all, and she has more vision than I did at her age." Perci spoke up with a lighter tone than earlier.

"Agreed, but five miles north of the port will run into a few old communities who are as prideful and stubborn as some in this room. However, if we..." Isela moved towards the map and placed the mall pins farther out where one of the tributaries could be shared without interaction. A compromise at seven miles. The original amount Anel had settled on during her final assembly meeting.

From the up and down head movements, another item had been checked off the list.

"*Progress.*" Chachan breathed deeply. Now there were two topics left to discuss, and from the hesitancy of both groups, they would be touchy subjects. Chachan thought it best that she break the ice. It had to be discussed.

"Our biggest challenge will lay in the cultural exchange that both of our citizens will experience. Some of the laws of Carcero, are well… to say the least, in direct opposition to the laws of our land. This port and the lands around it will be an experiment that we cannot let loose on the world until we can find common 'lawful' areas of interest. There will be all levels of magicians who will travel and barter with their goods and services. In an open economy, it's all supply and demand, and that's why we all have agreed that wages must be consistent for every worker. These 'common laws' that we will incorporate must also be consistent for every person. Any acts of violence, intimidation, discrimination against anyone will face our court of justice. We will be fair as it has always been in the history of our land. Our decision in any matter presented will be final."

FloAntal watched her friend take her seat. Chachan voting against her suggestion earlier had caught her by surprise, but the leadership she was exhibiting in this moment had been expected. It was the reason she had assumed the role of the Fifth.

Cusi scooted his chair back before standing. He picked his glass of water up and finished it before he spoke on what Chachan had just requested.

"We have come here to negotiate various items. The previous two have been more of this is what you *will* do, or this is what we expect. Have we been so far off in anything except perhaps egos? Elder Balent, your concern is great. Yes, we do have different cultural foundations, but we agree on law. Whatever rules and regulations for areas shared by our respected citizens will be included in those charters, but where we differ will punishment and recourse be your sole responsibility? We respectfully ask that like this assembly, two of our barristers, and two of your representatives determine sentences. We submit that if there are conclusions that render a split decision. The Fifth shall have sole power to determine outcome." Cusi took Chachans cue and cut through the chase. They could come to agreements on every item before midnight should this item be championed.

Perci chuckled and then laughed uncontrollably.

"Elder?" Chachan asked.

"Oh, oh, no, you must excuse me. I apologize, but doesn't Carcero have capital punishment on the books? What happens when the offense would require a sentence of death by your standards? Especially when it is dispersed in an inequitable manner? In fact, it has been seventy percent of magicians who have been executed by the law of your land, and they account for under ten percent of the population. We, in Ledoma, issue justice to everyone no matter their station, family, or race of being. Can your citizens be expected not to show bias?" Perci kept his voice light, but the words he spoke were accurate.

"What happens within our borders, according to our system of justice, has no bearing on what we choose in the separate but equal statutes of our partnership. Yes, we are purchasing a large amount of territory, and within those boundaries nothing changes for our citizens, but we concede as much as you do when we structure the laws to govern what we are creating together." Keeble matched Perci's tone and made clear the intent of the goal. Collaboration.

"It seems that we agree upon those terms, so let us table it and schedule an ensuing meeting between our legal counsels to create a list of laws and regulations." Perci saw no reason to pushback against the rebuttal. The laws of the port and surrounding areas would take time but were doable.

"Perceived currency manipulation. There it is, out on the table," Janae stated as a matter of fact.

"Perceived?" FloAntal repeated before continuing.

"There's always been a standard amount of the percent of copper, silver, or gold to be minted with each coin of value. Medellin, Ilens, and most nations have open trade. When there is a ten percent less amount of each substance used per each coin, then it does not have an equal value. How is that not actual currency manipulation? Our citizens pay 10 silvers for a transaction, which means compared to your valuation for same said item using your coin means that a loss is occurring, repeatedly. Now, those same coins make it back to Carcero to be recast and redistributed, not only have we lost the ten percent, but you've gained an additional percent, so we'd call that manipulation of currency and bad business," FloAntal finished. All the break-throughs they had found common ground on were doomed to fail if the valuation of money was not addressed.

Carcero, being as large of a nation as it was, created different trade policies with those lesser nations who depended on them. Ledoma was not one of those nations.

"All of the payments we receive for the land in question must be received by true standard weight and value. Those purchasers of goods, once this endeavor is complete, must also have full disclosure of the difference in value of coin. When you purchase items from our tannery, distilleries, or metal forgers, you pay one Carcero coin plus one copper, do you not?" Isela continued where FloAntal had left off.

"Those are mostly rumors. The services we provide, the goods and services that continue to be transported to the surrounding areas, what these lands agree on contractually shouldn't be your concern," Janae addressed Isela without pause.

The advisors who had accompanied the delegation from Carcero could be heard murmuring amongst each other, whispers which had those sitting at the main table focusing their eyes onto them. Shifting their attention away from Isela and Janae who had maintained eye contact with each other the entire time.

"If any of you have something to say, after thirteen hours of negotiation today… at this point, just spit it out." Keeble looked over his shoulder at the advisor closest to him.

"Well, ambassador… if we recalculate the figures for the purchase of land, including the cost to repair 'their' port, while losing money on the funding and completion of the Bagrah canal, another ten percent is not acceptable to our assembly," the silver haired man added a major objection to the project.

Chachan stood from her seat and walked away from the table to stare out the window. The late night was amongst them, and she was certain much clearer and fresher minds would help chart the next best course of action.

"Elders, perhaps we should take a respite and reconvene tomorrow mid-afternoon again. We have made exceptional progress today. With the enormous amount of time we have spent together today finding common ground, I am sure a solution to this consideration can be found." Cusi seemed to be on the same accord as Chachan.

"Yes, I think that best right now." Anri chimed in. He had gone much longer in previous negotiations with Anel Improvi, but even he knew that the issue on currency valuation would take a considerable amount of time. Perhaps another twelve plus hours on this subject alone.

"Does either party have any objections to continuing this mid-afternoon on the morrow?" Chachan asked as she returned to the table.

"No objection from our delegation," Cusi stated as he placed his hands onto the table.

"None from us," Anri concluded.

Chachan watched everyone slowly exit, except Isela who simply stared at the before and after maps should an accord be met.

"So much is happening, so fast. Are we giving up our autonomy and joining the pitfalls of man that we have avoided for centuries?" The intellect in her eyes was matched by the wisdom of her question.

Chachan didn't have an answer to the question posed. She and Iver had long discussions over this very topic. Were they being influenced by the changing world? With those from Medellin and Carcero injecting themselves into both political and G'la business, Chachan knew she had to pay close attention to what each party wanted to take away from Lake Ledoma and what they offered in return.

CHAPTER THIRTY

Keeping Up Appearances

Whal was extremely both tired and exhausted, but within three days, everything would come to a head.

Whal had not slept well after the inquisition by his Council of Elders on why he had the Creator's Glass in his possession. It should've been archived with other artifacts when he first returned to Ledoma with the other ancient relics. He had retrieved harsh words about his breach in protocol, but in the end, it was only his bruised ego that had suffered—that and a lack of sleep for several days.

Whal paced the floor of his old home, trying to quell his frustration. Just like he assumed, the other seniors had allowed their spiritual convictions to guide direction. Now, the Matriarch had assumed the leadership role in the investigation. The remains of the Soachim were in the hands of an entire team comprised of Petals and other qualified alchemists. Had he not thought to bury two additional jars in a remote location, his plan would be ended. Instead, the anger inside him raged, making it an easier decision to destroy anyone who stood in his way.

"The sacrifices one makes for the betterment of all." Ricka Ohm raised her glass to all those gathered. Basil Kern and Lyl Wazin toasted with her. They had been incorporated and groomed a long time ago before they joined the Senior Assembly of Ledoma.

Whal handpicked each and manipulated them to believing Lake Ledoma needed to be transformed. He finally calmed down over the course of the hour. Anger could cloud judgment, and the steps to execute his plan were critical over the next several days. The ceremony to introduce those who were now seniors was to be held on the night before the first day of the festival.

The outdoor stadium was built like a semi-circle with the stage front and center. The backdrop of the arena provided a majestic view of a mountain range that extended for tens of miles. Whal would ensure those from Medellin were present when he reanimated the Soachim. With the three seniors in his presence, and another four secured to join their insurrection, they would counteract any magic being performed to stop the evil creatures from completing their task.

'*Anri.*' Whal thought the name. He wasn't sure what his old friend would choose. In either case, with or without him, Elder Anri Batelle would not be viewed kindly when the history books were written. As he moved to the table along with the others, he let his thoughts venture back into the moment.

"Our conviction has never been clearer; we are bartering off bits of our land for money. We have allowed foreigners to take up residency in our sanctuary and place their needs above ours while many of our assembly members sniff behind them like house-broken pets. We will lead Lake Ledoma into the future, give what we can, and take what we want." Whal adjusted his glasses before pouring a glass of ale.

"Until the children return." He raised his glass.

"Until the children return," they replied in unison.

The next few hours were reserved for going over the plan in detail, where each one was to be stationed and who was to make sure none from Medellin could escape. He would find the Matriarch in all the commotion and kill her before she knew what was happening. The whole plan depended on misdirection, and the Soachim would be more than enough distraction.

"We will have a test run tomorrow to leave nothing to chance. Go about like you always do. Know that in just a few days, life as we know it will forever be changed." Whal watched as they exited his home. He secured a cane and made sure he had tabac in his pipe before leaving to go and lend a hand with the other alchemist studying the ashes still.

When he arrived, there were more from Medellin than those from Ledoma conducting tests or doing research of some kind. The Petals acknowledged him with cool stares and then continued with their various activities.

"Elder Stanjz, just the person I wanted to see." Senior Mereth Langs approached him. Langs was the only other person Whal believed competent to make any discovery he had overlooked. She was accompanied by a Petal he had not seen before. Her red hair matched the gem dangling from her necklace. She spoke directly to Whal but did not make eye contact as she wrote on something onto her pad.

“Elder, my findings so far are consistent with your conclusions.”

Whal squinted, not knowing if her words were meant for him.

“Excuse me.” Whal had not expected a direct verbal exchange between the Petal and him.

Mereth spoke in her stead.

“She has studied the history of the creatures that once walked this planet. These remains are not like the other ones. The mere fact that water did not drain them of the dark matter is the first indication, but the amount of heat one would have to exhibit would rival that of the Matriarch.”

Whal watched as Mereth turned and walked to a table that the minimal remains were spread across still being studied.

Whal was unsure of the Petals age as her skin seemed flawless; it was her green eyes, intensely deep that held his attention.

He allowed his focus to shift towards a table surrounded with special energy stones on each corner of it before he saw the spell written beneath the ashes. He was briefly mesmerized by the precision of the casting. It seemed to draw out whatever portion of magic that was left behind from the Soachim.

“It took two of my sister’s, but we found traces of western magic in the scarcity of actual substance left behind, but it’s much more darkness than even the nation from the west has harnessed. Without the Creator’s Glass, the energy of this magic would still be accessible to a Class One G'la." The Petal picked up one of the containers still being examined.

Whal took that as an opportunity to continue his business.

"Thank B'nobi that we now have a means to get to the bottom of this. It seems that this mystery is in good hands. Mereth, if there are additional questions or assistance required, I will be in the sanctuary for the next few hours." Whal bid them all farewell, but all the while, he was thinking he needed something additional to make sure the 'revolution', as he called it, would be successful.

He found his way to the sanctuary. Needing to keep appearances up, he participated in evening prayer and counseled Inez and others on how to use their disappointment in not passing their rites of passage to encourage them on their retest in three years.

As the business-like activities faded into the night, a far more festive atmosphere took shape. Children were no longer seen playing joyfully. Once the city's night lights were fully on, children were to be back home.

The grown-ups were now free to do as adults did. The gambling quarters had patrons waiting to be seated at a table. The ale houses providing entertainment for a variety of tastes were full. Even the dancing venues, where both men and women performed various acts, including those of various sexual proclivities, were being frequented by both residents and guests of the city.

Whal decided not to leave anything to chance. He made sure you that he was seen by many before disappearing to find his way back down into the old hidden storage area.

'*Something else but what?*' He scanned each item that he had become familiar with since he had lost the vote to First Master but, more especially, over the last decade. There were some items that he knew needed to be left shelved. Items with energy he could not control, unlike the control of magic he would exercise with the reanimation potion.

'*That... that would kill everyone.*' He shook his head as he scanned the space. There were articles even a trio of Diviners would be unable to control, items only those with the power of the Ancient Ones would even attempt to unleash.

He was startled by a noise behind him. A book unfamiliar to him had fallen and now laid on the floor.

"How did this..." The words left his lips before he saw a dark mass move slowly out of the storage area.

'*I must be tired.*' He shook his head, believing his eyes were simply weary. He retrieved the book, a bound manuscript that had been destroyed, or so everyone thought—a manuscript of forbidden magic.

Whal secured the book on his person and exited the storage space. He doubled back upon the same route he had taken earlier to make sure he was seen by many. Once he returned home, he placed a ward on his home and opened the book to see what spells, if any, were at his disposal.

CHAPTER THIRTY-ONE
Fading Innocence

Ransa was tired. She had been more exhausted than she imagined after passing the test. The fact that she was no longer an apprentice would be kept secret until the ceremony the next day. Whether or not she would be revealed as a Petal was not known either.

"She calls me daughter and welcomed me into the Order, but am I really a Petal?" She still had questions about everything but decided to allow things to come to her in their own time. For now, her only goal was to spend time with Imani and Naiyan. New responsibilities would never take away the intimate connection she had with her two sister-friends. As she approached the Balent farm, she noticed the twin boys splitting wood with Zuni sitting down watching them from the stomp of a larger tree already cut.

“So, the young ones do all the work, slacker?” she yelled across the small incline path worn down by decades of traveling.

“That’s right, Rags. Ziri didn’t give me assistance when it was my turn. Besides there’s two of them…” He paused and laughed aloud uncontrollably as she pointed at him for using her old nickname.

“Imani and Naiyan are out back by the pit. “The bossy one” has them peeling potatoes and cutting carrots. It’s not bad enough that she has us trying her new fashion. You should see the new shoes she’s making for us.” Zuni started laughing again as Ransa shook her head back and forth. She understood how adamant Imani could be about something once her mind had been made.

Ransa continued to the back side of the property and walked a short path to the area her friends occupied.

“Ahh, there she is. You know just because you got your colors, that doesn’t mean that you can just leave all the hard stuff to us.” Naiyan rocked forward from the stone she sat on and hugged Ransa.

“Yeah, especially when we agreed to enter one of the festival cooking contests together this year.” Imani tilted her head for Ransa to kiss her cheek.

After being pulled in several different directions over the past month or so, Ransa accepted the love immediately until she eyed the sack of onions needing cut.

“Oh, so, I get the onions. You two are bogus… just bogus.” Ransa held a big smile as she sat down and reached for the sack and knife. There was no other place that she would rather be.

The late afternoons had become hotter each day over the past month, and today was no different. The small creek they sat near had been their first playground as tiny children when their biggest concern was how long they could play together without being separated.

The time passed, and much of the prepping for their food was done, but they still had time to gossip.

"My ma came home with a headache last night. I guess we are going into business with them, damn silly to me, especially when they hold so many prejudices against us."

"Well, there's a pretty big obstacle to overcome," Ransa interjected. She looked around to make sure only her sister-friends heard her before continuing.

"Do you know their coins are not an equal value to ours, or any other nations trading in the union? I don't know the exact difference, but I *heard* it was ten percent," she finished. The business of the Fifth was shared with assembly members, but Ransa had no problem sharing with these two. All three had witnessed first-hand conversations between Anel and Chachan on multiple accounts, so they understood some rules were meant to be bent.

"So, not only do they despise us, but they want to rip us off. Thirty miles of land is substantial, and they wanted to short-change us too." Imani wasn't too happy with the visitors from Carcero.

Naiyan leaned forward waving her knife in the air. She had something to add.

"And that naked woman flaunting her… stuff to any and everybody." She reached for more carrots to slice and sat back.

Ransa and Imani looked at each other and laughed. They understood their friend more than she understood herself.

"I think the only person who saw her perky breasts and long legs was Ziri." Ransa stood and walked to the creek as she still chuckled. The onions were diced, and her hands needed freshened. She walked down a small embankment and dipped her hands into the cool water.

Naiyan, slightly embarrassed, had not thought about her slip of the tongue. Was she jealous? Was that what she had been feeling all along?

Movement from the creek caught her attention. Ransa used her magic to move the small parcel from the creek to a container of potatoes nearest Imani. As the water flowed into the bowl, both Naiyan and Imani stared at their friend in amazement. Over a month ago, Ransa transformed into someone with stronger magic, and it was still taking time for them to adjust.

"Don't go showing off on our account." Naiyan approached Ransa still at the creek's edge. She turned back to face Imani and winked at her.

"You know with all this magic you have…" Naiyan reached down for support as she descended the small slope to stand next to Ransa by the streaming water.

"It's our job to make sure you remember how to have fun!" Naiyan pulled her friend into the creek and began splashing her with water.

Laughter filled the property, and before long, the twins joined in the fun after carrying Imani into the stream with them.

The time had passed, and sundown was a couple of hours away. Ransa still had a few tasks left.

"I have to go and be taught; it never stops. I never know what to expect, and *everything* is different." Ransa dried off as much as possible, but Milos splashed her one last time.

"Good one, good one. I owe you, you little shit. There will be seats in the front row of the pavilion for the two of you. You have an extra advance notice, so please, don't be late. I don't think the Matriarch would like that." Ransa looked back over her shoulder while walking away. Her life was changing, but these souls were the foundation of everything she was grounded in.

"Your mother would've been proud of her." Imani didn't say another word as Naiyan pushed her down the path and back to the main home. Imani had already picked her outfit to wear. She made a specially designed white sleeveless dress with a green skirt. She stitched blue thread on the seam of the dress to honor Ransa and her magic.

Naiyan had not put much thought into her attire for the celebration. Realizing just how significant it would be, she asked Imani for ideas.

Imani gave her a separate style tabard to wear, not as fancy as her white sleeveless one.

"I've got a pair of those fancy breeches you made a few months back. They'll definitely make some eyes widen." Naiyan watched Zuni herd the sheep into the barn as Milo took over Imani's roll-chair.

"Maybe think about tradition for the ceremony and forego the breeches." Imani hinted that a dress would be more appropriate, but Naiyan ignored it.

I've gotta go. I need to take a long hot bath and untangle this." Naiyan pointed to her braids needing redone.

"I thought you were going for the gypsy look," Imani called out to her friend watching Naiyan walk away on the dirt path with her middle finger raised.

...

Naiyan entered her home from her mother's entrance. She had become more accepting of leaving the door open between the two adjoined cottages. At times, still expecting to hear her mother's voice, she exhaled and removed her shoes.

She lit candles for fragrance as she took a few heating stones to warm the basin in her mother's space. She found a bottle of detangler root that Ransa had concocted mixing coconut oil, pure honey, and olive oil. It worked wonders.

Naiyan sat in her mother's rocker and scanned the room as she took out her braids. She would tell her two sister-friends the day of the ceremony of her decision to leave—a decision that weighed heavy upon her shoulders.

She got up and walked into Anel's private quarters. The room was still immaculately clean with small bits of random dust particles building on the floor.

'*It will remain this way.*' A set of her mother's dresses and cloaks hung in the corner, all made of fine material.

Anel's ceremonial daisy-yellow hooded mantle hanging in the corner is what she had worn to each meaningful celebration. The green and blue pearls that tied together at the neckline were handpicked by Chachan and FloAntal when Anel ascended to the Fifth. She removed it from the hangar, and Anel's *lifestick* fell to the floor.

'*Can I gift this to Ransa?*' The thought quickly faded as she grasped the wooden rod. She was overwhelmed with energy from the mere touch.

Naiyan fell to the ground and began convulsing. Images flooded her. Not like those that forced themselves into her dreams. These were deliberate and focused. She saw the land of the giants again, along with the Tree of Life. Her mother sat amongst them along with who she recognized as Arjunai, Rose of the Garden, but they didn't have substance.

The image abruptly shifted to fields of dead bodies and the water of Lake Ledoma blood red. She couldn't control what entered her mind. As quickly as the images had surfaced, they had passed.

Naiyan regained her composure and returned the cloak and *lifestick* to the rack. She walked back into the front space and sat down again. She had never had a seizure before and wasn't looking to have a second one. Slowly Naiyan stripped to take a bath.

She heard someone barking orders in the distance; the night patrol was forming. She had lost faith in so many things like the ability of the armed group gathering to protect the city or the seniors protecting its citizens against those who would wish them harm.

'*My mother would never give in to any of their demands.*' Naiyan adjusted herself in the tub of water and laid her head back. Carcero wasn't to be trusted.

She thought about all the hardships Ransa had endured her life. The Medici and seniors, who tried to keep her from becoming a healer. The internal struggles she had for not knowing her parents or where she came from. This was one of the reasons for their strong bond, a similar history.

The sound of music pushed lightly into her home. An acoustic trio was playing as an orator told stories. She had listened to this act two nights in a row and found them entertaining.

She leaned her head back against the head rest. The heat in the water was blissfully good against her skin.

She dozed off knowing that nothing would stop her from seeing the joy across her sister-friend's face when being introduced to the world as Senior Ransa Ansar in two days.

CHAPTER THIRTY-TWO

Intersecting Points

The pavilion had been built close enough to the sanctuary that it could be clearly seen in the background. The areas set aside where goods were bartered and exchanged were situated centrally so that the businesses and smaller carts could be accessible. Although the carts were heavily present towards the commoner's homes where the streets were narrow, it bustled with activity.

New inventions of old ideas were being panned off as 'improved' while staple items like jewelry and clothing were ever present. The space was filled with shoulder-to-shoulder patrons positioning themselves to buy their items.

The closer one ventured into the city proper, the more the streets widened, and stores had their own small walkway into their shops. A smaller variety of items were offered in this space but of much higher quality. These family business owners had built a reputation over centuries and reserved the right to keep this strip devoid of two person carts who were granted space by paying a small fee.

Once the business section was passed, there was an enormous field for gathering. Several options could be used for access. The area had once been a staging platform for over forty thousand troops.

The interior pavilion was stacked with long bench seats situated in a semi-circle. From the large field, the amphitheater stage could be viewed clearly, and in this mostly green grassed area, both citizens and visitors were setting up for the ceremony.

Some of the performers set for the festival were chosen to perform in front of a crowd that would score in the tens of thousands. For the first time, in a long time, the thought of tragedy hadn't been in the forefront of everyone's minds.

Some seniors walked amongst the crowd and others sat down with those in the field to answer questions or simply be a part of the many activities taking place.

A few Petals had garnered a large following as they spoke on their life in Uteri before the insurrection. There were some who kept questioning certain parts of their testimony, but in the end, it was enlightening.

Chachan and Isela were ensuring that Ransa was unblemished. Her clothing had been selected by Erri and FloAntal. Her hair was being done by Jain, the personal attendant that had stayed by the Matriarch's side nearly all the time.

Ransa watched another bring two separate types of shoes to choose from; it was Chachan who determined which pair she'd be wearing.

"Always the comfortable ones during ceremonies. You'll be on your feet for a minimum of two hours, and how you are presented today will be the beginning of the stories and myths people will make up about you." Chachan excused the attendant as Erri put finishing touches on Ransa's makeup.

"My face feels like it's caked on, literally." Ransa objected to so much being done for her.

"Stop moving, or we will have to bake another one on your face. Don't take this lightly, sister; very few have been tested by the Matriarch. Whether you believe it or not, you are special." Erri stepped back to look at her work.

"Perfect."

"Yes, it is perfect daughter." The Matriarch entered the room, and everyone stood attentively.

Uncontrollably, Ransa laughed.

The Matriarch was wearing breeches that Imani designed for a business to sell on consignment. They were beautifully designed but intended for much younger people to wear.

The Matriarch looked sternly at Ransa and held her gaze before laughing with her.

"Should they be this tight around my waist?"

The mood in the room became light again. The Matriarch asked everyone to leave except Chachan, FloAntal, and Erri after she removed the pants to garner a more traditional dress. They would be the three to stand and witness Ransa's oath in front of the large crowd gathering near the pavilion.

"Many of those who have come before you have forgotten the oath you are about to take. That which was shown to you in the shadow of the First Mother holds your truth. I will guide you along your journey as I have done for your sisters, but your path will always be your own."

...

Whal walked the streets and spoke with people enjoying the pre-celebration. He knew that for some of them it would be one of the final conversations they would ever have. He saw some of the seniors who supported his action were already in their designated areas. He was anxious but would see this plan to the end.

'*Ledoma deserves better, and I will give better.*' Whal touched the small pouch at his waist that contained the reanimation potion. He would wait until the ceremony began to unleash his creatures against those who had a narrow vision.

He had not spoken to Anri in several days. Whal had no malcontent towards his old friend because he knew Anri had not betrayed him.

'*He may not be participating, but he didn't turn me in for inquisition, and if he had, I'd be in shackles right now.*' The distancing was all that Whal could expect from Anri at this point.

Whal decided it was time to secure the two jars he had left buried remotely. The re-animation potion would bring them to life, and in theory, the magician who performed the task would have complete control over the two to do his will.

The sun had already begun to descend, but the warmth it had brought was still present. A few crowds congregated around the new sweet delicacies being sold from a husband and wife. They had a two-tier cart, with a form of refrigeration device to ensure their concoctions didn't melt away in the heat. Their timing was impeccable as some families came early to carve out a location to watch the ceremony in the large grassy area that looked down upon the pavilion. Whal smiled at the couple. They weren't citizens, but they seemed familiar.

He took a second path to steer clear of anymore distractions. Once he arrived where he had buried the items he needed, something overcame him.

It wasn't a physical attack, but it wasn't welcoming. It was as if the air thickened, and the breeze that had circulated all day was gone. It felt lifeless.

He saw the fruit bearing trees had aged faster than normally. Where the Creator's Glass held the remains of the Soachim, the grass had died, and rotten fruit lay on the ground, untouched by the usual insect scavengers.

Whal opened himself up to the energy within him to loosen the dirt beneath his feet. The top of the jars could be seen, but there was a black resin leaking out the lids. The smell of it was like rotting flesh. He looked closer to see any dangers and saw none.

‘*What did you expect?’* he thought while wiping the excess of the resin on a cloth he carried. Whal retreated to prepare to return Ledoma to its rightful place in the world.

…

Janae lay naked across her bed staring at the ceiling. The negotiations were difficult, but all the items save one had been agreed upon. The currency difference was close to being complete. The proposal for coin valuation would have to be approved by Speaker Odward herself.

Keeble and Cusi had done exactly as she had been forewarned. Janae used the information to her advantage to make herself a critical component in the process. She was satisfied—well, at least in the task she had been sent to perform.

“Ambassador, the seating arrangements are set. However, there aren’t any roped off areas for dignitaries to travel without hinderance. It seems our guests believe that tonight is all about the people and who serve them. The seniors will walk amongst the common folk, and so must we.”

A beautiful, pale skinned woman walked into Janae’s sleeping quarters. The familiarity between the two was apparent as the woman moved her long red hair to one shoulder and sat down on the bed next to Janae. Her clothing was minimal and revealing.

“This will be such fun. I’ll have little tales to write in my diary. Those two old farts will probably stay behind for fear of everything.” Janae reached down and touched the woman on her hand.

“When we return to Carcero, secure me an audience with my cousin before our formal meetings take place. There’s another player buying land South of Ilens, and we have no idea who they are or represent. I'll need to change more appropriately to walk amongst the people as you say."

Edyth understood the request as she retrieved more comfortable clothing and shoes that still adorn regality.

. . .

Whal had waited long enough. The sun had set, and only the city's light source brightened the streets. Mostly everyone was near the pavilion, with a few stragglers making their way. He smiled at them and continued walking with the assistance of his cane.

'*Some must be sacrificed for the benefit of the many.*' The thought was a simplified version behind his reasoning, but it would suffice.

"Oh, shit, I'm sorry." Naiyan appeared from a smaller walkway nearly running into the older man. She jumped to avoid him at just the last moment.

The two hadn't seen each other, and both had been startled.

"Ahh, Naiyan Amitsa..." Whal paused to look closely to her attire. She had taken the liberty of wearing her mother's ceremonial robe.

"I see your mother's mantle fits you a little better than your second name." Whal didn't mean it as an insult. In fact, he held pity for Naiyan. She had no 'real' family, and under the weight of the name Bearer of Harmony, she would crumble.

Naiyan was at a loss of words. She wanted to respond, but nothing came to mind fast enough.

"Thank you." She regretted those two words as soon as they slipped through her lips.

Whal chuckled dismissively and continued forward with his cane. She was a minute distraction to what he was about to accomplish.

She watched him walk away without further comment.

'*He's one of the biggest assholes.*' She thought of what better responses she could have mustered as she hurried to retrieve her mother's *lifestick*. She was going to give it to Ransa if it was allowed. If anyone deserved it to have it, it was her friend.

Naiyan rushed into her mother's space, picked the wooden rod up from the bed, and wrapped it up in a simple colored sheet for concealment. She picked up two traveling straps to secure it across her back before racing back out of the cottage, so she wouldn't miss one moment of the ceremony.

CHAPTER THIRTY-THREE

A Night to Remember

Guards were stationed in groups of eight to ten every fifty yards or so to ensure their visibility would keep the crowd under control. The open area where people congregated was being cleaned by keepers. An assortment of trash from what was purchased for consumption was scattered, but by the end of the celebration it would all be cleared away.

From a vantage point at the top of the amphitheater, one could see to the far end of the park. Most of the guests who were granted seating privileges had arrived while some seniors led the two who had passed into their classification across the stage. They waved at the thousands gathered, who responded in great cheer. The atmosphere was joyous.

"Danju and Repa," Imani whispered their names as they could be seen in the distance bringing up the rear of the Senior's procession. They had been the two who had passed.

'Ransa is much more than they will ever become.' The thought came to mind as she searched for her old companion.

The sound of horns rang out into the night to announce the two of the three who had passed their testing. The crowd roared as Danju and Repa walked onto the stage. They were guided to separate locations to sit as the ceremony began.

"Honored guests we celebrate you." Perci raised his hands above his head and clapped as he used an amplifier to make his voice reach the entire area so that all could hear.

"Tonight will be a night unlike all others before us. We witness the last transition before the new millennium." He shot fire out of his hands in multiple direction before clapping his hands again. The crowd roared.

Ziri made eye contact with Cheney as they sat behind Elder Rax who kept playing to the crowd.

Cheney shook her head back and forth, indicating that it was little over the top. Ziri smiled and began clapping his hands to mimic Elder Rax. He saw Imani in the front row in a cushioned roll-chair next to an empty seat where Naiyan should have been sitting.

Ziri wondered why she hadn't arrived yet, and as if she could read her brother's mind, she shrugged her shoulders to let him know she had no clue either.

...

Janae had been proven wrong about her two male counterparts attending the ceremony. In fact, it was quite the opposite of what she had assumed. Both Keeble and Cusi had mingled among those in the seated area and had also drunk several beverages with spirits.

"This is quite exciting. We aren't breaking any laws by enjoying this, are we?" Janae shouted out while dancing. She watched as other seniors joined Perci in a display of magical fireworks for the crowd's pleasure.

"No, not at all. This is diplomacy at its finest!" Cusi shouted back, holding a glass of libation above his head.

Keeble passed her a container with clear liquid in it that he had been enjoying.

"If you think you can hang with us." He nodded with a genuine smile.

Janae took the glass container and took an ample sip. She coughed and looked at Keeble before taking another large swig.

The sound of stringed instruments broke through the noise. Ziri and Cheney, along with all the other seniors who were not elders stood and made their way off the stage. They relocated along the edge of the stage between the first row of seats.

A bright illumination was seen coming from the entrance of the sanctuary. The radiant glow moved toward the amphitheater while the stringed instruments were accompanied by drums and the horns still playing.

The cadence was beating into the ground, and it brought a heightened expectation. As the light drew nearer, the crowd could make out the outlines of people walking in the light.

The Petals were leading the way with the Matriarch behind them. Next in line was Ransa, followed by Erri, Chachan, and FloAntal. The rear of their procession walked the three bald women. This was what Erri and FloAntal had discussed with the Matriarch, a near replica of someone passing into the Order of Petals.

Ziri glanced back over his shoulder toward Imani. Naiyan's chair was still unoccupied.

. . .

Naiyan knew she had to take a shortcut to get back in time. The crowd gathered would be too difficult to navigate. She scampered with the *lifestick* on her back and her shoes in hand.

The horns in the distance told her she needed to move faster. Naiyan came out on the backside of the amphitheater in between the sanctuary and the stage; it was the most direct route she could take to avoid the large crowd.

'I won't hear the end of this from Imani.' Naiyan knew how critical her friend would be if she didn't get back soon.

Naiyan pushed through the last brush and came out as the ground beneath her feet vibrated. She thought she could make out the waves of magic moving within the very ground itself until she saw the bright lights surrounding a group of people moving from the sanctuary.

She hurried past the guards who were posted near the stage who recognized her, and as the Petals walked onto the stage, Naiyan took her seat next to Imani.

"Really? Thanks for showing up." Imani shook her head in disbelief as Naiyan slipped her shoes back on.

Ziri made eye quick eye contact with Naiyan and smiled before turning back towards the procession who had arrived at the stage.

The Petals parted and allowed the Matriarch to walk up the few steps, followed by Ransa. She was decked out in a most extravagant dress with her hair fashioned. She didn't look anything like herself. Ransa, typically in worn clothing and tattered shoes, looked regal and of stature.

"She's so beautiful." Naiyan sat in amazement.

"She is, but she's also so nervous." Imani gripped Naiyan's hand.

Ransa walked slowly as Erri had advised. Those in attendance would be speaking of this night forever, and Ransa Ansar's entrance would always be remembered.

Chachan, FloAntal, and Erri took the stage after Ransa. The Matriarch prayed over the ceremony before asking for calm.

"Those that you see before you are filling a path walked by many before them since the beginning of time. Blessed to walk in the light, we present the three before you." The Matriarch turned and motioned for Danju and Repa to come forward to stand on the opposite side of where Ransa stood.

What sounded like loud applauses drew everyone's attention to the top of the small incline slope of the grassy areas. Naiyan and Imani yelled out loudly too while clapping, but they soon realized that something wasn't right.

The cheers from the top of the grassy knoll were not jovial.

The Petals rushed the stage to surround the Matriarch who wasn't sure what was happening until she saw the first of the evil. Her attention quickly moved to another portion of the crowd, and she saw two additional creatures of the dark, killing everything in their vicinity. She looked around the stage at the seniors of Ledoma who were slow to act, except a small handful.

Perci was first to identify the threat and moved with haste as he and a troop of thirty armed guards hurried to meet the challenge. Chachan and FloAntal saw the enormous crowd scampering toward the arena. People were being crushed under foot as they ran for their lives.

Chachan saw Naiyan pushing Imani behind the staged area. She returned her attention to the three Soachim who had not slowed their onslaught.

A large silhouette could be seen in the distance in the night sky. A winged creature was descending downward, headed straight towards those in the seated area which had been overrun by those attempting to flee.

"Kendra and Jusie give those people respite and create a barrier between those out of their reach. Myl concentrate on the right flank. The rest of you are with me." The Matriarch gave orders while keeping her eye on the winged creature who could also be heard as its shrieks permeated the night sky.

Chachan, FloAntal, and Erri moved with the group now leading the charge against the giant six-legged canines who had not been engaged yet. These were extraordinarily larger than the ones that had killed Elder Improvi. Chachan continued forward to join Perci in his defense. The other two women redirected their attention to a group being preyed upon by a second pairing of the six-legged canines.

"They will not pass!" The Matriarch pointed to the two Soachim closest to their position.

A group of Petals separated and reached into their magic as they attacked the animal.

Perci and the soldiers were engaged with the third creature who pushed forward against them. In its wake, dead bodies lay, some ripped in half and other simply trampled.

It was pure chaos.

The Petals who were first to engage the first two Soachim had one of them under control and were using their powers to forge magical weapons to rip it apart. It was taxing, but as the nine women worked in tandem, one dark creature was killed.

Chachan saw seniors who had not taken up arms against the Soachim but were instead casting magic to shield the remaining creatures from the magic being used against them. Half of the troop accompanying Perci had been slaughtered. Chachan directed her magic at those seniors who were working in agreement with the dark master's chosen.

'They cannot serve two masters.' She concentrated on the two she had witnessed launch blind attacks against the guards. Chachan's intent was not to kill because answers would be needed, but the amount of force she used was overwhelming as their legs were cuffed by earth. She wasn't completely sure that she had not intended to rip the femoral arteries, but she was positive she could live with it.

...

Perci watched the head roll toward his feet, unsure how two of his fellow assembly members had fallen.

Chachan moved to his side to help him with the dark creature he opposed.

"We have some of our own working against us!" Chachan used the earth to wrap around the legs of the Soachim, and Perci released his fire magic to burn the creature. Although it slowed, it would not die.

The three bald women, the Diviners, glided towards Perci and Chachan and formed a circle around the Soachim who roared out defiantly.

Chachan had been taught this technique in practice, and now they would channel their energy together and direct it at the beast. It would be a delicate collaboration intertwining various magic, but as the three women began chanting, Perci and Chachan could feel their magic being redirected.

...

Santal Culdris had read about this winged creature while a young student in the Garden. How it came to be, was not as important as to pulling it away from the thousands still present.

"FloAntal... Erri, behind the stage! We have to get it away from these people!" The Matriarch pointed into the sky, and without warning, a reddish hue appeared around her body. She was lifted into the air and got the wyvern's attention with a simple fireball.

It sensed the greater threat, and now that it had a clear singular target, it changed course. The wings of the creature spanned an easy twenty feet, but it was the barbed tail that created the most danger.

The Matriarch shot two additional fireballs before flying away towards the streaming water behind the arena. Like she had hoped, it continued to trace behind her.

It closed the distance as she landed with FloAntal and Erri already waiting to engage.

Erri caused the currents in the air to shift downward in variations of drafts across the back of the creature. The force being exerted could be observed by everyone in their eyesight.

FloAntal dove into her magic and pulled the earth from the ground around to form shackles across the only two visible legs. Thankfully, unlike dragons, the front legs were fused to its tremendous wings. The wyvern could not lift upward, but it had reached a stalemate with the three women.

Its shrieks rang out into the night as it struggled. It put a strain on both Erri and FloAntal to maintain the little bit of control they had over it.

The Matriarch spoke an old spell she had learned in the Garden. In essence, the spell she wove would draw out the force supplying the creature with energy. She had never performed it, but she had no other viable options because it would take much more magic than the three of them to kill it without her *lifestick* which she left in her room; but even then, that was no guarantee.

CHAPTER THIRTY-FOUR

First Blood

The delegation from Carcero ran like everyone else. Keeble had suggested helping fight the beasts until he saw them devouring those in their path.

Janae had kept her head; it was the only thing preventing her from hyperventilating. She scanned the area for a place to retreat and recognized any direction they took would bring them closer to the fighting. The guards who had accompanied them were not allowed in the seating area and had engaged with the others confronting the abominations before them.

Janae saw Naiyan pushing Imani in a roll-chair behind the stage at the stadium. She grabbed onto Keeble's arm and pulled him towards the side of the front stage.

"Come on! This may be our only chance to survive!" she yelled.

Cusi, seeing his counterparts scampering along the edge of the stage, followed closely behind.

"This is what magic does; it's destructive..." Cusi attempted to scream but was interrupted.

"It is, but now is not the time for that discussion." Janae kept moving as they rounded the back of the amphitheater. She stopped suddenly, and both Cusi and Keeble ran into her back, causing her to fall face down onto the worn dirt.

"Why did you stop? We have to..." The words stuck in his throat as they watched a wyvern being combatted by the Matriarch and two others.

"Fuck, let's go this way!" Keeble pointed in an opposite direction which led deeper into the woods.

Cusi and Keeble changed direction, but Janae was stuck on her hands and knees. She was frozen with fear. The most powerful magicians remaining were at an impasse with the winged creature, and they were visibly tiring.

The wyvern seemed to be gaining altitude, flapping his wings with great force. From the corner of her eye, Janae could make out Naiyan still pushing the roll-chair on the path less than fifty yards away. She was attempting to get to the sanctuary.

Janae pulled herself from the ground. She was witnessing a life-changing event. Her attention was drawn to the sound of people screaming. Scanning the area, she saw two bodies being tossed into the clearing, and that's when all chaos erupted.

One of the Soachim had found its way to their location. The other portions of the two severed bodies that landed and bounced separately were dangling from its mouth. It shook those remains and zeroed in on the two humans fleeing. It pivoted to take a straight line for them.

Janae, unsure what to do because she was in the same line of sight, froze in her tracks. Keeble and Cusi had abandoned her, and she was without a plan.

A piercing shriek was followed by a loud booming sound, the noise like a size-able incendiary device shaking the air upon blast.

FloAntal and Erri had been overpowered. Both were thrown backwards nearly ten feet, and the wyvern was able to rise into the night sky once more. The Matriarch was glowing crimson red, drawing in the elements around her. She had to attempt to give the other two women time to recompose themselves and engage again, even at the risk of losing control of her magic.

The Matriarch, as powerful as she was, would not last much longer, and that's when she saw the evil canine rumbling quickly toward the two younger defenseless women, but there was nothing she could do about it as she struggled against a creature that had been wiped from existence a thousand years ago. The howling from the Soachim could be felt in the ground as its six appendages stomped away, but she could not let go of the wyvern, or all would be lost.

. . .

Imani had not said a word as Naiyan pushed her quickly towards the sanctuary. There were some protective wards that would prevent the Dark Master's beasts from entering. At least she hoped this was the case. She saw the wyvern more clearly as they neared the confrontation. The skin of the creature looked like an intermittent design between leather and scales. The razor tail seemed to move haphazardly, but Imani ascertained that the Matriarch was minimizing its attack.

An ensuing boom made Naiyan turn back to look at those fighting the wyvern… They were losing. Naiyan slowed, watching FloAntal pick Erri up after being driven into the ground.

An even louder howl startled both Imani and Naiyan, causing them pause in their route, a darker shadow emerged from the other side of the arena. It was barring the path to the sanctuary, releasing the content of its mouth.

Naiyan had no viable option for retreat, and if they were going to die, she had made up her mind that this evil would have to go through her first to get to Imani.

She pulled her mother's *lifestick* from the bundle in Imani's hands and stood between them and the beast.

Something shifted in her as the beast came barreling down at them. The vision of her mother dying at the lake resurfaced from these same creatures. Naiyan noticed her feet tingling. She felt the vibration in her hand from the *lifestick* increasing. The six-legged canine closed the distance.

"*No*!" she yelled into the night, and a beam of white light emitted from her *lifestick* into the Soachim. The chest cavity of the beast exploded with a hole the size of a cantaloupe in the center of it.

Imani watched in awe. The fear that she had was replaced by an emotion she had never known.

Naiyan had emitted white light, an electrical magic that none had seen in these times and ages.

She held her breath as Naiyan rose high into the night sky next to the Matriarch who had tired considerably. The wyvern was breaking free of her magic.

The stream of water erupted around them as two interlocking liquid chains were formed and rose forty feet into the sky to bind the legs of the wyvern. A more formidable wind was directed to press onto the creature to force it down as Erri had performed just moments ago. A second beam of white light was directed to one wing. It cut through it like a hot knife to butter. The second intense emission of light disemboweled the creature which then fell to the earth in a loud thud.

The Matriarch lowered herself to the ground and glanced up at Naiyan who was scanning across the field at the chaos in the grassy area of the arena. The canines with six appendages were killed, but so were countless others who had come for a celebration.

The night air was thick as the magic subsided.

Erri had not stopped moving once the wyvern was downed. She was performing an incantation as she walked towards the defeated descendant of dragons.

The Matriarch, composure regained, formed fire chains with her magic to cut through the tail of the wyvern.

"Mother, its heart, you must remove it before it's too late. It will give us answers!" Erri moved closer as she released a form of magic FloAntal had not seen before, and without haste, the Matriarch's hands became dark red, and the flames shot from her hands into the leathery skin.

The Matriarch pierced the tough skin of the wyvern and burned its flesh away while pulling the heart from the beast. With it in her hands, answers would surely follow when the alchemist reversed the spell.

The intensity of the fire magic blew Imani's dark hair from her face, scorching her skin but she had yet to take her eyes off her friend.

"Naiyan!"

As if called back from a trance, Naiyan looked down, and the fear on her face could not be erased. She began falling, but FloAntal was there, using her magic to catch Naiyan before she bounced off the ground.

…

Janae had watched it all, without blinking. She found herself running towards Imani to push her when Naiyan took a position in front of the Soachim. Her instinct drove her towards danger.

Keeble and Cusi were cowards, and now that the slaughter was over, she found the eyes of everyone staring.

"You're glowing," Imani called out to Janae who had not decided if she should stay or go.

"It's the makeup they used; it's a new reflective that does that at…"

"No, child, you are one of us." The Matriarch held the bloody heart in her hands.

"Erri and FloAntal, take all three of them to the sanctuary. They are my guests until I can figure out what's best for them." The Matriarch's amber glow shifted to show the magic she was controlling was still being utilized. Slowly, she lifted back into the air to seek the three bald women. She had an immediate task to handle, but she knew until she had an answer about Naiyan's ability, the safest place was with her.

Janae was staring at her hands. They did seem to be glowing, but before she could understand, Erri was barking orders at her.

"You, push the roll-chair."

FloAntal and Erri took the side of Naiyan to help her walk. She could barely stand.

"I feel sick." Naiyan slumped while still holding onto the *lifestick*. She pulled away from them and threw up where the wyvern's tail had been separated.

"It is not safe for you or any of us now, Naiyan Amitsa." Erri kept the group moving into the safe wards of the sanctuary.

FloAntal prepared a special tea to help G'la in moments like this when they overexerted their magic.

Erri sat across from Naiyan without saying a word. Her eyes were calm, but she was tense.

Janae couldn't think straight, but she would not let them see the complete fear she held at bay.

'How can I have magic?' The thought was overwhelming. Would she be welcomed back into Carcero even after she had helped finalize the sale of land? Would her family accept her? How could she accept herself?

She refused the tea that FloAntal had offered.

"It's not a request. You are one of us whether you like it or not, Janae Fiah. This will help." FloAntal put the cup into Janae's hands.

"Drink."

Janae reluctantly took a sip. It was a pleasant taste, but she wasn't as trusting with these women just because they said she had glowed with magic earlier. Being overwhelmed with the presence of death would not make her lose her senses now. There had to be an explanation.

'Those fuckers left me.' The faces of Keeble and Cusi flashed in her mind as a keeper walked away from Erri who still sat quietly glancing at Naiyan every now and then.

The door to their room inside the sanctuary opened, and both Ransa and Ziri walked in. Ransa had wiped all the makeup from her face and changed into simpler garments. A few more Petals appeared, exhausted from the battle, and the Medici, who had not been maimed or killed, could be seen carrying multiple people to an area to address their critical wounds.

Ransa took a straight line to her friends.

"You just had to go and become G'la." Imani smirked at Ransa as she shook her head back and forth.

"Erri and Ransa, you are needed immediately." The Diviners appeared next and spoke in unison. As soon as they appeared, they had left. The first words the three bald women had spoken.

Ransa did not hide her resistance to being pulled away, but she had responsibilities now as a Senior, Medici, or whatever her designation would be. She pushed the thought away as she and Erri moved into the hallway, following the route the women had gone.

Ziri simply nodded at his sister and Naiyan to acknowledge they were not hurt.

The two young women nodded back that they were fine. He did not know why either of them had been sequestered, but he didn't have time to concern himself with it.

He sat down at the nearest chair and spoke lowly.

"There were seniors who were working in tandem against us. Our mother killed two, and a third traitor, who was severely injured, is being kept alive to be interrogated. There are more than a thousand dead. I saw those three women cast a spell to slow the decomposition of the dead to prevent disease; at least I hope that's what it was." The strain in his voice relayed just how exhausted he was.

Imani shifted in her roll-chair. The cushion she sat on also needed adjusting, so Naiyan helped as Ziri lifted her a bit.

"We will not rest until we have answers! Everyone will be tested for truth, and those who fail will be sent to the inquisitors. There are innocent dead bodies that we were responsible for, and it was our ignorance to continue with this celebration and festival when we held no answers on the attack in which Elder Improvi was murdered as it seems." Perci's voice could be heard loudly before his physical presence was made walking through the hallway.

Cheney looked in the room occupied by Naiyan, Imani, and a few others. She saw Ziri and motioned for him.

"I'll be back." Ziri excused himself to see what she needed of him.

Naiyan watched the two of them leave with speed, and for the first time she noticed Janae sitting by herself. They made eye contact.

"I can't stay here. I need to leave!" Janae tried to force one of the Petals who was charged with keeping the three situated until the Matriarch returned. She was losing her composure and continued to voice her opinion to everyone in earshot.

"I am not a citizen of this god-awful land, and I do not live under the rules from the states of Medellin. This is kidnapping, political suicide, and at minimum, you're holding me against my will." Janae did everything short of engaging in a physical confrontation.

"Please, ambassador, have a seat. Once Mother decides what to do with you, you will be the first to know."

Janae grew even more agitated and was unsure why the two additional Petals took an aggressive stance until she looked at her hands as she waved them back and forth while she talked.

She saw the glow extending from her fingertips again. Janae recognized the tingling sensation in her hands from moments ago when the Wyvern was killed. The small hairs on her arms stood up like lightening surrounded her. Realizing her actions were being taken as a threat, she retreated and sat at a separate table from everyone.

"She is a whole bunch of extra," Naiyan whispered, so only Imani could hear.

Imani could understand the frustration with Janae, but she also knew why her friend didn't like the naked antics of the ambassador with Ziri.

Naiyan needed to be honest with herself.

"We should give her a break. She just found out she has magic, and it goes against everything she has known her entire life..." Imani paused to reach for Naiyan's hand.

"And you, you have magic too."

Naiyan had not thought about this fact. For the first time, the memory that had been blocked the morning hell's beast touched the Lake of Faith had become clearer.

"I have something," Naiyan stated flatly as Chachan walked into the room. She spoke with Janae who seemed reluctant at first to follow the elder, but seeing there were no other options, she made certain everyone knew it was against her will.

"What do you think they're going to do with her?" Naiyan asked.

"Find the truth," Imani answered.

...

Chachan led Janae along with two Petals into the assembly hall where the three bald women waited.

"We must make certain of a few things." Chachan told Janae as she walked her towards a small section of marble flooring. "Stand there and do not move."

Janae had just gone toe to toe with this woman when negotiating, and she didn't like the tone, nor did she not like having a say in what was going on. She realized at the same time she needed to have this answer, so she did as was told.

The Diviners raised their hands and pulled energy from the columns to direct towards Janae.

Her truth had been revealed. She indeed had magic. Strong magic.

Two of the Petals then took Janae to a separate room where the Matriarch had been waiting with her *lifestick* in her hand.

"I have questions for you, and you will answer them completely with truth. Is that clear?"

Janae thought about pushing back, but with everything happening earlier, she thought it best not to poke the bear.

The Matriarch called her forward and had her place her hands onto her *lifestick.*

"Were you aware of your magic before this night?"

"I was not," Janae replied.

"Do you have any knowledge of those involved or participated in the evil of this night?" the Matriarch asked.

"I do not."

"Good, good. You will remain our guest until we can decide the best course of action with you." The Matriarch motioned for the Petals to find her new accommodations and to secure her belongings from the quarters she had last occupied with the others from her homeland. She was escorted out, noticing for the first time the line of people standing in the hall.

Janae looked back and noticed the stained blood on the floor and walls. When the next person was brought in to be questioned, she finally understood just how close to death she had been.

. . .

General Roner and Iver were still sorting through those dying or laid dead in the large grassy area. No words needed to be spoken. They had witnessed a massacre.

General Roner put groups of soldiers to work to find any survivors while those who laid lifeless were given final rites to ensure they passed into the next life.

Dozens of Medici had sprung into action and were preparing many to be treated.

"We will have to burn the majority of these…" Iver began to say.

"I know… I know." Merico was short in response.

The moans of those still dying could be heard as the night still held its grip over the land. Merico bent down to check the vitals of someone who had portions of her body separated but was unaware. There was nothing that could be done to save her. He took his double-edged, short blade and ended her life to stop the suffering.

Iver didn't like it, but he understood. He also knew that Ledoma would never be the same again. The people would never be the same again. For nearly a millennium, their way of life had been intact. Now, now he wasn't sure what was left.

They had been unprepared.

"Iver, Master Iver!" A Medici was followed by three soldiers ushering someone towards the medical station.

Iver froze. His heart missed a beat.

Zuni was being carried by the soldiers; he had been injured badly indicated from the amount of blood dripping from the cot he was dangling from.

"He landed the killing blow, but he was damaged before the beast died. We need you to follow us now. He will need your blood!"

"Father… Father!" Ziri was scrambling towards his father and brother. His eyes showed panic as he approached. He had a deep gash across his chin.

"Zuni, is he…"

"He will be fine; he needs blood…" Iver kept moving forward as he chose his next words carefully.

"You have a responsibility to these people, Senior Balent. I will care for you brother." Iver pointed to a section of people unattended, and Ziri followed his father's words.

Iver was very concerned about Zuni. The loss of blood was a concern, but if the wound had been infected with the Soachim's poison, a blood transfusion would not be sufficient enough for a cure.

…

Naiyan and Imani waited for what seemed hours before Erri returned with Ransa. Their clothing was covered in blood, and even though they had been washed, their hands seemed stained.

As they walked in, Ransa moved towards Imani and took hold of her roll-chair. She pushed her out of the room and down the hall. She looked back over her shoulder at Naiyan.

"You must follow."

Naiyan met her friend's eyes and could not make out what message she was attempting to convey. Naiyan stood and moved past the Petals to walk side by side with Ransa as she pushed Imani down a long corridor.

When they emerged from the hallway, they were moved into the grand assembly where only the Matriarch and the three bald women stood in the lower section. Chachan, FloAntal, Isela, and Perci were also in attendance.

"Good luck." Ransa spoke before Naiyan was motioned to stand on the large marble tiling in the center of the assembly hall.

The tiling began to shimmer as soon as she stepped foot on it, and the speckled columns went white, devoid of any specks of color. There was a vibration pulsing from beneath their feet before the marble floor Naiyan stood turned as white as the columns surrounding them all. The small wooden connections that had emerged when the columns revealed their energy had turned white.

The Matriarch stared in amazement as the columns suddenly danced in all four variants of magic. Solid blue and greens mixed with shades of red and amber. The last time she bore witness to this was when she was in the Garden and King Hasinho had been tested.

The three bald women fell to their knees and placed their foreheads to the ground before standing again.

Erri stood fast, but her eyes were full of awe.

Naiyan emitted a bright light from the tips of her fingers that traveled the room and then through the roof of the assembly hall and spread across the space.

As soon as the display started, it had suddenly ended.

Imani gripped the side of her roll-chair with Ransa standing behind her. Chachan and FloAntal flanked the Matriarch who stared intently at the younger woman.

"Naiyan Amitsa." Chachan let the name slip from her lips as an acknowledgement of her magic. The Matriarch agreed as she moved past the three bald women to take Naiyan by the hand.

"There is much for you to learn and much for us to teach, in such a short time."

...

Whal slowly had awakened from being treated for injury. He was unsure how everything got out of hand so fast. The reanimation potion was supposed to give him two creatures under his control, but as he mixed the remains of the Soachim with the liquid, three times as many were formed. That wasn't the greatest surprise.

Seeing a wyvern form before his very eyes frightened him, and as the dark beasts forged ahead towards the ceremony, Whal had sentiments of regret about his plan for the very first time. He watched from a distance as scores of onlookers were trampled and torn apart. Those who fell to the ground as the crowd rushed over them were compressed. He saw those who had conspired with him fulfilling their pledge, but they had been recognized to be traitors.

He winced, watching Chachan decapitate a senior who had once been a sitter for her two youngest twin boys.

His contemplation had been to flee or to find the remaining accomplices and kill them before they spilled his secret. He chose the latter.

Knowing where each team was stationed was the easy part. Navigating the dead bodies wasn't as simple as he had imagined.

"Elder, help us please!" a child's voice called out as he tried to pull his mother from under a mound of bodies. Whal remembered making eye contact with the young boy but kept his pace.

He remembered the wyvern under attack towards the back of the staged area. His attention was drawn to the onslaught of magic being wielded against each Soachim. The creatures were dying, but Chachan was barking orders to keep one alive.

Ricka and Basil had been closest to reach. He had cast his magic against them before they knew he had turned on them.

"Chachan!" Whal called loudly, directing the woman's focus onto the two younger magicians who were casting spells towards her.

Whal wrapped the tendrils of his magic around Basil's throat, cutting off his air supply and making the man's face swell with blood.

Chachan encased Ricka in a mound of earth and constricted it around the younger senior like an anaconda.

The last Soachim was no longer able to use any of its legs after they had been separated from its body. Its long canine teeth were shattered. A bone curdling yell from behind the amphitheater drew everyone's attention.

Whal, in his momentary lapse, was stabbed by Basil who had survived the suffocation. Whal turned his body at the last moment but had not been fast enough.

"You betrayed everyone!" Basil mustered.

Whal, bleeding from his abdomen, evaded the younger man as best he could. He wasn't fast enough. He was stabbed in his thigh and as the blood flooded out, Whal unlocked the hidden blade in his cane and pierced the young man's chest cavity.

Whal lost consciousness, and when he woke the first face he saw was Anri's.

One of the Medici were tending to his wounds, but his small cot was surrounded by Petals who had put cuffs on him to thwart his magic.

"Brother…" Whal hoped Anri would give him an explanation although he already knew his insurrectionist plot had failed, and he had been found out.

The Matriarch walked into the room with her *lifestick* already pointing toward Whal.

"Remove him from his cot and drag him by his injured leg if necessary…." She paused, and a scowl formed on her face.

"You will answer my questions."

His inquisition was about to begin.

…

Keeble and Cusi had made it back to their rooms for safety the night before. They ordered their attendees to make ready for departure at first light.

"She could be dead for all we know, and I am not sticking around this horde of death one damn minute longer than I must." Keeble was ready to go, but there was another hour before daybreak.

Cusi held the same idea that Janae was probably one of the victims of last night's massacre.

He looked out the window and saw groups of fifty troops patrolling the streets. A scarce few people could be seen from his vantage point. They appeared to be the keepers doing their best to return the area to its previous state.

Cusi could see smoke rising in the grassy area where so many died. He had no doubts that magic was being used to burn the bodies that could not be claimed. It was emotionally taxing, and he was grateful to be returning home soon.

Cusi made sure all the negotiation agreements were secure, but he couldn't help to wonder if Janae was one of those being cremated with the others.

CHAPTER THIRTY-FIVE

Delicate Balancing

Four days had passed since the madness. Citizens huddled in their homes more than they did out in the city. Those who had fled from Patin and Trivoli were now accompanied by many who had come for the ceremony and festival. They all had lost loved ones, and now without shelter or a means to travel home, they made do with whatever assignments they were given.

The Assembly of seniors regrouped and ensured the city was secure and safe. The Medici worked non-stop in treatment.

Smaller groups of seniors with stature had requested an audience with the Fifth that seemed to become tense.

"The wards have been set around the main access points to the city. Many have already shown their displeasure of being given papers to show their affiliation after being questioned to enter. But they have nowhere else to go." Yolan paced the floor of a side chamber in the sanctuary. She spent most of her time on scholarly studies and thus understood the ramifications that history would paint them in. These protectors of ancient magic could not prevent a massacre, and even with the Matriarch, the most powerful curator of magic, they were unable to lessen the loss of life almost a week ago.

"Our task has been, and is, the same. Use our gifts to protect the less fortunate. There are lineages who have been erased from this earth in the span of one night. Those incoming refugees had similar stories of horror. We all have been naïve." Cheney Joli saw clearly, and any other pushbacks were objections not meant to serve their purpose. She would not silence what little voice she had.

"So, are we to give up our lodging to foreigners? Are we to become strangers in our own land?" Perci posed the question.

"No one mentioned anything about our lodging. We have the ability to provide shelter for an additional fifteen, maybe twenty thousand souls," Yolan countered.

Chachan studied the faces of those who had lost just as much as anyone else. They were supposed to have all the answers. Watching Yolan finally sit down, she realized the task before them was more monumental than families claiming their loved ones and the ensuing mass burials.

Creating a haven for the thousands still within their borders, while repairing the physical properties that could be fixed, was near the top of the list. Giving comfort was more important than the previous.

Tracing the complete origin of the creatures of evil had proved beneficial. The main antagonist was found out. Whal's ignorance of the reanimation potion unleashed the evil winged bird of prey. Now he was in chains being drained of his magic and mentally broken down by the three bald women with his deepest life secrets being revealed.

The Matriarch had ordered every senior to come to the light to be questioned. There was no room for hidden agendas when they had been pulled into an unforeseen battle. In a sense, the revelation that Whal had only done it for ambitious reasons and not as an agent of the dark master had relieved a bit of anxiety.

However, he had been found to be the inspiration of the insurrection and forced to reveal more secrets of the partnerships with powerful magicians he had formed when last traveling in the wilderness. The partnerships he had forged over the ages were in possession of items with extraordinary magic, like the Creator's Glass. The consensus was Whal had engaged with those from the wilderness knowingly.

The hidden access that Whal used to the old storage was surrounding by new spells and wards after the Petals sorted through as many artifacts as they could to return with them for further study.

Somehow Basil, the co-conspirator, had survived the massacre initially after stabbing Whal but succumbed when he was put to the light for questioning. Anri had not known of Whal's specific plan, and it was the only reason he wasn't in a cell next to his over ambitious traitor of a friend.

The seniors who had lost their lives in the attack were honored as were all that died.

Erri along with Ransa dealt with the more seriously maimed. Ransa had learned more in the past week than she had over the past years working with the young shaman.

Emotions were scattered between the seniors occupying the smaller gathering room, and it was beginning to come out in the dialogue.

"Elder Yolan, those people will find commonality and comfort in knowing that the people they are surrounded by are no different than themselves. If a small piece of paper is the sacrifice, so be it." Chachan walked forward. She admired the elder, but she had a role to play in leadership.

She had more pressing matters to attend to; Zuni was still recovering under the watchful eye of the Medici. His wound was from being swiped at by the Soachim while he landed the death blow was healing slowly. His twenty-four-hour consistent care was required until there was no trace of poison in his blood, and the dark energy had to be countered.

"It's more about our affiliations…" Chachan paused before standing at the fore of the room with all eyes on her.

"There will be no secret spell or magical remedy to our most challenging obstacles. We have a collection of knowledge and the tools that the Creator gifted us with. We are only but water from the source. Those of us, assembled now, have been true to our oath. The perpetrators who harvested this great tragedy are no more. The First Master's will convene in two hours to discuss the roles your houses will play in recovery. General Roner will update us now." Chachan motioned for the general, who had been waiting patiently.

Chachan had hoped to see Iver at his side during this debrief, but between scaling up plans, overseeing repairs, and spending time with Zuni, he barely had time to sleep.

Merico Roner had been leading the armed troop for over fifty years. He did not answer to the seniors. He understood the balance between magic and the military force. They both were needed, one not more than the other.

"As mentioned, every major access point is now stationed with a minimum of one hundred soldiers. Our city patrol during the day is adequate, it is my request of this council that two seniors accompany each patrol during their night shifts." Merico heard a few murmurs before continuing.

"I understand that there are some in this assembly who have received foreign items in the past. We have placed a limit on what items will enter our city. Any shipping vessels making their way downstream will drop anchor and be boarded before being allowed to our docks. Those shipmates who wish to enter our city will have the same investigation done as any traveling by foot. As you know the Medici have been overwhelmed for nearly a week, and although they are doing the best they can, they need more assistance. Those seniors who have some background in secondary care are required to assist."

"Required?" Anri looked confused.

"Yes, required. I have spoken with members of the Fifth, and they have agreed that portions of martial law must be instituted. Curfew, business hours of operation, and yes… the so-called identification required. Under these provisions the military has taken control in these areas, all other activities will remain the same," General Roner finished. He met the eyes of those he knew would be against his plan. He had respect for each member gathered, but there was not one inch of acquiescence in him.

Chachan saw the looks of hesitation in some and knew she needed to address them.

"Yes, we have agreed to institute this now until we are certain that there are no more threats. We will not fail again. The alchemists are discovering more each day that they spend dissecting what's left of the wyvern and the other filth. The stain of domestic terrorism upon our land is on each of us, but the initial attack on Elder Improvi was from an unknown perpetrator. We are at war." Chachan seemed reluctant to speak those last four words.

"At war, with whom? The only culprits we are certain of are our own. Surely not the with the Nation of Carcero; we didn't even pause the negotiations. How do we know they didn't instigate this whole fucking thing?" Anri was getting hot. He believed, at the very least, the partnership between the two lands should be postponed.

"I didn't believe it to be true, but you really are that shallow. With all due respect…" Isela interjected.

Anri went to respond, but Merico had something additional to say.

"It's always leverage; we have it, and they don't. They will bring with them additional security forces, and that means we will not have to supply our own people. The coin from the sale of land will aid in the rendering of our repairs. We need people thinking about other things than the stain of death on the grounds that lay within eye shot of this very assembly. We must have money to make repairs. We have always had those who wished us harm, but these unseen enemies have acted against us. Perhaps Carcero is part of a plan to destroy us, and we simply don't know. But what I do know is that we now have refugees who will need to earn money. It will help prevent an increase in crime, wage disparity, and hopefully lessen the discrimination some have had to deal with. We need allies… We must rebuild trust from our community that we have their best interests at heart. We must rebuild the trust we have in each other. If there are no questions, I have to make sure we have a nation left to defend." He walked out with haste; he didn't have time for petty squabbles. Anri stood up as he walked out to address those present.

"Everything keeps coming back to coin. We are selling land for money, and we are expanding labor for money, so are we simply whores with magic?" Anri asked without care of offending anyone. He looked around the room, shaking his head negatively and then departed.

The uncomfortable silence that ensued was interrupted by Chachan.

"Your assignments will be known for the night patrol after the Fifth meets in a couple of hours. We all know the challenge before us, and it was you who accepted the positions you have. Don't let down the people who need us most," Chachan finished and sat down in a newer cushioned chair.

The heads of the elemental houses excused themselves while Ziri and FloAntal stayed behind.

A few newer seniors were hesitant to depart, like they wanted additional information, but FloAntal dismissed them with a wave of her hand. Now was not the time.

“That could’ve been worse.” Ziri closed the door behind as the last few walked out. He had been worn thin over the last week like everyone else, and his concern for his brother had not waned.

“You mean worse than martial law?” FloAntal shook her head and joined Chachan in the sitting area.

“Martial law isn’t our biggest concern. Our biggest issue is the unknown factor of dark magic. We have no idea what to expect. Martial law is our ally.” Chachan was conveying a direct message to them with no expression to read on her face beyond tired.

Chachan and FloAntal had earned Class One status from the Matriarch’s testing. It didn’t mean that they assumed leadership, only that more would be required of them.

“I will arrive on time for the Fifth.” Chachan stood suddenly. She was going to see Zuni and the slow progress he was making. She didn’t tell Ziri because she needed space to think. She walked out the door leaving her friend and son to speak on any details left to be ironed out with the night patrol rotations.

CHAPTER THIRTY-SIX

Change Is Inevitable

'It's always easier when the choice is yours and not made for you,' the Matriarch thought as she opened the door to her personal space. The old study was now fixed with a comfortable bedding station and a full body water basin for her as her attendant had already released the fragrances from the potpourri bowls.

"Ahh, that is pleasant, especially after the stench of inquisition." The older woman had overseen the most recent session against Whal, who had not been completely broken of his magic, but only a trickle remained.

She sat down and slumped back into the cushioned sofa.

“After evening meal with the families I encountered today, I want them entertained as well. Lemon water and sweet mint bread with some sweet wafers will suffice. We will have a small firework show that I will lead, so ensure the field is clear,” the Matriarch finished, allowing her clothing to drop to the floor before stepping into the basin.

This was the first moment in weeks she allowed herself to exhale. Pushing both Chachan and Flo beyond their comfort level was taxing. She hadn’t put that much strain on herself in years, but it was necessary to make sure she had a viable delegate to leave in Ledoma. She had two now. She let her thoughts flow to Yolan who had agreed to take to the road with them, but she made it clear that she would not be taking orders from anyone.

As Santal relished the warmth in the water basin, she spoke to herself.

‘Everything is changing.’ She took the washcloth and laid it flat across her face.

“Mother.” Jain announced herself as she returned several minutes later with the older woman’s attire for the evening. The clothing she would wear to dinner was embroidered with the sigil of the Garden and the seal of the Matriarch. The cloth was from the finest linen, woven with magic filaments mixed from the tree of life itself—a secret only a handful were privy to.

“Let’s go with something a little less… regal,” the older woman suggested.

“Bring me one of the new outfits, but no breeches this time.” As the Matriarch watched Jain performing her tasks, she realized over the past decades she and Jain had become close. The

Matriarch had just realized, more importantly, that Jain might be the person she trusted most.

"I have secured another attendant to help in my daily tasks. Naiyan is returning to Medellin with us, and you are to keep a watchful eye on her while teaching her a few of your responsibilities."

"Mother, may I ask if you are relinquishing me of my post? There will be no honor to my family's name if I do not meet the expectations set by Arjunai, Rose of the Garden. Have I made an offense?" Jain asked with sincerity in her voice.

As Santal dressed, she paused before responding, "Jain, after these years we've shared, you have become more than my attendant and advisor. You are my family. I worry about the people. The lands have begun bickering over titles and power. My every breath is faithful to the Most High, and thus, my actions must match my faith. I will tell you this. I believe that the Creator is moving us, moving kingdoms and people into position, and readying us for another confrontation with the adversary. Your role will be much more important, and right now I am employing a few that may be suitable to follow your lead when the time is right. For the record, I think your honor is of the highest standard, but what does an old woman know?" She paused to wink before continuing.

"Tomorrow you are to secure dried goods, smoked meats, and handpicked vegetables and berries. Benja Lucsan has a farm near the lake and was a close friend to Anel Improvi. We will need as much as possible but no more than what we can consume in thirty days. After that, take whatever time you must to categorize some of the new items collected in the old chamber Whal had kept hidden.” The Matriarch selected a dress with a much shorter hemline that showed the lower portion of her knees.

“Modesty seems to be weakening.” Jain couldn’t help but to make the comment.

“As does the magic keeping the evil from spreading across the land.” The Matriarch sighed and adjusted the top of the dress before walking to host a dinner party with new associates.

CHAPTER THIRTY-SEVEN

Goodbye and Farewell

Naiyan soaked in her complete surroundings as she passed by the gambling district and felt an emotion she tried to push down. The upcoming talk was not one she looked forward to, but it had to happen. She was having her sister-friends meet her at Crater Pond. It was time to let them know of her decision to leave with the group from Medellin. She had cried off and on, all day, not knowing how to navigate the emotions she underwent.

She waited until they had completed a session of *'haishu'* before she told them.

"My entire life, it's been us. Every moment of joy and grief, and all the crazy other one's in-between, it's been us..." Tears began forming in her eyes.

Ransa reached into her magic to form a small barrier around the three. She pulled them all closer until they were within an arm's length.

"We know; we already know." Imani reached out for Naiyan's hand. She couldn't help herself and joined in the tearful moment.

Naiyan was caught off guard with the revelation.

"Yes, we know already. I am around a group of women who gossip, and I hear things. It was not my place to bring it up to you." Ransa reached for her other hand.

The three pulled each other closer until none could distinguish the water surrounding them and the wetness flowing down their cheeks.

"It's only for three years of service, and I can figure out the rest of the symbols my mother left behind. Besides, there are other things that I fear *she* can only teach me." Naiyan sighed.

Imani grimaced the closer they waded to shore. Gravity had a way of reminding her that water was only a temporary fix for her ailment.

"We have some things for you. It didn't take a mastermind to figure out this is what you wanted to tell us," Imani finished as Ransa shook her head in agreement.

"So, here are half the winnings..." Ransa pulled a medium sized hand-purse from her clothing on the bank, but she was interrupted by Imani.

"Half?"

"Okay, here are the winnings from the last two years." Ransa reached into a second pocket to retrieve a second satchel equivalent in size.

Naiyan stared at Ransa. She had no words.

"I can't take…"

"You can, and you will. She doesn't require it anymore. She's stuck here with the rest of us. She's important now. Like you…" Imani hesitated. "And I-I get to dress you all. Trust and believe our couriers will be arriving in Medellin with full ensembles of clothing every three months." She tried forcing a smile out as Naiyan began shedding tears again.

"It's only three years, and you can visit. I think I can come back to visit at the end of each calendar cycle." The tears weren't only of sorrow but of familiarity. Each one understood that their lives could no longer be the same.

Naiyan would find more answers to questions, but most importantly she could learn who she really was. Was she blood of the First Mother?

"I have these for both of you." Naiyan retrieved a small tin box. Inside were the keys to her home.

"No outlandish parties." She handed one to each.

They didn't understand the gesture initially, but Imani caught on.

"So, we have to keep an eye out on your stuff, huh? Well, if so, I've been wanting to decorate your side since you put that hideous set of lamps in there." Imani nodded her head as if to say I told you so.

Naiyan frowned.

"That was over four years ago." Naiyan calculated.

"Well, you loved them because Ziri gave them to you, but honestly, they're unsightly," Ransa interjected.

Naiyan squinted her face at her friends. They were only a gift he brought back from visiting Hanibar, a budding city east of Ilens.

'*They were nothing special.*' Naiyan didn't say the words because they were special because they came from him.

The next hours seemed to pass quickly as they walked through the business districts and old paths surrounding the sanctuary. Every place they stepped, there were stories to be remembered.

Bittersweet was an insufficient word to use in this moment. It was coupled with fear of the unknown, along with the possibility of truth.

Naiyan and Ransa dropped Imani off at her home. There were still a few days before their lives would be altered, and the fact was Imani was emotionally exhausted. Her brother was still battling death while her dearest friend was leaving.

Naiyan walked with Ransa toward the sanctuary. She noticed the slight change in Ransa after she had joined the Assembly of Seniors. She still had the joy of life about her, but the weight of responsibility seemed to accelerate maturity. As Naiyan listened to Ransa, she realized nothing would ever be the same again.

"Times have changed over the past eighteen years. Domestic terrorism by members of the Assembly. You and I have forms of magic not known in ages. The demons from Sitini walking within the boundaries of our home. We must do everything in our power to protect those we love. Three years will give you knowledge to bring back to help build what we lost and even greater. While you're there, it's important to form bonds with those who can trace lineages and figure out the truth. I believe you are of the First Mother. I believe your mother did not leave your scripts and scrolls behind as mere happenstance. Like Chachan said, *we are at war,* Naiyan."

Naiyan had not expected what was just spoken. The heaviness of it. What she said was true. It made Naiyan think back to her mother's words. '*Your mind could be as brilliant as a diamond with enough pressure.*'

Was this the result of pressure? An advancement into adulthood. It wasn't the dialogue either wanted to have, so they hugged as Ransa moved towards the old guest's quarters to attend to her business with the Petals.

Naiyan nodded at a few seniors who were meditating outside the sanctuary. She was grateful that no one knew of the power she wielded the night of the massacre. How the Matriarch had accomplished the feat would've been thought of as impossible. But after Chachan had sealed their lips after reading her scrolls, Naiyan knew almost anything was possible with magic.

She found herself walking towards the senior quarters. Something had moved her to seek Ziri out to let him know of her decision to leave.

Naiyan had not thought of Ziri in the fashion that he wanted, at least she didn't believe so, until she had small bits of jealousy knowing he had seen Janae naked. Now she questioned if her ignorance was self-inflicted and her feelings had more meaning.

As she approached his door, she hesitated.

"Hey."

The voice startled her.

Ziri had walked up in the opposite direction. He looked exhausted, but his face lightened seeing Naiyan.

"Oh, hey. I was just about to knock."

"I can see that." He had stacks of papers in his hands that shifted, a few pages almost falling out.

"Can you grab my key and open… the door?" He nodded toward his waist pouch.

"Oh, yeah, of course. Why are you carrying all of that anyway?" She retrieved his key and opened the door, stepping to one side to allow him entry first.

"Grunt work. I have to post and maintain each patrol for the next sixty days while martial law is enforced. The crazy thing is we are no closer to knowing of any magician strong enough to have recreated the original Soachim the morning at the lake…" He paused purposefully. It was not a subject that Naiyan needed to recall. He placed the stack of papers onto a long rectangular desk and gave her a hug.

His home was a mix of old ways and new technology. He had traveling water when needed and an open hatched roof with durable screening to prevent animal's entry. But his artwork were classic pieces from different eras. All the furniture, from the cushioned seats and tables to his bedding, he had made by hand.

"Did Imani have you come check on me? I haven't been able to go home with everything, and I'm closer to Zuni being here. So, tell her she can handle two teenage twins without me for now. Besides, she is always telling people what to do, so now should be no different." Ziri looked around his quarters for a bottle of spirits he had left. He popped the cork and took a swig. He extended the bottle to Naiyan without thinking.

"Oh, I'm sorry. I know drinking wine is your thing… not the stuff that makes you grow chest hair." He mustered a smile and pulled the bottle back but not before she took hold of it.

"Well, some things change." She took twice the amount he had and coughed. She tapped her chest as the spirits burned going down.

"Good… good… that's good stuff." She barely got the words out as she finally caught her breath.

Ziri stared at her, wondering what was really happening in the moment.

"So, this might be the first time you've come to visit without one of your two friends. What's going on? Do you need my help with something?" Ziri took another sip before motioning for them to sit down.

Naiyan wasn't sure how to tell him, so she blurted it out, "I am leaving with the Matriarch and spending three years in Medellin."

Ziri's eyebrows raised as he took a deep breath in and out. He nodded when he acknowledged her words.

"So much has happened to you in less than two months, and if it were me, I'd probably make the same decision. I am scheduled with the next rotation to Medellin in one year if that's still a thing between our nations."

Naiyan could see the weariness in Ziri, but like his parents, he would not stop until his responsibilities were complete.

She saw a shiny piece of jewelry laying under the chair he was sitting. Right away, she knew the design of the gems were created in Carcero.

"Do you have a thing with Ambassador Janae?" Naiyan discovered her neck getting hot and wasn't sure why, but she was going to get an answer.

Ziri wasn't sure where the question came from.

"What? Why would you ask that?" He shook his head back and forth, not knowing how to answer.

"It is a simple question. That little ambassador woman should be showing her body in the entertainment section and not in your home, leaving her gems behind." Naiyan didn't care if she spoke ill of Janae. She felt…jealous.

"No one's been naked in my home. What are you talking about… and why do you even care? You've always known how I feel about you. Never have I overstepped because you made it clear years ago when I told you that I could see us married that it would never happen."

Naiyan couldn't form the right words to speak, but she moved closer to his seat and kneeled. She reached under his seat and pulled the necklace out.

"So, what's this?" she asked and dangled it in front of his face.

Ziri looked confused until he remembered that Edyth, the ambassador's attendant, had brought it to him as a thank you for all the help he had been during the negotiations.

"Naiyan… listen. Janae Fiah is not my type, and that—that was a gift, and that's all I'm going to say. Perhaps the stress of leaving has you acting like this, but I'm too tired to entertain this nonsense…." He paused and thought about what words to share next. His plate was full of tasks, his heart was filled with concern for his brother still being cared for. He hadn't slept more than two hours a night for over a month, but he would not be unkind, especially not to Naiyan.

Naiyan didn't know why she was asking questions about another woman or why she even cared.

'*Stop lying to yourself.*' The thought surfaced, and all she heard was the last bit of his sentence.

"I'm sure we all are going to miss you, especially me."

Naiyan didn't know why after he had said Janae was not his type, she had the urge to kiss him. So, she did.

It was much different than she imagined. In many ways Ziri had been like an older brother, but the way they kissed and the emotion in it, Naiyan felt butterflies in her stomach. She welcomed his hand moving up her neck while his other rested on her hip. His mouth was sweet, and the movement of his tongue created weakness in her.

Ziri had been caught completely off guard by Naiyan's impulse. The few thoughts that had surfaced when she moved closer faded as their lips locked. He allowed the emotion in it; the feelings that he had suppressed over the last two years had emerged again. He had always been in love with her.

When they pulled away, they stared into each other—past the fear, past all the reasons why she had never entertained his words before. She stood up and undressed.

Her braids fell across the back of her shoulders, and her cocoa brown skin was flawless. Her eyes looked to him for acceptance because this was completely new for her.

"Are you sure?" He didn't want any regrets to follow. He needed her to be certain that it was him that she wanted and not simply because she was leaving.

Naiyan had never been with a man, but this felt right. She stepped into him for a second time, crossing a threshold that she had not imagined existing.

CHAPTER THIRTY-EIGHT

A Paradigm Shift

The chamber had taken on a new personality with the full Assembly of Seniors. The Fifth sat on one side of the lower section, and opposite them were Jain, Erri, and the three bald women. The Matriarch had just given a speech outlining the various times in history that war had come and gone in her home of Uteri. She gave a short description of how they were forced to flee after Arjunai, Rose of the Garden had been ousted and stripped by the widowed queen of any status pertaining to Uteri. It was much more than she intended to share, but she understood the necessity of making sure those she left behind stayed active. Her last acknowledgment created a stir in the chamber as she revealed the elevation of Chachan and FloAntal as Class One G'la.

“Class One...” Anri was beside himself. He had lost face the day of their arrival to Lake Ledoma, and now he was being told that both women were considerably stronger than he was with magic. He glanced toward Isela who seemed just as shocked as he and many others were.

The Matriarch asked the two women to rise and come forward.

“Upon this date, you have been revealed to the world. This is a time for rejoice and a time to reflect. Rejoice in knowing that the Creator has found favor in those in attendance. Reflect that we must honor the oath you have taken for the greatest good. This Assembly of Seniors is only as strong as its weakest links, and through investigation and inquisition we have determined and dealt with those who failed their duties and created this domestic terrorism. The magic is strong in Ledoma, and the conviction of this assembly’s resolve must match it. In less than three years, a new age will dawn. We must stand ready as we have all born witness to the madness. Upon my return to Medellin, we will ensure our houses instruct their magicians to learn more about combat. Short of a decree to enlist in the basic training classes, they will understand war philosophies and the history of nations. I suggest these items be considered within your city. FloAntal and Chachan are my daughters, as is Ransa Ansar. They will serve Ledoma well.” The Matriarch ushered the two women forward and had them kneel. Jain waved Ransa forward to join the other two women. She walked out to greet them with their *lifesticks* in her hands.

“You have honored us, and we shall honor you.” Jain gave one to each woman before departing the way she had entered.

"FloAntal Yusi, Chachan Balent, Ransa Ansar—you are given all the rights and privilege as Petals to the Garden." The Matriarch had them rise.

Silence followed this acknowledgment. The others in attendance were speechless. It was Cheney Joli who yelled out, "Until the children return!"

"Until the children return," the Assembly replied in unison followed by claps and cheers.

The Matriarch kissed all three on each cheek before leaving the seniors of Ledoma to conduct their business. Her time there had finished.

Chachan waited until the Matriarch and the Petals had left before speaking to the Assembly about the details of the final dealings with the land of Carcero, along with the updated total of those still in the care of the Medici. It was strange to hold her own *lifestick*. It looked like a normal wooden rod, but she discerned the power in it. It was intoxicating.

The Assembly dismissed with FloAntal and Chachan being congratulated again as they left first. Some congratulated Ransa, but most of those already risen to the status of senior hadn't come to terms with her elevation. The Matriarch wanted them to see her right after the event.

When they walked into her quarters, the room had already been cleaned and put back to its original state. They had already packed and looked to be getting ready to travel immediately.

"What's happening?" FloAntal spoke what both she and Chachan were thinking. Ransa simply observed.

"We must leave this afternoon. There's a bit of urgency to return home. We have stayed much longer than intended. Even though we are a beacon for humankind and magicians alike, we too have political agendas working against us." The Matriarch had been standing by the oval window staring out into the city.

She moved towards the two women and took them by the hand.

"Class One G'la, but what's in a name? I wish I could tell you that everything was going to be okay and eventually go back to normal. It is not. There are no deals to be made in the face of darkness. Lake Ledoma has changed. Your Assembly will never be the same, but you can make it better, stronger than what it once was. You two must lead." She released their hands and walked into the interior of the room. On the table were two leather bindings.

"Jain has documented the important findings from the alchemists. The other is what I was able to interpret of the first language. There seems to be a room of reflection with traveling mirrors in this land. The only way they can be accessed is with the blood of the first. Unfortunately, it was only a small clue, and the location of the room is unknown. We all know that the safest place for Naiyan is under my care. Whether she is or is not… will not determine how she is treated. If she can access her power upon her will, she will be one of our greatest assets. She will be pushed, and I pray the she has half the will of her mother. She will need it."

FloAntal retrieved both bound transcripts.

"We will send messages by the birds as you requested," Chachan informed the older woman. Communication was going to be a required act. Until the source of the evil was found, there was a threat of repeated attack.

"Yes, by birds, but I think we can do better than that." The Matriarch moved back to the outer room. She retrieved an item covered with a dark cloth.

"We will be able to speak with each other through this. It is tuned to your magic, and it is a direct link to the set I have." When she removed the black linen, a viewing mirror was revealed.

Chachan was hesitant to approach it. She had used one as a neophyte, and she wasn't sure how it worked.

Ransa had only heard of this mode of communication in her studies. This was a first for her.

"You must use your *lifesticks* to make a connection through it. We will convene in five weeks as soon as we return to Medellin. We are building a network with Ilens, Medellin, Lake Ledoma and…" The Matriarch paused, hearing a knock on her door.

Jain walked in, followed by Janae. From the look on the ambassador's face, she seemed defeated.

Ransa had seen that look before.

"Good evening. I have decided that the best place for me to be is with you. If there were any other calculations that made sense, I would have chosen those." Janae looked at Chachan and FloAntal. She was beginning to see them in a different light, not complete adversaries. She was puzzled about Ransa being present until she saw she had a *lifestick* in her possession.

"A wise choice." The Matriarch excused everyone except the two elder women.

Ransa would find her two friends and let the adults engage.

She heard the Matriarchs voice as the door closed behind.

"If you have anything to ask, now is the time."

Neither woman had any requests. They had more than their hands full with the assembly and the military.

"Good. There's one more bit of housekeeping to address."

Now was the time to have the elder who raped Ransa explain himself and determine the punishment for the offense.

. . .

Erri was a little out of place as she watched Ransa, Imani, and Naiyan saying their final goodbyes before Naiyan departed. They laughed and cried. Erri had never known a bond as deep as theirs. It wasn't jealousy but a reminder that her life would always be different.

"You what!" Imani said loudly.

"How does that happen? I mean… You did not." From the look on Ransa's face, she was also in shock.

"I did, and I'm okay with it." Naiyan finished as she glanced toward Erri.

"He hasn't said a word to me, but then again, we only had a moment to ourselves after we visited Zuni. He's been so busy. I can't believe you… you did it." Imani shook her head, still in disbelief.

"Well, that's two of us, and one left to go." Ransa tapped Imani on her shoulder.

"Actually, it's two left to go," Erri added. She knew they were speaking on Naiyan and Ziri. Erri held no shame in the fact that she too had never had sex. She changed topics to something that each of them had an interest in.

"The history of treatments I am leaving behind has some information how to minimize the pain in your joints. To be honest, it could be an ailment that I've seen only once before leaving Uteri. Your condition may not be permanent," Erri stated casually.

"I promise you that if there is anything in this history of treatment that I find, I will use it to erase the discomfort and pain my sister has dealt with for most of her life. Sister, you have been more insightful than any Medici's that I have studied under. I wish we had more time, and maybe we could have solved this together." Ransa acknowledged her counterpart by keeping it simple.

Hearing Ransa call Erri sister reinforced how much everything had changed to in such a short period of time.

"I am going to check with the sisters before we depart. Please don't be late. She hates that if you haven't already figured out." Erri said her farewells to the three friends, and as she walked out the door, Iver and Chachan were approaching, carrying a basket of some sort.

They nodded to acknowledge the young shaman in passing.

Imani stared at her parents who seemed to have been crying. Naiyan had been like a daughter to them, and she understood this moment was like saying goodbye to one of their own flesh and blood.

"Naiyan Amitsa, I will not have you shedding weight again. There are Calizi squares, some jerky, and caramel apples included. There isn't enough to last the six weeks, but it's enough that it won't spoil with the small, refrigerated mechanism."

Iver moved past his wife to hug Naiyan. He only had a small window to come see her before his final counsel with Commander Ghamrod and General Roner was scheduled.

"You are an amazing soul, Naiyan. Your mother would be extremely proud of you. I am proud of you, and I will miss you dearly." As Naiyan hugged him, he allowed himself tearing up.

"It's okay, Iver. Real men do cry." His wife tried to make things lighter in the moment. He waved his hand at her as he turned and walked out of the cottage to speak with the guards posted.

Chachan went over the belongings Naiyan had packed to ensure she was not in need of anything. She couldn't believe that the girl she had helped raise could be a descendant of the First Mother. The older woman had no doubt that the best place for Naiyan to learn about her powers was with Santal Culdris, the Matriarch of Medellin.

"Where are your…?" Chachan referenced her scrolls.

Naiyan had packed them first, beneath all her other belongings. She had left most of her important items behind to be cared for as they cared for her home.

Chachan reached out to hug the younger woman.

"I haven't discussed them with anyone. It was not my place. Elder Vane will be accompanying the party. If you must trust anyone, she is worthy. You are more than what it seems, like your mother always said. I have no idea if you are Blood of the First, but I am absolute in sharing that the magic you possess is the greatest I have ever witnessed," Chachan whispered the words into Naiyan's ear before releasing the embrace.

Ziri was seen walking swiftly towards them with a small bundle in his hand, wrapped tightly with strong green twine.

"I didn't know you'd be leaving so soon." He bypassed everyone else present and stood face to face with her.

She was slightly embarrassed, believing everyone knew what transpired the previous day, but as she listened to him, it all faded away.

"I wasn't sure when we'd be leaving, but I am glad to see you before we…."

Ziri cut her off by handing her the bundle in his hands.

"I have always known that you are special. These are what I have journaled over the years attempting to manage my emotions… about you. I have never shown anyone because these are my intimate thoughts, but they have always belonged to you." He extended his hands for her to take the letters.

Naiyan reached slowly. She had an emotion she couldn't recognize easily.

The rest of those gathered simply watched until Milo and Milos spoke up.

"You *love* him back?" They asked in unison.

Naiyan placed the bundle next to her belongings before walking into Ziri's space.

She kissed him, passionately.

"Oh, my…" Iver couldn't help the words. He had known all along that his son, did in fact have deep feelings for Naiyan. Now was seeing Ziri in a different light as more than an Assembly member, and more than a brother or even son. Ziri had become a man.

The momentary silence was followed by a tremendous amount of laughter.

"We will take these to the wagon to be loaded and give you some time." Chachan had the twins carry the wardrobe chest Naiyan had filled but left the bag with the brown satchel. It always needed to remain in her possession; too much was at stake.

Imani and Ransa were seeing the transformation of Naiyan. She was fearless for leaving behind all she had ever known to fulfill whatever destiny her mother had charged her with, but they saw braveness in their friend for finally allowing herself to show the emotions on display now.

"It's kinda weird to see you two kissing." Imani laughed when Naiyan took hold of her roll-chair.

"It's actually about time if you ask me." Ransa carried one of the two bags left behind.

Ziri ignored them both as they walked towards the grassy area near the amphitheater.

The wagons that had been confiscated in Patin were occupied with a portion of slavers that had been caught. These were the hardened criminals who could not remain behind to live out their lives in the prison colony, and they had many more answers to provide.

Whal was seen amongst the group. It was strange to see an elder of Ledoma relegated to a man shackled by hand and foot.

"I still can't believe all of the shit that happened was because of his ambition," Imani said, twisting her skirt in her fingers.

"Well, he had others following him, so it was more than ambition." Ziri reached out to slow Naiyan from pushing the roll-chair. He pulled her a few steps away and removed a bracelet he had received from her mother when he became a senior.

"This is part of me, and her. I want you to have it."

Naiyan went through an overwhelming emotional sensation, and she could not prevent herself from crying as he placed it on her wrist. She was more than content being patient and willing to take whatever came next, both from Ziri and her upcoming journey. Happiness seemed just out of reach for now.

"I... I don't know what…"

"You don't have to say anything. Your actions speak loud enough. I love you, Naiyan Amitsa." He leaned into her with a kiss before excusing himself to help with the final arrangements for transport.

She reached and grabbed him as he turned.

When their eyes met, there were no walls to prevent the vulnerability in this moment.

"I love you too." The four words felt right when they left her lips.

Ziri smiled and kissed her again.

"I know." He hugged her one last time and left.

"Who are you?" Imani laughed as Naiyan continued pushing her forward.

Ransa saw Erri speaking with a few of the Medici she had grown fond of. Over the course of nearly two months much had changed, including the way the Medici had regarded Ransa. No longer was she an outcast apprentice. She was much more.

"Sister, of all the people I will miss, you are at the top of the list." Erri excused herself from the healers to say her farewells to Ransa.

"Thank you for everything that you have pushed me to become…and for the other 'thing'." Ransa was sure no one else knew, besides the Matriarch perhaps, that she was in possession of the book of forbidden magic.

"You have pushed me in equivalent fashion, sister. I never thought I would have someone else like me." Erri watched Ransa, paying attention to her two sister-friends.

"It's imperative though for both her and us to have answers. She will be protected at all cost you have my word." Erri followed Ransa to help Naiyan into the carriage she'd occupy with the Matriarch, Jain, and herself.

"You are with us." Erri took her bag and handed it to a guard to tie atop their wagon. Naiyan held onto her brown satchel and journal letters from Ziri to be read as they traveled.

"Don't just throw my stuff around like that!" Janae's voice was loudly barking orders. She had made the decision to travel to Medellin under duress, but that did not mean she would be happy about it.

"She's going to have a long trip if she behaves like that; the three bald women can be short with patience." Erri laughed and excused herself, leaving the three friends standing around as everything else was loaded and prepared for departure.

"We have survived much more than distance," Imani said as her two friends got awkwardly silent.

"I know it's what has to happen, but it doesn't mean that I necessarily enjoy watching our best friend leave without us." Ransa shook her head once more and hugged Naiyan deeply.

"Don't go about eating all the Calizi squares in one sitting and get sick." Imani didn't want to create any additional emotion, so she kept her goodbye short.

"Yes, I know. I know," Naiyan replied as she bent down the embrace Imani one last time.

The Matriarch had been walking from the sanctuary with Chachan back at her side. The members of the Assembly trailed shortly behind them.

"It seems we have everything in order." The Matriarch thanked the keepers for their assistance with their elongated stay. She made sure that they were compensated considerably above their standard rate.

Chachan detoured toward the three younger women while the Matriarch spoke with Ghamrod and Merico.

"So, this is it?" She placed her hand on Naiyan's shoulder to gain her attention. A portion of her was happy to know Naiyan would be learning more about who she was, but she acknowledged a second loss. She could see Anel whenever she looked at Naiyan, in her mannerisms, in the way she laughed and spoke.

"Yes, this is it, I guess." Naiyan straightened her face to minimize her expression. She was frightened and excited in the same breath.

“You may have a few visitors before you realize.” Chachan shook her head affirmatively and stared into Naiyan’s eyes.

“You are prepared for any obstacle that comes your way. You are the daughter of Anel Improvi and a woman of my family.” She kissed and hugged Naiyan as Erri called out that it was time to go.

Imani asked them to help her up to embrace in one last combined hug of friends. She watched Naiyan step into the carriage and the door close behind. Ransa stood behind Imani’s roll-chair as the lead horses began to move forward.

Ghamrod mounted his horse and rode next to the Matriarch’s carriage while the slavers were secured in wagons they once used for profit. For the next five weeks, this party would take a different route in returning to their homeland. Time was of the essence with discord running amongst the elemental houses in Medellin, threatening a peace that had lasted centuries—especially with the Age of Prophecy approaching.

About the Author

A. **V. Smith** is an athlete turned writer. During the mid-2000's, he was a featured poet at the Columbus Arts Festival and also won second place during The Great Debaters poetry slam in Columbus, Ohio as Oprah Winfrey's movie was being released nationally.

With a passion for storytelling, he paints with words that draw readers into the story. A.V. writes on an emotional level to empower readers to engage in deeper conversations about their past, their relationships, and their connection with The Universe.

With his first book, *Madison God's Fingerprint 1.618,* he won the Author Academy award for Best Romance in 2019. Since then, he has released *Madison: In the Presence of God* and *Madison: Vengeance Is Mine*. He has also written two crime novels, *OHIO 10* and *OHIO 10 Book II*. Each book has earned Amazon's #1 Best Seller Rank

Normal Chaos: Ledoma Book I is his first fantasy fiction book. He loves to stretch his own limits of creativity by dabbling in various genres of fiction.

Through life and love, André has learned our journeys are temporary, yet intensely meaningful. This understanding led him to donate a kidney to his younger brother. As the father of three children, his desire is to see his children overcome the fear of success by being the best version of themselves; therefore, he strives to lead by example, at times falling short, but understanding human beings are still a work in progress. When he is not engaged in his passion, you can find him with a fishing pole in his hand, coaching youth level football, or attending a local artist event.

For more information or to contact A. V. Smith, please visit www.warpedwritingandpublishing.com.

OTHER BOOKS BY A. V. SMITH

Madison: God's Fingerprint 1.618

While in College, Madison befriends a second-generation Colombian who gets bullied until she steps in. Madison receives more than a simple warm welcome when her friend takes her to visit Colombia for his family's gratitude. Unbeknownst to Madison, a familial bond is illuminated that changes her future. Love dares to awaken Madison's soul; however, with the darkness that surrounded her teenage years, she has constructed walls of protection.

As passionate, erotic themes and emotional conflict shift her vision of the world, she is forced to face the event that paralyzed her father and sent her parents to prison. The murder of a family of three combined with a harassing phone call at work puts Madison on a collision course with the man who had her friend's father assassinated, and who tainted the narcotics found in her father's possession the night her life was forever changed. Madison is a woman with a tumultuous past struggling to escape her demons all the while blindsided by love at a poetry event. Longing to feel normal, Madison attempts to balance her desire for justice with her need for swift, deadly punishment. With the help of her grandmother and sister-friends, she discovers who she really is as well as the courage to let love in.

> ***"Madison: God's Fingerprint 1.618*** *by A. V. Smith is a suspenseful romance with shades of a thriller. Madison has had a painful past and she still suffers from trauma... This is a spellbinding novel with a strong female protagonist. Madison is written with a solid background and it is interesting that most of her actions are determined by the trauma she experienced. The plotting is ingenious, the characterization plausible, and the atmospheric prose enriches the reader's experience of the story. A. V. Smith creates characters that are psychologically rich and complex. Madison goes through a lot of challenging situations and is portrayed with normal reactions to these problems. While readers will maintain their interest as they follow the romance, they will be awed by the author's spectacular skill in writing about deeply flawed and believable characters, as well as the thrilling suspense that was generated. Madison is a hauntingly beautiful tale."*
>
> **—Readers Favorite Book Reviews**

Madison: In the Presence of God

Madison continues on her journey of vulnerability and intimacy. She learns to submit to her fears as things between her and Kendal take a turn. Madison explores the depths of her sexuality with a man who pushes her physical limits, but intimacy requires trust. Is she ready? Is she willing?

In the meantime, tragedy strikes, and Madison is forced to defend her family. In so doing, she is steps closer to revealing who her true enemy is and why.

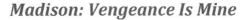

Madison: Vengeance Is Mine

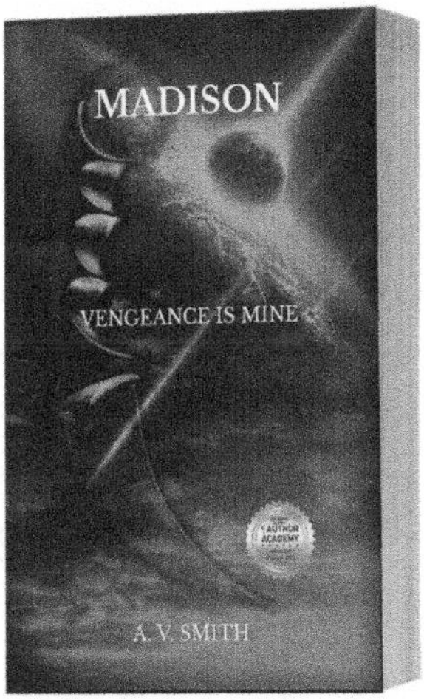

Madison and Kendal's love affair continues to ignite; however, Madison still wrestles with wondering if she is worthy of love. Will Kendal be able to handle her deepest, most intimate secrets? Will their passion continue to heat up or will Kendal run away?

For the first time in more than 20 years, Madison believes she can have it all, but will the Universe find a way to redirect her purpose?

In a turn of events, Madison crosses paths with those who seek to take the life of one of her sister-friends to help cover up a homicide. Will Madison be able to stop this heinous act? The battles rages on as Madison strives to defend her family and seek retribution.

WHAT OTHERS SAID ABOUT A.V. SMITH'S *OHIO 10* BOOKS

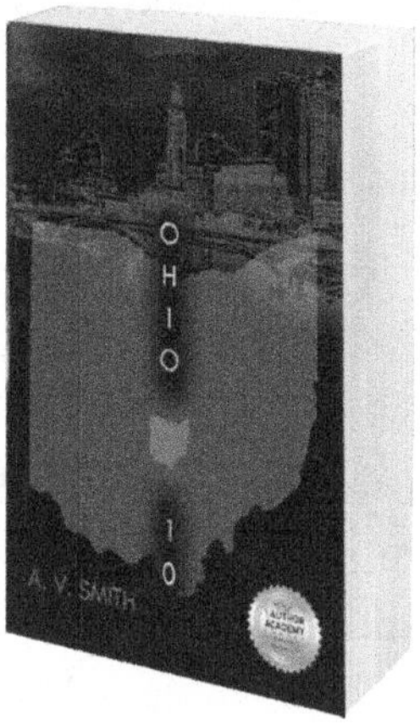

"...fans of procedurals will enjoy this novel's complicated relationships, false leads, and personal vendettas. An engaging...crime tale."

—Kirkus Reviews

"It can be tricky to maintain the suspense of a good mystery novel for the whole length of the tale, but author A. V. Smith does an impressive job of maintaining both pace and mystery in this intriguing and action-packed tale.... I'd certainly recommend Ohio 10 to fans of immersive crime dramas with atmosphere and complexity aplenty."

—Readers Favorite Book Reviews

OHIO 10

A story about good cops versus bad cops amidst a crooked, criminal, and political regime. Based in the capital city of Ohio, the stories surround a diverse group of Columbus detectives. Against all odds the team takes on the inestimable task of maintaining integrity and staying alive while bringing the city to justice from top to bottom.

OHIO 10 Book II

In part one of OHIO 10, Author A.V. Smith acquainted readers with a team of Columbus detectives and the cases they closed. In OHIO 10 Book II, everything escalates with even bigger stakes at hand.

Personal challenges mount for each member of the team as they investigate City Hall, and the crooked law enforcement officials that oversee the city. Two detectives are tasked to go deep in an undercover assignment. Will they be discovered?

Pressures increase for Captain Montgomery to stop investigating cold cases. As the team wars against crime, they learn their toughest battles aren't on the streets, but in the rank and file. The same people who swore to uphold the law are in the pocket of a criminal mastermind. Will they each survive or find out that the force they battle is too great?